torn

ALSO BY
AVERY HASTINGS

feuds

rival

torn

AVERY HASTINGS

st. martin's griffin
new york

TORN. Copyright © 2015 by Paper Lantern Lit. All rights reserved. Printed in the United States of America. For information, address St. Martin's Press, 175 Fifth Avenue, New York, N.Y. 10010.

www.stmartins.com

Designed by Anna Gorovoy

The Library of Congress Cataloging-in-Publication Data is available upon request.

ISBN 978-1-250-05927-7 (hardcover)
ISBN 978-1-4668-4533-6 (e-book)

St. Martin's Griffin books may be purchased for educational, business, or promotional use. For information on bulk purchases, please contact the Macmillan Corporate and Premium Sales Department at 1-800-221-7945, extension 5442, or write to specialmarkets@macmillan.com.

First Edition: July 2015

10 9 8 7 6 5 4 3 2 1

torn

I

DAVIS

The rocking sensation of the ferry should have put Davis to sleep, but all of her senses were on high alert. The guard had led them down in the dark, single file. Davis's eyes had barely adjusted in time to see the stairs that she stumbled down, and when they did, the trapdoor above her had slammed shut, allowing only narrow beams of light to filter in through tiny gaps in the wood. She could hear the water lapping against the side of the boat, just a few inches from where she sat. Smells and sounds compensated for a complete lack of light in the small cabin. The space was dimmer than dim, and the faint smell of mildew was inescapable. The air in the room felt oppressive, yet Davis had been shivering uncontrollably for at least an hour, from shock and fear.

There were no beds, only rows of benches, and there were so many sick passengers that children were piled on top of others' laps, and some sat on the floor. Davis felt lucky to have a surface to sit on and a wall to rest against. The sharp elbows of the people next to her jabbed her rib cage in rhythm with the boat's movements. She hadn't had food or water for hours and wondered how long it would be before they were fed. She felt dizzy, weak. Sweat and the sounds of moans permeated the air around her, and with each rise and fall of the boat, Davis's stomach lurched. She was a carrier of Narxis. She hadn't died right away like Priors who'd contracted the disease, but that didn't mean she wouldn't eventually.

A faint lapping sound and the echo of footsteps above suggested that they were in the lower level of the ferry. And the smell. It was unmistakably the scent of dead bodies. It was immediate enough that Davis suspected they were right there in the cabin with her. It took everything she had not to gag at the smell, but at the same time, a sense of hopelessness overcame her. This was how the dead were treated? She couldn't believe her father would stand for something like this—though, it suddenly occurred to her, perhaps he didn't *know*. She didn't believe respect should stop the second a person took her last breath. All of this—this *casual* treatment—left her horrified and confused.

When a hand wrapped itself around hers, Davis jumped. It was possible, in the dark anonymity of the room, to forget about human contact. But something in her craved it. She didn't move away. Instead she gripped the hand in return, moving toward the light that cut a slim path across the floor. The beam of light was maybe six inches long, a centimeter wide. Through it she could see his knuckles, the tips of calloused fingers.

The hand was large and strong against her own. Comforting. It squeezed hers before removing itself. Then it moved more directly in front of the beam of light. Davis saw it form a circle, thumb and index finger touching. Then another hand reached from the dark to grab hers, folding her palm closed and drawing her own index finger against the circle, forming a line that intersected the perfect shape his fingers made. Then a figure leaned toward her—a shadowed, masculine form barely illuminated. The figure kept a tight grip on her hand. Davis's heart beat wildly, but something told her not to be afraid. She moved closer, resting her forehead against his shoulder for a brief moment as she relaxed fully into the tears, allowing them to bring her relief.

Then his voice, a faint whisper in the dark, meant only for her.

"Hope," he said. A single word before the boat hit a wave, the motion pulling him back into the darkness as his fingers were ripped from hers.

The passage of time was incalculable. Davis could tell some hours had passed; the sliver of light was waning. She dozed off briefly, only to awaken to pitch blackness and an eerie silence punctuated only by the deep breathing of sleeping passengers around her. She nestled on the floor, stretching out her legs as far in front of her as she could. She thought maybe she'd fallen asleep again. She couldn't tell; it was impossible to tell what was real and what was a dream. She'd never felt so lost.

There'd been a moment when, boarding the vessel, the guard herding her in had lifted his hand from her wrist. She'd been bound, but it wouldn't have mattered. The urge to hurl herself off the plank and into the water below, hands and feet tied tight, had been more than tempting. It had been nearly irresistible. She still remembered the air, crisp against her skin. It wrapped its tendrils around her cheeks, beckoning her forward into the placid water below. The water had looked cool, inviting. Peaceful, even. It could have all been over then, this suffering and overwhelming despair.

And then she'd thought of the people she'd miss.

Her sister's face flashed through her mind. Fia's soft curls brushing against her face in the morning, when Fia snuck into her bed for a snuggle. Cradling Fia close while reading her a story—enacting the voices the way Fia always begged her to, and dissolving in giggles along with her little sister, until they were both gasping for air. Her heart ached at the thought of never seeing Fia again. She couldn't give up when Sofia's fate was undecided. She couldn't be responsible for causing her little sister any further pain. It would be too great a betrayal.

But Cole was dead.

She couldn't stop replaying the image of him reaching for her, cupping his hand around her neck and kissing her on the hospital roof deck—the way the sun streamed through his hair in the morning light as she rested her head against his chest. That moment— their night together—had been perfect. It had been the first time they'd told each other how they truly felt. She'd known for sure by then that she loved him. When she watched him fight in the FEUDS, she experienced every punch, as if Brutus's fists were hitting her, and not Cole, square in the heart. Loving Cole had always been beautiful and painful at once, but she'd never have traded it. Losing him was a loss of a large part of herself—the part that felt wide open and innocent.

She was grateful in some ways for that lack of innocence. It was impossible to tell where she was headed, what would happen once she arrived. Whether she'd even still be alive tomorrow, or the next day. She realized she might never know what really happened to her mother. Everyone around her was dying; how long would it be before she followed them?

A creaking noise broke her train of thought. Then the craft jolted, and Davis slid a few feet from her spot against the wall.

"Sorry," she said to no one and everyone. "I'm sorry." Then Davis heard the sound of hinges, and a broad door in the ceiling swung open to reveal a uniformed guard outlined against the twilight.

It was dark, but the light of the just-rising moon illuminated the room around her. She was prepared to see others like her—thirsty, grasping. She wasn't prepared for the bodies. She wondered how she'd adjusted to the smell.

She recoiled, leaning against the thick, damp boards that lined the boat. She pressed a hand to her mouth, sickened and empty, and felt tears slipping silently down her cheeks. It was as though she'd entered a new world in which nothing and nobody really mattered.

She thought of her mother, and what her mother had been through. Her mother would want her to be strong. The thought gave her courage.

"Everyone up," shouted the guard, holding a gun at his side like a threat. "Form a line! Single file!" Another officer emerged from behind him and used his own gun to shove them into a rough approximation of a line. Davis moved between a middle-aged man and a woman holding a baby, before the gun could touch her. She shuddered, narrowly avoiding a body slumped against the ground. A hand reached up for her and she grasped it in her own, attempting to hoist what looked like a twentysomething woman up and into the line, but the weight of the woman's body nearly pulled Davis down, too, and she had to let her go. She prayed that the guards would help the sick.

Davis allowed herself to be shepherded roughly up a ramp and through the gate to a narrow dock. A white sandy beach stretched out beyond the craft, trees rising beyond. The wilderness sloped gently upward, and she could just make out several crumbling stone structures beyond. Narrow paths cut through the trees, linking the buildings to the beach. They seemed to be on some sort of island that would've been beautiful if it weren't so creepy. Where were the houses, the other people? Davis felt cold, shivery. She moved with the line toward two officers standing ahead.

"Men that way," one of the officers called. "Women, there!" One woman fell and Davis tried to help her stand, but she shook her head and cried. She pulled away from Davis, her eyes wide with fear and her hair matted like animal fur. As a guard approached from behind, the woman turned and ran.

Davis watched as the woman pushed her way through the crowd, kicking a guard when he tried to grab her. *Where will she go?* Davis wondered. The woman broke for the water and ran in, her torn dress pooling at her waist. Davis watched on, her heart accelerating and her hands growing moist.

But the guard trampled through the waves and grabbed the woman's arm, yanking her back on shore. She struggled all the while, and when they reached the group he threw her to the ground.

"You can't go anywhere," the guard announced. "None of you. You are contagious, and by order of the Territories' Center for Disease Control, you are to stay on this island."

"Until when?" a man's voice called out.

"Until I say so."

Davis felt as if the ground had split open, leaving her to hurtle down an endless black void. It was an island. They were trapped. Wordlessly, the woman allowed the guard to haul her back to her place in line.

Shaking, Davis looked back toward the boat and saw several other officers hoisting bodies from below onto stretchers. She turned back ahead, quickly, frozen in fear. Her eyes panned the line of males, pausing on a muscular boy with blond hair and a broad frame. He held her gaze, drawing one finger to his lips. Then he used the other hand to form a circle, striking the circle in half with an index finger.

Hope.

Davis jumped, her whole body alert. And then he was gone, pushed into a wagon marked *TOR*.

Davis's own wagon was just ahead, already so full of female passengers that the door on the side refused to close and women hung from the sides. Her wagon, too, read *TOR*. Davis allowed herself to be lifted and shoved inside the wagon. She would have fallen if there hadn't been such a crush of people in there already. She clung to the wooden frame of the cart, one of the last to be loaded, as the engine revved and the vehicle swung into motion. Davis looked back toward the other wagon, already moving ahead on one of the dirt-lined paths. She tried hard not to fall as it bounced against rocks and moved into the thick of the forest, the beach—and the bodies—disappearing behind her.

2

COLE

Bang. Bang. Bang. The sound of fists on the door grew louder, more insistent. Cole jerked out of his reverie. He'd been in that curious space between sleeping and waking, where dreams are jumbled and begin to feel like reality. He moved from the corner where he slept on a narrow pallet, and reached for the door, a mere three feet away. Now he was fully awake, and he remembered. He remembered running from the police. Getting lost in the chaos of the riots. Using the violence and mayhem to his benefit, in order to slip away. Michelle, one of his oldest friends, agreeing to help him fake his own death. It was the only option, she'd said. She'd been right.

But most of all, he remembered losing Davis. And now there was no way he could think of to save her. He'd had the radio on almost constantly over the course of the three days he'd been in hiding. He'd stayed up late at night, hoping for news of Narxis or Davis—allowing himself to succumb to sleep only when he was powerless against the drooping of his eyes. He'd been attentive, but he'd gleaned nothing. The lack of news was killing him. He *needed* information. If they'd taken her back to Columbus, it was nearly impossible—no one was allowed in or out anymore. No one, for any reason. The guards were three deep around the border. Cole peered out the tiny peephole he'd fashioned in the door of the ramshackle house where he was squatting. Thomas Worsley stood outside, holding a bag.

"Come on in." Cole held the door open just a crack, concealing himself in the shadows behind.

"I brought you food."

The smell was tantalizing. It was all Cole could do not to rip the bag right out of Worsley's hands and tear it apart.

"How is it out there?" Cole opened the bag and eyed its contents. Mashed potatoes. Roast beef. "Where'd you get this?" Gens—or "Imps," as Priors called them—*never* got feasts like this. Their rations from Columbus proper, where the Priors lived, were usually close to expiration and limited to castoffs. Beyond that, they relied on what they could grow themselves. The Superiors controlled everything. Their wealth controlled everything. It was how they'd been able to afford genetic enhancements in the first place. It was why they'd felt the need to segregate themselves from those who were imperfect.

Cole felt himself seethe, even as his gratitude to Worsley overwhelmed him. And besides, all Priors weren't the same. Davis wasn't the same. She had her own mind and heart, even though she'd spent her whole life absorbing their beliefs. The scent of the food wafted toward him, making his mouth water. He looked to Worsley for an explanation.

"Bribed a border patrolman," Worsley said. "Gave him something he needed."

Cole didn't ask. He didn't want to know. He knew the natural enhancers Priors used had been scarce since the riots broke out, and many Priors were desperate for enhancement pills. Even amid the medical hysteria, they still craved the pills that would make them "better."

"It's a shit show out there," Worsley muttered, his normally bright eyes angled downward to match his frown. "All the Priors are getting tested weekly, even though the virus has been contained. There's always a new rumor—food contaminations by a cook with Narxis; nannies who've passed it along to children. Tainted water. The disease *is* contained—so far, anyway—but nobody believes it." It was ironic, in a way, that the mutations that had given the Priors every advantage were now causing an epidemic that could destroy them.

"The other territories?"

"Nothing's been reported. All instances have been within New Atlantic so far. But no one's getting in and out. Security's tripled."

Cole shook his head, sitting back against the makeshift bench he'd fashioned from plywood and two cinder blocks. The bench creaked under his weight. He shoveled in the food. It seemed like it had been a forever since he'd had good, hot food, but in reality it had only been a few days since he'd gone into hiding. Still, meat had been rationed since the riots, and most Imps were eating whatever they could grow themselves, supplementing it with occasional handouts the government transported across the border in sterile packs. This was a luxury—something Worsley likely had brought him to keep his spirits up.

"There's something else," Thomas said as he sat on his haunches across from Cole, watching him chew. "I . . . I think I've hit on something." Cole's head jerked up. Worsley seemed tentative—nervous, even.

"A cure?" Cole's heart stopped. A cure would solve everything. Davis could come home. He could have her back. More than that, he realized: a cure could potentially allow them to be *really* together in a way that had never been possible before. It could mean an end to the divide between Priors and Imps. It could force everything to change. Worsley was a Gen. A cure found by a Gen wouldn't just mean salvation for Davis and everyone she loved—it was exactly what Columbus needed to arouse Prior sympathy for Gens and to lead to full integration. Cole's head swam with the implications.

"But I'd need a baby," Thomas said haltingly. "A Prior baby. Actually," he said, casting his eyes downward, "a pregnant Prior woman. I'd have to test in utero."

Cole stopped, fork in midair. "Well surely you know how crazy *that* is," he said dryly. He wanted to be mad at Thomas for getting his hopes up, but Thomas looked so discouraged that Cole didn't bother. Worsley already knew how hopeless it all was.

"There's no way I can even get into the city," Thomas said, resting his head in his hands. "Even if I could, how would I bring someone back here and convince them to let me work on them? I'd have to basically kidnap them. I could see that going over really well. It's not like any Prior would willingly volunteer. They only think of themselves."

"This is *about* them," Cole reminded him.

"They won't see it that way."

"You'll figure it out," Cole assured him, trying to sound like he believed it. "Don't worry." Inside, he too was worried. But it wouldn't benefit Worsley to know how little faith Cole had in his ability to solve this thing.

Worsley was standing to leave, dusting off the back of his pants, when a piercing shriek rang out. Both men dashed from the ramshackle hideout before Cole remembered that he wasn't supposed to be seen.

There in front of them, no farther than ten yards away, was the crumpled and bloodied form of a woman. Just past her, a man darted away, making a sharp left turn down an alley.

Cole and Worsley ran over to crouch next to the woman, who was screaming after the Imp. "Thief," she called out. "Come back!"

Cole recognized something in that tone. His voice caught in his throat. He turned the woman gently toward him, and she didn't bother to resist; she was clearly weakened from the attack. When she rolled over to face him, his eyes widened in recognition.

"It's you," she whispered through cracked and dirtied lips. Her eyes were wide with terror. "They said . . . you were supposed to have died. You're dead." She recoiled, trying to move away from him, her face ashen. She seemed confused and disoriented.

"Vera," he said gently. "Don't be scared. It was all a mistake. The news got it wrong. I'm okay." He reached for her hand, and she looked at it for a long minute before accepting it. He squeezed it gently, feeling his soul move for the poor, panicked girl. He lifted her up, tucking her torn and dirtied dress—once, from the look of it, a delicate shade of pink silk—under her knees. He turned to Worsley. "We've got to get her back inside, now."

"You know this girl?" Worsley's eyes were wide with disbelief. "We can't take her! You're already in enough trouble."

"No one's looking for me," Vera muttered into Cole's chest. "They left me here. They don't want anything to do with me."

The men exchanged glances; it took less than a minute for Thomas to nod his assent and the three to move quickly in the direction of Cole's hideout. Once there, Cole laid Vera gently on the thin pallet he'd been using as a makeshift bed. He brought her a glass of water. Vera eyed it warily.

"It's been filtered," Worsley assured her. Then, less sensitively: "Besides, you have no choice." She nodded and drank quickly, taking it down in enormous gulps, not bothering to look up until the entire glass was drained. Cole waited as long as he could—which turned out to be about two minutes.

"Have you . . . ," he paused, racking his brain for a delicate way to phrase it. "Do you know anything about Davis?" he asked, flushing at his own callousness.

"Cole! Let her rest."

"I'm sorry." Cole took a breath, moving to the sink to wet a towel for Vera. Her face was covered in sweat and dried blood from being scraped when she'd fallen. He glanced back, taking her in. In such a short time, she'd fallen so far from the gorgeous friend of Davis's he'd first seen at a rooftop party only a few weeks ago. She'd been laughing and whispering with her boyfriend—some uptight Prior named Oscar—and she'd seemed as untouchable and perfect as Davis had to him then.

Now her blond curls formed a chaotic halo around her shoulders. It was obvious Vera was still beautiful—still a Prior—even at the height of her exhaustion and fear. She wore a pink silk sundress that nipped in at the waist and fastened demurely at her chest with a row of opalescent buttons. She'd been dressed conservatively when they kicked her out. He wondered where she'd last been— at a cello recital? Davis had said she was brilliant with the cello. How could they have thrown her out like she was nothing? Fury ran through his veins; he had to take several breaths to compose himself before turning back to her. He ran cold water over the towel and moved back toward Vera, patting her face where he spotted the largest clots. She winced when the towel hit her forehead, and pulled away slightly.

"We're going to need to ice that," Cole told her. "I don't have ice here, but Worsley can bring some soon. Are you hungry?"

Vera nodded. "I've been here for two days," she said. "They threw me out with the credit card that guy just took, and a little food, but it was barely enough to last through yesterday."

"Who did?"

Vera stifled a sob. "My parents," she said.

Cole swallowed a hard lump of anger in his throat. "I don't have much," he told her, moving toward the small stash of provisions he kept in a garbage bag in the corner, just in case. He was never sure exactly when Worsley would or wouldn't show up. He tried to temper his impatience—to focus on helping Vera—but his whole body burned with the desire to know where Davis had been taken and if she was okay.

He brought her a few crackers, some peanut butter, and a bruised apple.

"It's all I have," he said, a note of apology in his voice.

"Thank you, Cole." Vera looked up at him, meeting his eyes. He could tell she was touched. Only a couple of months ago she would have shuddered at the idea of eating Imp food.

"Can you tell us what you know about Davis?" Worsley spoke up. Cole startled; Worsley had been so silent the whole time that Cole had half forgotten he was there, sitting on the bench in the shadows. Vera shook her head, her mouth smudged with peanut butter. She was shoveling it in by the spoonful, ravenous.

"I only know that she was taken to TOR-N. I haven't heard anything from her."

"TOR-N?" Cole looked at Worsley for clarification, but Worsley's eyebrows were knitted.

"TOR is the Territories' Operational Research facility," he said. "But what's the *N*? Oh. . . ." It dawned on them all at once.

"Narxis." Worsley answered his own question before Vera could reply.

"Yes." She nodded. "Columbus has been sending Narxis victims to TOR-N every day. They go by ship. It's supposed to be an incredible facility. I went to Davis's house, spoke to her father. He said it's a large, island campus—almost like a luxurious resort, with state-of-the-art technology. He said it's the best place for her, that there's a world-renowned chef, a studio for her to dance in—every luxury she could want, in addition to top-notch medical care. But I haven't heard a word from her since they took her."

Cole felt relief to know where Davis was, at least. Relief to know she wasn't dead. Probably. Not yet, anyway. They were studying her. But why hadn't Davis gotten in touch? Surely if the facility was that advanced, staying in touch would be easy, and Vera was her best friend.

"Have any survivors come back? Anyone who was cured?" he asked.

Vera hesitated, then frowned. "No," she told him finally. "None that I can think of. But it's not really talked about. Nobody wants to think about it. It's too scary. People just—" She stopped, choking back a sob. "People can't believe it's happening."

"How are you?" Cole asked, softening his tone and reaching for her hand. "What happened? Why did you . . . end up here?"

Vera hesitated before responding.

Cole glanced up at Worsley, who had been oddly quiet the whole time, observing their interactions from where he sat. Now the two exchanged a look of concern. Cole turned to Vera, who met his eyes, tears welling in her own.

"I blew the Olympiads," she whispered finally. "Oscar wouldn't have me."

"Your parents dumped you in the Slants because you blew the Olympiads?" Cole's mind raced. None of it made sense. The Olympiads were crucial, sure. And he remembered Davis telling him Vera had been a shoo-in. But to disown their daughter over this failure?

He'd had no idea the kind of stakes they were up against. No *wonder* Davis had been so worried, so tense. Always under so much pressure. But what did she mean, Oscar wouldn't have her?

"No," Vera broke in, her voice hesitant. "Not just that."

"It's okay," Worsley reassured her. "You can tell us."

Vera inhaled deeply. "I blew the Olympiads," she said, her voice quavering, "because I was . . . distracted. Oscar and my parents sent me here for a different reason."

Cole waited, steeling himself against what she was about to say. What could have been so horrible that they'd dump her in a place widely considered to be untouchable?

"I'm pregnant," she said.

Cole felt his eyes widen. He opened his mouth to say something— anything to let her know everything would be okay—but Vera held up a hand to quiet him.

"I'm pregnant with Oscar's child," she continued, "*and* I screwed up the Olympiads." Her voice was trembling, and she let out a choked sob. "Oscar might have married me if I'd only passed the Olympiads. After that, I was a disgrace. He didn't want me. He didn't want the baby. My parents were humiliated."

Cole felt his hands clench in anger. He was shocked, horrified that any parent—any *boyfriend*—would do what they'd done. He moved toward Vera and wrapped an arm around her. "It'll be okay," he said, drawing her head to his shoulder. "We'll help you figure it out." Cole vowed to keep his promise. Vera was Davis's best friend. Davis would be heartsick at this news. He had to keep Vera safe.

"I can see why she was so crazy about you," Vera whispered, her body sinking against his with relief.

He let her cry and sniffle into his shirt, and eventually her breathing slowed. When she finally fell asleep, Cole stared hard at Worsley. "What are we going to do with her?" he whispered.

Worsley smiled for the first time that night. "Don't you get it? It's perfect. It's like the solution fell right into our laps."

Cole looked down to where Vera was lying against his lap, and smiled a little at Tom's joke. Then the significance of the word *solution* dawned on him.

"No," he whispered.

"Cole. *Yes*," said Worsley. "We've been given a chance, don't you see? It'll help her. It could change everything." He leaned past Cole and shook Vera's shoulder gently. Her eyes stirred as she began to wake up.

"Time to get up," Worsley told her. "We've got to move you."

She sat up, stretching and rubbing her eyes. "Where are we going?" she asked groggily.

"To my work space," Worsley said. "You'll be safe there for now."

Cole tried to catch Worsley's eye. It was all so much upheaval for Vera to handle in such a short time. She was fragile, and he worried that Worsley was too fixated on the end goal.

"Can I talk to you?" He motioned to Worsley, who nodded and followed him to the opposite corner of the room.

"She's never been in the Slants," he whispered. "She's terrified. You can see it in her eyes. Please be careful with her. She's Davis's best friend."

Worsley put a hand on his shoulder. "Her well-being comes first," he told him. "The rest is secondary. I swear to you."

Cole nodded, though he wasn't completely sure he believed his friend. Worsley didn't know Davis like he did, so he couldn't know Davis's love for Vera or feel the responsibility he felt. Still, there were few options. He'd just have to check in on Vera as much as possible.

Worsley turned back to Vera, then crossed the room and knelt by her side. "I care very much about keeping you safe," he said. "You can trust me. My clinic is very comfortable, and Cole will check in on you, too. Are you okay with that?"

Cole saw the crease in her brow softening. Worsley did have a good bedside manner; his voice was calm, compassionate. Vera nodded in acquiescence, allowing Worsley to help her to her feet. "One more thing," Worsley said, as he wrapped a supporting arm around her waist. "How would you like to give birth to the cure?"

3

DAVIS

The hardest part about the island was that there was no escape. The second-hardest part was being strong among the weak. Davis could take the stiff mattresses, the scratchy sheets, the chores they were forced to do every day to keep the place in running order. It was nothing like the gleaming medical facility her father thought it was. It had once been luxurious; that much was obvious. Davis had heard rumors that it had been an old beachside resort, and some of that glamour still remained—gilded windows, a sweeping staircase that led to the dormitories. Big computer rooms for patients, now empty and pillaged, with loose wires dangling from the walls. Large dorm rooms stripped bare and outfitted with far too many beds and boarded windows. Little shared cabins that probably once had been storage sheds. None of it had been maintained, and Davis could imagine why not. After all, how could the government have anticipated a need for TOR-N until recently?

Still, she couldn't forgive the fact that they could have done more and didn't. Nothing was clean. It was as if they hadn't inspected it before throwing people in. You could see the beauty under the surface, but just barely. Her dad would never have sent her to a place like this—squalid and gloomy, with poor-quality food for all the patients—if he did know. She assumed he'd been sent information containing old pictures from its times of former glory. Part of it was humbling—it was what she imagined Cole's life had been like. But people died every day here, and that was the part she would never get used to.

She felt overwhelming fear, deep in the pit of her stomach. She didn't know if or when she herself was going to die, only that she seemed stronger than most of the rest. And that gave her the faintest bit of hope.

Before TOR-N, she'd never seen so many people suffering from illness. It just hadn't happened in Columbus . . . until Narxis came along. And even then it was somehow possible to pretend it was all a bad dream. She'd still been surrounded by the healthy and the beautiful. She'd still had her comfortable bedroom, with her down bedding and her loving family. She could still, to some degree, feel untouched. It was the memories of her family that kept her going, that made her believe they'd find a cure and she could go home. She had to believe.

Davis made her way to the hut of Margaret, a woman who had held her while she cried, the first night of their arrival. Only, since then, Margaret's sickness had progressed far more rapidly than Davis's.

"Margaret," she whispered, knocking on the door of the shared cabin. "It's Davis." The shades were drawn in the cabin, and the other occupants had cleared out. The smell of sweat and waste assaulted Davis's nostrils. Her stomach turned over. But she took a deep breath and entered the room. Sunlight streamed through the open door, illuminating Margaret's face. It was easy to see that Margaret had been beautiful once, with high cheekbones and violet eyes. She was probably only a few years older than Davis—midtwenties, if Davis had to guess. But now her skin was dry and patchy, cracks already beginning to form. She'd aged years in the past few days. Davis was afraid to move closer, even though she had been assured that, once you contracted Narxis, your strain couldn't worsen with exposure to another strain. It just was what it was. She wouldn't get sicker from being near Margaret.

Davis pushed herself forward into the room and sat down beside Margaret's bed.

"Here," she said, digging into her pocket, from which she produced four seashells she'd collected from the shore. "I know you like them."

Margaret's lips cracked into some semblance of a smile and she weakly held out her hands. They shook as Davis carefully placed the shells into her palms.

"Beautiful," Margaret whispered.

"Here, let me help you arrange them," Davis offered, too uncomfortable to remain seated. Margaret handed back the shells and Davis placed them in a row on a nearby windowsill, drawing back the shades a little.

"Thank you," Margaret whispered. The sound of true gratitude in her voice made Davis want to cry. The thought of being reduced to such a state, and still finding beauty in the small things, reminded her that there was hope in even the gravest of circumstances.

A few minutes later, Margaret was drifting to sleep, so Davis snuck back out of the cabin, closing the door carefully, and heaved a huge sigh, grateful to be back in the fresh air again.

"That bad, huh?"

"Worse," Davis muttered without thinking. She jerked her head up to find herself eye to eye with the boy from the boat.

"Mercer," he told her. "The other one who's semihealthy around here."

"For now," Davis told him.

"Well, aren't you just the picture of hope?" he said. "What's your name, Ms. Positivity?"

"Davis." She sighed and leaned back on her heels. Who did this guy think he was? He had no idea what she'd been through.

"I know what you're thinking," he said. "You're thinking who the hell am I to talk about being positive, am I right?"

Davis shrugged. "Kind of."

"Well, I'm the guy who's Narxis positive," he said. "About as positive as they come."

Davis met his eyes, which were sparkling just a little, even as his face remained serious. She wiped her forehead with the back of her gloved hand, and for the first time in days—or maybe weeks—she smiled.

Davis stretched across the windowsill, pulling her body all the way into the sterile, sparsely adorned facility. A funky smell assaulted her nostrils—some sort of mix of cleaning fluids and whatever putrid scent the fluids were meant to extinguish. The windows to the facility were never locked—they were high enough off the ground to deter most intruders, and nearly everyone at TOR-N was too weak to do much anyway. Davis trembled from the exertion of cre-ating a makeshift platform from discarded lumber and hoisting her-self into the building. She was sick of being left in the dark.

Once there, she hardly had time to recover; an alarm sounded before her feet hit the ground. Fingers trembling from weakness, she coded in the password she'd seen Dr. Grady enter to deactivate the alarm during their most recent morning appointment. Davis had shown up early on purpose, trailing him into the building as he un-locked the doors. Always watching, searing everything he did into her brain. Smiling and nodding while he talked about the weather and the supposedly great new changes to the dining facility—changes that included the addition of "fresh" vegetables—the semirotten produce that couldn't be sold in stores.

The alarm silenced, Davis edged into the office, squinting against the dark. The only illumination was a narrow beam of moonlight that filtered through the vaulted window. Davis leaned against the wall of the office, trying to catch her breath. The facility was tiny; Dr. Grady didn't need much more than a treatment office, a surgi-cal area, and a storage room, she guessed. Still, where was all the money she was certain her father was paying for her to be there? The space was clean but devoid of any trimmings, and even some of the equipment looked a little dated.

Davis clasped her trembling hands together, feeling her way into the even darker space that she knew held official documents and rec-ords. She'd walked past the room often enough on her way in to know exactly where it was, but she was unprepared for how difficult it would be to see anything at night. She reached for the light switch, her hand hovering over it. Maybe she could risk turning it on for just a few minutes. It was late; no one would even be awake to see. Still, something held her back. She was about to go for it—to flick it on despite her reservations, because the trip would be wasted otherwise—when a beam of light flashed from behind her. Davis screamed before she could stop herself.

"Shhh," someone said as a hand clamped around her wrist. "Calm down." It was someone young—not the voice of a night guard. Davis wrenched herself from his grasp as the hand loosened, turning quickly to face a guy about her age, blond and attractive despite his gaunt cheeks. He flashed the light under his face to illuminate his chin, giving him a ghostly appearance.

"Mercer?" It came out as a question, but she'd known who it was—she'd met him outside of Margaret's room several weeks ago. They stared at each other, and Davis found herself fixated on the specks of green in his hazel eyes. "What are you doing here?"

"Getting into trouble," he answered. "Looks like I'm not the only one."

"I don't know what you're talking about." She rubbed her wrist self-consciously. It still felt warm from his touch.

"You don't?" He raised his eyebrows, indicating the room with the beam. "I guess I misunderstood the situation." The corner of his mouth lifted in a wry grin.

"Are you following me?" she hissed. She felt her face flushing, but she wasn't sure if it was out of anger or something else. Who was this guy, this other one who didn't seem to be succumbing to the disease?

"Would you mind if I was?" he asked.

Davis let out a sigh and started to walk past him, threatening to leave. Whatever she'd planned, it wasn't worth it. She'd been watching him, but despite her curiosity, Davis wasn't sure she could trust him. Why should she?

"Okay, okay. Let's say I *was* following you—hypothetically, of course. . . ." He shrugged here, and smiled in a way that showed off the line of his jaw. "I figured you'd need help. I'm better prepared. If you hit those lights, someone will see us in a second. It's only midnight. Dr. Grady is just turning in. I know, because as I said, I'm the kind of guy who's prepared."

"So you know the alarm code," Davis challenged.

"No," he told her, smiling. "But I knew that you knew it."

So he'd been watching her, too, because they were the same. Positive for Narxis but showing barely any of the signs—seemingly healthy Priors sent here to TOR-N to waste away.

That's why she was here now—to find a way to get another message out.

"Why are you really here?" she asked him.

"Same as you. To get answers."

It was a vague answer, but it was honest. She knew what it felt like to be totally powerless, enduring a series of medical tests and never knowing what it all meant.

"Fine. Let's see what that flashlight of yours can find us," she said.

As they worked—rifling through the low cupboards that housed slim, digital files—she felt herself relaxing. Why shouldn't he be curious, too? Why should she be the only one brave enough to look for answers? Realizing that they had this in common—a curiosity, a drive to seek something beyond what they were offered—made her feel strangely close to him. When he reached into a drawer and extracted a slim hard drive, extending it to her, she took it.

The case read *Morrow.*

"It was in the correspondence bin," Mercer told her. "Nothing for me, alas. Guess my family doesn't miss me."

"Don't say that," Davis told him.

"Hey, it's not a big deal," he told her. "It's probably taking a while to put together my massive gift basket."

He had a joke for everything. Davis wondered if it really wasn't a big deal to him, but she moved on and scanned the list of contents written on the outside of the hard drive.

"This video chat is dated three days ago." Davis furrowed her brow. "I wonder why they haven't given it to me? And wait. The mailing seal's been broken."

"That's weird," he said, examining the cracked seal. "Didn't realize they'd be vetting our mail. Here. Let's pop it in." He slipped the hard drive into a wall-mounted computer, which made a whirring noise and flickered on automatically. Davis's stomach clenched at the sight of Fia's, Terri's, and her dad's faces filling the screen.

"We miss you, sweetheart," her dad said, causing her eyes to fill with tears. "Can't wait to see you as soon as you've made a speedy recovery." Davis's eyes welled, and she fixated on the screen, mesmerized.

Beside her, Mercer let out a rasping cough, jolting her from her reverie.

"I just can't understand why they wouldn't have given it to me," she said again.

"Because of hope," he said. His eyes shone hazel against his pale, sallow skin. "They don't want us to have our messages because then we'll have hope."

Davis let out a nervous, loud laugh. "That's morbid," she said. Though this whole place was morbid. She felt goose bumps on her skin and crossed her arms in front of her.

"Hey, listen, Morrow. I didn't mean to freak you out. They probably—"

"How did you know my last name?" She realized she didn't know his, and took a step back.

"Like I said. I keep an eye on the good ones."

"I find your attentiveness a little disconcerting."

"Well, when you're trapped on an island with a bunch of sickly old women, and one pretty, semifunctioning girl breezes into your life. . . ."

"Semifunctioning?" She hated that she smiled, but she couldn't help it.

"You start to take notice. Now that you got your gold," he said nodding to the hard drive, "let's see what else they've got hidden up in here."

They filtered through the drawers, falling into an easy silence. The space around them was punctuated only by their raspy breathing. *Soundtrack of a sick teenager*, Davis thought. For a moment she thought this might be hopeless, but then she found something that made her pause.

"Mercer," she said, holding up a video chat that was still sealed. "This is from the Columbus Health Department. Dated a month ago."

"They didn't open it?" His eyes knitted together under the beam of the flashlight.

"Nope."

"Shall we?"

"Won't they notice?"

Mercer shrugged. "Maybe. But they're not gonna know it was us," he pointed out.

They inserted it in the computer, and the face of Peter McNamara, the renowned head surgeon at Columbus General, filled the screen.

"Dr. Grady, Peter McNamara here. We're missing last month's progress update from TOR-N over at Columbus General, and we'd like a comprehensive update within the next two weeks. Maybe we got overlooked in your mailings. Please check in with your status by the fifteenth of the month. We'd also love to hear more about these murmurings that patients with a Neither status can contribute to the creation of a Narxis vaccine. What's that about, Grady? Call me back." Then his face cut out and the screen went black.

"*Neither* status?" Davis repeated, staring at the black screen.

Beside her, Mercer sighed. "It means not fully Prior nor fully Gen, but genetically somewhere in between."

She turned to him. "Am I . . . Are *we?*"

Slowly, Mercer nodded. Then he turned back to the files. "There are more than a dozen in here," he said. "Look. These are all unopened. All from hospitals across New Atlantic."

"So they're not sending any information out. But why?" Davis was puzzled, still trying to wrap her head around what Mercer had explained. *Neither.*

"Maybe this is why." Mercer clenched his jaw, scrolling over a thin tablet marked *Annual Report.* "Jesus," he whispered. "This is nuts. Check out the money they're getting! Durham alone invested four million in the facility. That's where I'm from."

Davis peered over his shoulder. There it was: a million from Columbus, a million and a half from Seattle. All in all, TOR-N had received over fifty million dollars in funding. And yet, the patients were eating food that was barely fit for consumption, and they were sleeping on hard wooden bunks in rooms filled with four or more people. There was no air-conditioning, and Davis often felt like she could taste the air, thick and leaden with germs. There was a vast swimming pool just begging for use—and supposedly it *was* for patient use—but it had been restricted ever since she'd arrived, for fear (as the doctors said) of contamination. Yet the doctors themselves used it. It didn't seem fair.

"Grady," Mercer whispered. "Did you ever notice how he dresses? The watch he wears?"

"You think they're skimming?"

"I'd bet my life on it," Mercer said. Davis watched his jaw clench and unclench. "And did you hear what he said about Neithers contributing to a vaccine? I'm willing to bet he doesn't want to aid research because he wants to *keep* skimming. He doesn't want the clinic to go away."

Davis frowned at his words. If he was right, that made the doctors here corrupt. It made them monsters.

"Here's your personal file," Mercer told her, setting aside the annual report. "I can step outside while you listen, if you want." But his eyes returned to the drawer, betraying his reluctance to leave.

"No," Davis said quickly. "Stay." She suddenly felt scared to be alone.

As she switched on the file, which was just audio, Mercer rifled through the drawer, pulling out an envelope that caused him to wrinkle his brow. Meanwhile, Dr. Grady's voice echoed around the small room. They listened for five minutes while he described the symptoms she already knew she had. Still, it was painful and embarrassing to hear them recounted: nausea, sweating, and shakiness. Mercer must have sensed her discomfort; about halfway through he reached for her hand, holding it firmly until the end.

When they both heard Dr. Grady's final words, he squeezed it hard, breaking into a full grin.

"Ms. Morrow is expected to make a full recovery," Dr. Grady said, "aided in part by a strong immune system and a healthy, athletic build. Ms. Morrow likely contracted the disease while in peak physical condition, and thus should be able to ward it off within a few months with proper care and treatment."

"Did you hear that?" Mercer grabbed her by the shoulders, smiling full-on into her face. "You're going to get better!"

Relief flooded her entire being—leaving her queasier than before. Davis leaned over and drew Mercer into a hug. He stiffened, surprised, but then she felt him melt into her. She hadn't thought she would ever get better, and the return of hope was overwhelming. Everything felt brighter somehow. She would see her family again!

But when Mercer gave her a squeeze, Davis felt a rush of painful nostalgia. She missed Cole. She would have traded Mercer for him in half a second. She slid out of Mercer's arms, feeling guilty, and backed up against the wall. She sank down and hugged her knees to her chest.

"Hey, Morrow," Mercer said lightly, "I've got an idea."

"What's that?"

"Let's bust out of this joint."

"Right. I'll start digging," Davis said. But when she looked up, his expression was hard. She felt her forehead scrunch in confusion. "You're kidding, right? They'll send us home when we're in the clear, right? Why wouldn't they?"

"You think they're ever going to let us out?" Mercer asked. "They're happy to sap our parents for every dime they can get. Why do you think he didn't tell you himself that you're on your way to recovery?"

Davis thought hard. It was true that Dr. Grady had seemed concerned—even grim—at their appointment that morning.

"And," Mercer added, looking grim himself, "I found something while you were listening to the audio. There was a letter in the drawer from a doctor I've heard of from Durham. I opened it."

Davis gasped. How could they ever cover up their snooping now?

"It was already open," Mercer clarified. "Dated a month ago. The thing is . . . ," he trailed off, looking troubled. "The doctor—Dr. Hassman—said he needed blood samples from the Neithers here in order to complete a test that he thought would lead to an immediate cure. There are two other letters following up on it, asking Dr. Grady why he hasn't replied or sent the samples."

"It would be easy enough to send our samples," Davis said, following his train of thought. "So why didn't he?"

But even as she asked the question, she realized she had already figured out the answer. She stood up slowly.

"He doesn't want there to be a cure," she whispered.

Mercer nodded. "If there's a cure, the facility will shut down and the money will stop coming in. This whole thing is one big Prior lie."

The cure was being squelched here, not developed. She felt sick as the severity of it dawned on her. "What can we do?"

"We go there. We bring Dr. Hassman the samples. *We're* the samples. We can bring samples from before, when you were still contagious, and he can take samples of our blood now."

"This is *crazy*." Davis shook her head. She'd only wanted to see her file. A prison break? That was something else.

"Crazier than staying here?" He spread his arms out and gestured to the room around them and everything beyond it. "People are dying. There are armed guards. We have proof that these doctors don't give a shit. And you want to stay?"

"No," she said softly. "I'm just . . . I can't . . ."

"You *can*, Morrow. Come with me. What other person on this island can memorize sixteen-digit passcodes? Who else is ballsy enough to scale stacks of bricks and bust through windows? You're it, Morrow. You're my partner in crime."

Davis couldn't help but blush a little. Mercer wasn't exactly someone she trusted yet, but he was bold, and comforting—and he said things that made Davis believe. She hadn't felt close to someone since Cole.

Cole.

His death had left a void too big for anyone to fill, maybe ever. For the last few days, she'd been focused only on trying to get information. The rest of her—her heart and her body—had been numb, unable to accept the situation. Unable to imagine never seeing Cole again. It was like a thick black wall had gone up in her mind, blocking out the reality of his death. She knew the truth was there, just beyond the wall, but the knowledge of it was just a cold, dull thud, nothing more.

But this new plan . . . it was like a crack of light in the darkness. Almost painful, searing, but also invigorating. She felt as if a jolt of fresh oxygen had just gone to her lungs. They'd escape, and she'd get home to Fia and her family, and she'd help Thomas Worsley or one of the surgeons at Columbus General find a cure.

"I'm in," she said, feeling her voice waver—with excitement, with fear, with the realization that doing this meant having something to live for again, and also something more to lose.

Mercer broke into a broad smile. "I knew you would be. But in the meantime, let's get older blood samples. From when we first came to TOR-N."

The samples were kept in a refrigerator in the same office where appointments were held; many times, both Mercer and Davis had seen Dr. Grady draw their blood into thin vials and place them there. It was easy to obtain the samples, dated nearly three months ago. Almost too easy.

As they snuck out the way they came, Davis realized they hadn't gotten anything for Mercer. "What about you?" she asked. "Don't you want to see your file?"

"My file?" he whispered as they padded down the hall. "I'll see it eventually. And when I do, I want the first word I read to be *cured*."

4

COLE

Worsley had warned him against going out, but Cole went anyway. He waited until after dark, of course; but still, the cemetery was lit by the faint glow of the moon, and it was elevated on a soft slope that left him feeling exposed. A few laborers walked along the foot-path that bordered the cemetery—it served as a shortcut between the sanitation plant and the Slants's main cluster of housing. Had anyone been looking, they'd have seen his shrouded figure hunched behind a tree that arched above the gravestone marked *Cole Everest*. Cole knew it was risky; he'd half expected his mother to be holding vigil by the mound of fresh dirt that concealed some other guy's wasted, unrecognizable body. He was almost disappointed to find that she wasn't.

The cemetery had been empty when he approached, and now he cast furtive glances around him. It was only ten o'clock, but he hadn't been able to wait any longer. Some sick part of him wished he'd been at his own funeral—not to see everyone mourn him, just to *see everybody*. He missed his mom and Hamilton so much it hurt. He wondered if Michelle and Worsley had kept his secret.

Twenty minutes ticked by. When the road finally cleared of pedestrians and he couldn't see any more approaching from his elevated position, Cole inched from behind the tree and approached his grave site, just a few feet away. He could see there was an epitaph scratched into the stone, and he was morbidly curious to find out what it said.

HE FOUGHT WITH INTEGRITY; HE LIVED WITH HOPE.

Cole felt his throat tighten. His mother had chosen it, he knew. She'd always told them that of all the values she'd tried to teach them, integrity was the most important. The hope thing . . . that was different. She'd teased Cole about being perpetually optimistic since he was a kid. He was her dreamer, she'd said. The message she'd chosen was one he could be proud of.

A cloud shifted above him and something glinted against the dark soil. Cole reached down and grabbed the object, allowing the soft soil to sift through his fingers. When he grasped the round metal and rubbed the remaining traces of soil from it, he gasped. It was their great-grandfather's medal for valor, the one Hamilton had inherited before Cole had been born. Cole had always coveted it; it was pretty much the only family heirloom they had, and as a kid he'd often snuck it out of the shoebox where Hamilton kept his trea-sures, and had fallen asleep clutching it, until Hamilton awoke and took it back. He couldn't believe Hamilton had left it here for him now.

The tightness in his throat increased, and he blinked several times. His chest felt heavy. He so desperately wanted to come clean—to tell his family the truth—but he knew it wasn't possible. Not yet. He couldn't risk making them culpable. Cole took the medal and slipped it in his pocket, then pushed to his feet. He'd just started to make his way back down the hill toward the rusted chain-link fence surrounding the property when he heard a voice.

"Cole?" the voice called. "Cole, is that you?"

It was Brent. His best friend called his name repeatedly, begin-ning to jog toward Cole, who had frozen, his head down. Something in Cole wanted to own up to it, wanted to tell Brent everything. But then he remembered what could happen if too many people found out, and he snapped. Cole turned and ran in the opposite direction as fast as he could, hoping his baggy sweatshirt and hat had prevented Brent from getting a good look at him.

He looked back only once as he ran, pushing through trees and winding through the darkest spaces between the rows of modest homes that decorated the Slants. When he looked back, Brent wasn't there. Cole collapsed onto the floor of the shelter, breathing heavi-ly. He willed himself not to cry. The feeling of invisibility—it had been almost enough to convince him that he *was* dead. Just a ghost, hovering on the periphery of the town. After so much isolation, the relief of someone seeing him—recognizing him, calling out to him—was enough to devastate him.

He was just beginning to pull himself together when he heard a knock on the door. Michelle hovered just outside, her brown curls glowing against the backlight.

"Can I come in?"

Cole nodded, motioning for her to sit next to him. He breathed deeply, trying to steady himself. He couldn't lose control like this. He couldn't afford to let his guard down, not even in front of Michelle.

"Are you okay?" Her voice was cautious. She lowered herself to the ground next to him, then placed a hand on his.

"Not really."

"I know you went by the grave site."

Cole's head jerked up, and his face flushed.

"Don't worry," Michelle told him, squeezing his palm. "He doesn't know it was you. He said . . . he said he got spooked. Saw something he wanted to see. He thought it was a ghost at first. But he convinced himself it was just some straggler. By the end of it, he didn't know if he saw anybody at all. Why'd you go out there, Cole? You were taking a huge risk."

"I know," he said, his voice sharp. "Believe me. I know. I just . . . I had to see it. It was stupid," he amended. "You're right."

"I just worry about you. You've stayed alive this long. . . ."

"I know." He squeezed her hand. They sat side by side for a few minutes, neither of them saying anything. "How are they?" Cole finally asked, his voice tense.

"Your mom isn't doing so well," Michelle answered quietly. "She's grieving."

"Is she healthy?"

"She's holding up," Michelle said. "Losing you . . . it hasn't been easy on her."

"Hamilton?"

Michelle was quiet, picking at a small hole on the knee of her jeans. She didn't look up.

"Michelle. What is it?"

"He's having a hard time," she said finally. "He's taking care of your mom, going to work, but . . . he's just not himself."

Her words were heavy. Cole could tell there was something she wasn't saying.

"What's going on with him? It's better I know," he told her, his voice firm.

"There's nothing you can do, Cole. He just misses you. He blames himself."

"Why?" Cole felt light-headed, and his palms were sweating. He moved his hand from Michelle's grasp and brought it to his forehead.

"He caused the unrest. He provoked the Imps, got everyone agitated. The riots were partly because of him. And now everything's separate, which is maybe what he was going for in the first place, but you're gone. He's not dealing with it well. He feels like he killed you himself."

"Jesus." Cole didn't know how to react, what to think. "Michelle, you have to tell him—"

"I'm not telling him anything," she said firmly, crossing her arms. "The biggest hope you have for your family is to keep them out of it and keep yourself safe. That's the only way things are going to work out. But you're loved, Cole. You should have seen it today. I've never known someone so loved." She met his eyes, and hers were shining. She bit her lip, moving away slightly. He knew what this was all costing her. Her feelings for him were written all over her face. It was killing her to see all of it, to protect him, to love him. Who wouldn't he hurt in the course of all this? "Just stay out of it," she said again. "Do what you've been doing."

Cole nodded, resting his forehead on his knees. She was right. There were no alternatives.

"One more thing," Michelle told him, her voice hesitant. She stood, moving toward the door. "I'll say it quickly and then I'll leave. But first, promise me you won't do anything. You'll stay right here."

"Anything," Cole said, his voice raw. "I promise."

"Davis never got the note," Michelle said. Her face looked ashen. "I didn't get there in time."

"She never got it," he repeated, the question in his voice. But that meant—

"She thinks you're dead, just like everyone else."

Cole leapt to his feet. "No."

"You promised." Michelle's big dark eyes were pleading. "Don't do anything, Cole. Please stay here and keep yourself safe. Please. I'll never forgive myself."

He clenched his fists at his sides. "I'll stay here," he told her, looking her in the eye. She nodded once, and then she was out the door, shutting it gently behind her.

It was the first time Cole had ever lied to her.

If Davis thought he was dead, then there was no telling what she was feeling. He thought about Davis mourning him and he felt sick over the lie. And then he wondered if she would move on. He was suddenly seized with urgency—he had to get to her. He had to tell her the truth.

DAVIS

THREE MONTHS LATER

Davis dug her toes into the cold sand, stretching her calf muscles. Next to her, Mercer plopped down on his back, stretching prone across the shore in the blue predawn light. From this angle he looked like a blissed-out surfer. If it weren't for his TOR-regulation shorts and a white T-shirt, they could've been a couple of kids on the beach, just relaxing.

Ever since they'd initially discussed it in the medical facility, they'd captured moments here and there after dining hall cleanup and before lights-out to sneak off to the beach to brainstorm details.

But today they sat quietly. She turned back to the water and sucked in a breath as the first rays of light peeked over the horizon, illuminating the seemingly endless expanse of water in front of them. The sky had transitioned from hazy blue to a startling orange in seconds. This was the perfect way to start the day—a glimmer of raw, unfiltered beauty to make the rest of the island seem a little friendlier. It never got old.

"It's so beautiful," she told him. "When I'm out here, I almost feel normal again."

Watching the sun rise on the shore each morning had become her routine with Mercer, who was the closest thing she had to a friend at TOR-N, other than another female patient, Seraphina, a woman in her midtwenties with whom Davis now shared a room. Seraphina had been sent to TOR-N by her own husband, and now occupied the bed that had been assigned to Margaret while she was still alive.

"There was never a 'normal.'" His blond hair was thick and tousled, and it added to the scene: a general disposition of careless ease. "Unless you count a DirecTalk attached to your face as 'normal.'"

"At least you could connect with people," Davis said, frowning. "I haven't talked to my family or friends in forever."

"You'll see them soon," he said with a casual wave of his hand. He propped himself on his elbows and looked at her intensely. It was unnerving. She had to look away, into the horizon.

"How much longer do you think we'll be here?" she asked. "How long until we can leave, like we talked about? I feel well enough to go home, but . . ."

"But we're still contagious." Mercer's jaw flexed.

"What if we're always carriers?" Davis asked quietly. It was her greatest fear, but she'd never voiced it until now.

"Then we do it anyway. We escape, just like we talked about. We're both stronger now."

It was true. When she first got here, Davis could barely make the walk to the shore without coughing or having to stop. And she was so sad all the time. About her mother's disappearance and the futility of ever finding her. About everyone she left back home. About Cole . . .

"The doctors are better in Durham, anyway. I've told you this. It's part of the research triangle: everything that comes out of there is ten years ahead of the rest of New Atlantic. Even if I'm still contagious, they'll know what to do about it there."

It sounded like faulty logic. It worried her.

"Why did you come here instead of getting treatment there?" she asked. It was something she'd been too afraid to ask before.

"Durham doesn't allow Neithers," Mercer said, his voice bitter. "It wasn't an option for me. Once I was identified as a Neither, there was nothing my family could do. But if I manage to sneak back into the city—if their records show I'm here and not there—I might be able to find something that could help us. I have friends whose parents are world-famous scientists." At this, he trailed off, reddening slightly. "If you come with me, that is."

"I want to go," she said. "If there's a chance they can help us faster than we're being helped here, then I'd come with you. But I need to know I'm not contagious first. I won't leave here thinking I might infect someone else."

"I don't know if I can wait," he told her, sitting up and resting his forearms on his knees. He gazed out at the water, his relaxed demeanor suddenly tense and his brow furrowed.

She paused, letting this sink in. She knew he badly wanted to go back, that he felt nothing could ever compare to his old life. In that way, he was at a disadvantage. She'd seen more and therefore had adjusted better. She knew being a Prior wasn't as perfect as everyone thought. It would hit her hard if he went along without her—if he took away the one chance she had at fixing this mess. If they couldn't find a cure here, at TOR-N, maybe Durham was their only hope.

"Would it be hard for you?" Davis asked, changing the subject. She knew it was touchy, but she and Mercer were always candid with each other. She liked that about their friendship: nothing was hidden. "Going back to Durham . . . but having things be different than they were before?"

"You mean having everyone know why I left. That I'm a Neither."

"I didn't know I was different until just a few months ago," Davis told him. "I don't know how I would have felt if I'd known most of my life."

"I'm not *so* different," Mercer pointed out. "I mean, *neither* are you. . . ."

"Ha-ha," Davis said dryly. It was a bad pun he'd used every day for weeks.

"I'm just saying, the fact that you didn't know means something. It means you're way more Prior than Imp. You look nothing like an Imp. Plus, you're stronger and more developed than Imps."

"Gens," she corrected.

"Same thing. Gens are different from us. They're in a whole other class."

Davis remained silent. She loved her rapport with Mercer, but she'd heard him go off on this tangent before. It seemed really important to him to separate himself from Gens. She got it. She really did. She might have felt that way once, too. But not since knowing Cole.

That, however, was impossible to explain. She still hadn't told Mercer the details of what had led her to TOR-N.

Mercer's digital, facility-issued alarm rang, interrupting her thoughts. "Off," he ordered the metal dog tag hanging from his neck.

Davis pulled herself to her feet. "Time for my favorite part of the week," she said, making a face. She had an appointment with Dr. Grady.

"If he does anything shady, you let me know. I'll give him a real piece of my mind," Mercer told her as he made an exaggerated show of flexing his arms.

Davis laughed, then abruptly stopped. It was still strange, whenever she caught herself able to laugh. It caused a tumult of other sensations—some joyous and some incredibly painful—that she couldn't quite name.

As they walked back toward the treatment center, Davis looked reluctantly over her shoulder at the landscape that was disappearing behind her. The sun was high in the sky by now, and the foliage on the island was in full bloom. When she looked back like this, she could almost forget. It was when she looked forward—back to the path that led to the women's compound—that her stomach dropped. The island's natural landscape gave way to grim cement buildings, spare and dirtied from the dust that blew around the island. Worse, when she left the protective expanse of trees that separated the facility from the shore, her nose was accosted by a familiar, rank odor. It was the kind of smell that no disinfectant could conceal. It was the kind that sank into your hair, your skin, your nostrils—returning there from someone else's hair, skin, nostrils, like the remnants of one human were desperate to find another human to cling to. Davis knew she'd never get used to it; she didn't want to, because that would mean giving in.

"Your vitals are in a healthy range," Dr. Grady told her a few moments later, as she sat shivering on his operating table. Only a thin piece of paper separated her body from the chrome surface, and the air-conditioning was on full blast—likely to ward off the smell of decay. "Certainly not optimal yet, but you're getting there. A marked improvement from last month. Your natural antibodies are fighting the disease. I'd like to begin monitoring you weekly, with your consent." He winked, then removed his vitals reader from his neck and turned toward her chart, making a few notes on his tablet.

Davis shuddered. He'd winked, she knew, because her consent didn't matter. While she was at TOR-N, she was a ward of the state. Consent was a luxury she didn't have, she thought, staring out the window of the examination room. A sealed vehicle marked with a black cross wheeled past, taking a right turn down the tree-lined path toward the sandy coast: another pile of dead bodies to be incinerated. She felt herself shudder at the sight of it. She always did.

"Any questions?" Dr. Grady asked, tapping his finger against the tablet keyboard. A wisp of his carefully groomed sandy brown hair dropped in front of his eyes, and he pushed it back with his left hand. It wasn't the first time Davis had noted his barren ring finger. Dr. Grady was handsome . . . for an old guy. He was tall and in shape, with wavy, light brown hair. He had a few wrinkles in his forehead and near his eyes, but Davis was sure he'd been attractive back in the day, as weird as that was to think about. The only reason she *did* think about it was because it was so weird for someone like him to be drawn to a place like TOR-N. It was such a lonely, isolating life. Ferries only crossed to the mainland twice per day, and even then only to order supplies. Most staff lived on-site. The gray, ivy-covered forms of the research facilities and dormitories rose up from dark, ominous forests around them, and the sick and dead were everywhere.

In short, it wasn't exactly the kind of place where she wanted to spend *her* forties. If she made it that long.

"Not that I can think of," Davis started. "Well . . . ," She paused, uncertain whether to mention the latest. She couldn't tell if it was in her best interest or not to be getting better. "I can tell I'm building some of my muscle tone back," she mentioned. "I'm just wondering how long until—" Dr. Grady held up one hand to silence her.

"Davis," he said in a soft voice, placing one tanned hand on her arm. "We've talked about this. Be grateful for what you have. It's unlikely you'll ever be back in the shape you were." He winked again. "But you're still looking pretty good, in my book. We're keeping a close eye on you."

Davis's heart sank. She moved away, gathering her tablet. "Unlike the others," she mumbled. She'd seen so many people die by now that it was practically rote. In the three months she'd spent at TOR-N, she must have seen hundreds of bodies.

"Davis," Dr. Grady said again, his eyes widening in concern. "Are you doing okay here at TOR-N? Are you thriving?" Before she could answer, he moved his hand to her cheek. "So beautiful," he said, gazing at her. "Your eyes . . ." His voice was tremulous.

"What?" Davis froze, reacting in confusion. Dr. Grady was bending closer. Did he see something in her eyes? Some awful symptom? She didn't figure out what was really happening until it was too late. Dr. Grady brushed his lips against hers. Davis jerked back as if she'd been burned.

"What are you doing?" she gasped. "I have Narxis!"

"It's okay," he assured her, his voice throaty. "You're no longer contagious. You haven't been for weeks now."

"What?"

At first she thought she'd misheard him, but when he went for it again, repeating himself, it was all she could do to contain her ecstasy. If she wasn't contagious, maybe Mercer wasn't contagious. If they weren't contagious, they could leave.

She pushed Dr. Grady back with one hand, hard, and his face darkened.

"If I'm not contagious," she said to him, her voice cold, "I can go home. Right?"

"That's impossible," Dr. Grady told her stiffly, turning his back. "You still need professional supervision. We have more tests to run. You could regress. Your symptoms could reappear at any time. They can't offer you what we can offer you here. You'll need to stay at least several more months. In fact, your father mandated it." He was speaking quickly, stumbling over his words. He looked nervous.

Davis looked at his gold watch, which offered a startling contrast against the white of his medical jacket, and she knew. Mercer had been right. They were being held there not out of concern for their health but for their parents' money.

Seraphina knocked on the door to the examination room, a moment too late. They had a deal to bust in on each other's appointments if they didn't end within twenty minutes. They had each other's backs; no one wanted to be alone with Dr. Grady for too long. Seraphina ought to have come sooner, but her lapse had given Davis this important gift.

"'Scuse me," Seraphina called, poking her blond head into the room. "Davis is needed at the canteen. It's her week for dishes."

"No problem," Dr. Grady said, eyeing Seraphina. "I'll see you tomorrow, Sera."

"Seraphina," she said in a cold tone, and Davis stifled a smile. The woman had no patience for Dr. Grady's attentions.

"See you next week, Davis," Dr. Grady called after her, as she moved from the room.

"See you next week." Her voice sounded flat, even to her.

"God," Seraphina said. "He's such a creep. What'd he do this time? Details."

"Nothing too weird," Davis replied, her palms sweating at the lie. She and Seraphina had bonded primarily over the fact that they were both Neithers, but other than that, they didn't have a lot in common. She still didn't feel all that comfortable opening up. Especially not over a secret this huge. Seraphina had never even heard of Cole. Davis couldn't imagine how she'd react if she knew Davis was contemplating escape. She was a good girl—had faith in the system, played by the rules. She was a little timid, too. She trusted her treatment, mostly because she had to. The terror in her eyes every time Davis mentioned an alternative to the island was evident. She took joy in the small things, like the screening room that had been set up for the entertainment of the sick patients and that was still intact. She almost seemed to enjoy the sense of safety the island provided—there, she wasn't judged. She felt she was protected. If her only form of entertainment was interaction with other patients and a pseudo movie theater, so be it—that was her attitude. The two didn't connect on this point; Davis was convinced there was something better out there that could cure them and release them to their former, much richer lives. She would never give up on getting out.

Still, it was nice to have an ally. "Just, you know. The usual looks," she said in response to Seraphina's question.

"Such a letch." She rolled her eyes. "Wanna go to the screening room or hang out in my dorm room or something?"

"What about the dishes?"

"Davis. Please. Your naïveté is losing its charm."

"I'm actually going to go lie down inside," Davis lied. "Let's catch up at dinner."

"Okay. Wonder what it'll be?" she joked. It was almost always protein shakes, vitamin shakes, and—very rarely—actual milkshakes, along with the very occasional produce. Davis had nearly forgotten what it felt like to chew. Seraphina waved and walked off in the direction of her dorm. She was still a little weak, and as a result she hadn't earned enough merit points—amassed by cooking and chores. Merit points and burgeoning strength gave the patients more freedom to explore the grounds.

"Thanks for the save," Davis called after her, and the other girl smiled in response. Seraphina often acted like she wanted to enjoy the "resort" she pretended TOR-N still was. Davis knew it was all just a big game that helped her cope, but it seemed like, at some point, Sera had started believing the game. And maybe it was better that way. No one knew how long they'd be at TOR-N. They didn't know if they'd die there.

Davis walked down a narrow dirt trail in the opposite direction from where Sera had gone, keeping to the innermost side of the forest so no one in the upper clinic could see her. She kept going, jogging now, about half a mile, until she was out of breath from the exertion and excitement. She was getting stronger; she could feel it. All of a sudden, the world looked brighter and more hopeful. She *liked* pushing herself, feeling the ache in her muscles after a day of exertion. The rush she felt as she accomplished little things—like running a full mile straight—was unlike any physical joy she'd ever experienced before. There was something about succeeding when you were down that offered an incredible boost. She'd never *been* down, not until she got Narxis. She'd always been ahead. She'd never known what it was like to truly crave something and work for it, knowing the odds were stacked against you. She wondered if it was how Cole had felt. The thought made her heart surge with admiration.

She was tired of lying in bed, of "resting up" and obeying doctor's orders. She'd started sneaking out during the late evenings—when the doctors and staff turned in their badges—about a week ago. Since then, she'd gotten bolder, sneaking out every chance she got. It was how she'd found the laboratory.

She moved faster, knowing she was closing in on the clearing.

When she was moving like this, with the smells of the tropical forest and the damp soil sticking to her shoes and the green blurring past her, it was almost possible to see this place the way Seraphina tried to. It was almost possible to feel free. Then, heart pounding, she broke through the trees into the clearing. This was how she'd found it last time: running, delirious with the feeling of freedom and returning strength. She'd literally burst upon the abandoned building and into the patch of overgrown grass and weeds, totally by accident.

The structure was ancient, crumbling. It didn't look like it had ever belonged to the TOR-N program. Maybe it had been devoted to the research on some other disease the government had covered up—who knew? Or maybe it was left over from the golden days, the days before genetic mutation. Its crumbling cement surface and cracked windows spoke of neglect and a million hidden histories. It gave Davis chills every time she saw it.

At first, she'd been afraid to go inside. She'd feared it would crumble in on her, or that she'd catch some other, even worse disease by exposing herself to its musty air. But then curiosity had seized her and she'd first peeked into the windows and later ventured through the door—its bolt had snapped easily, practically rusted through. And then she'd seen the space.

To someone else, maybe it would have seemed like a surgical wasteland: rotting mattresses atop rusty cots, old metal instruments discarded and half covered in dust and cobwebs. But to Davis, it was a studio.

It had taken her several hours—snatched here and there between appointments and lights-out and mealtimes—but she'd managed to sneak away a broom and use it to clear the place of most of its dust and cobwebs. Then she'd moved the operating tables against one wall and shifted the rest of the clutter to a series of built-in shelving units . . . and she'd danced.

She'd been dancing ever since, every chance she got. When she did, she felt light and airy, even though she knew she was only a shadow of what she used to be, physically. The way she felt, though, running through her old warm-ups—it was the kind of happiness a starving child might have felt at the sight of his first warm meal. It was a joy that made her feel like she was flying, even though her muscles were limited, her body softer. Davis could do it all day, every day. But she made herself stop after only twenty minutes each time. Twenty minutes was the perfect amount of time, to not arouse suspicion. Anything more would be dangerous, and the thought of this little freedom being stolen away from her was enough to leave Davis breathless.

Now she opened the creaking door and smiled. Light filtered into the room through the panes that she'd wiped clean with an old kitchen rag. She stripped off her regulation booties and placed her bare feet against the floor, standing and flexing her toes and calf muscles. It was hard, leaping around on cement without ballet slippers. It hurt a lot. But she barely noticed the pain or the subsequent bruising.

Davis hummed a little, some basic Mahler, as she began her warm-up. She started with the basic positions: *écarté*, *effacé*. She did this for a few minutes—an abbreviated version of a warm-up—until she felt her time waning and couldn't stand it any longer. She moved right into a bourrée, then a *déboule*, her body spinning so fast she felt like she was flying. Her movements felt soft and free and joyful, despite the harsh surface of the floor impacting her bare feet. She was about to move into an entrechat, when she heard it: the unmistakable sound of footsteps crunching through the underbrush outside.

Davis stopped so fast she nearly toppled over, her heart pounding. The footsteps drew nearer to the door. She scanned the room but there was no other way out, short of the ancient, jagged windows. Seeing a broken test tube, she grabbed it, hoping its broken edges would act as defense if it came to that. She dropped beneath one of the surgical tables, her pulse beating faster than it should have after a simple workout. She touched her face and felt its dampness. She was flushed, nervous. She closed her eyes and waited, trying to keep her breath as silent as possible. Then the door opened and a figure stepped through. Davis leapt out from under the table, letting loose a high-pitched shriek, ready to hurl the beaker at the intruder.

"Holy crap," the figure shouted. "Wait a second!"

Davis lowered her arm, her whole body trembling. It was just Mercer.

"Don't do that!" she yelled, swatting him playfully as he laughed. "Jesus. You scared the crap out of me."

"You're just an easy target," Mercer teased. Davis couldn't help grinning up at him.

"A new shipment's arriving tomorrow," he told her now, grinning wide. "Are you ready?" He said it every week. And every week, she told him it was impossible. They had to wait until they weren't contagious. And now she wasn't.

"I was born ready," she told him, hands on her hips. "This was my plan, after all."

She laughed as his face went white.

"Wait—you're serious?" He was so used to her telling him no.

"Mercer," she told him, running to him and wrapping her arms around his neck. "I'm not contagious anymore. If I'm not, surely you're not, either. Our health has improved at the same rate. They give both of us free rein at the facility. He said I haven't been contagious for weeks. Let's do this. I'm ready." She pulled back and walked over to the air vent in the corner of the room and pulled out the map they'd been crafting for weeks.

"Everything's set," Mercer said, eyeing the map. "It's foolproof."

"Is it?" Davis asked, standing up to stretch her legs. She knew from experience the dangers of assuming anything was foolproof. She moved across the tiny room, doing a series of stretches, and finally, a running leap. When she landed, Mercer was in front of her; he lifted her up, using the momentum of her leap to hold her over his head briefly. She giggled and squirmed out of his grasp.

"Looks like you've got some ballerina in you," she said to Mercer, laughing. He smiled, but it was solemn.

"You look beautiful when you dance," he told her. "You're perfect."

Davis felt the full weight of the word, and it was like a cloud descending over them, illuminating instead of obscuring her current physical state—weakened from Narxis, a shell of what she used to be.

"People like us can never be 'perfect,'" she told him, unable to keep the bitterness from her voice. They were both Neithers. It was the one thing he should understand. *Perfect* was the one word he should have avoided.

"You know what I meant," he told her. "You're perfect to me."

Davis smiled, turning away awkwardly. She knew he was waiting for a response, but she didn't know what to give him. Sometimes when he made those comments . . . it was like he was pushing for something. But she was still dealing with Cole's death and trying to shake the feeling of inadequacy she had only just begun to grow used to. She couldn't consider it. She wanted his friendship, that was all. At least for right now.

There was so much else to think about. She still couldn't believe there were so many Neithers out there. The fact that Priors and Imps had relationships often enough for an entire population of Neithers to exist blew her mind. It also gave her hope for a future in which her romance with Cole wouldn't have been doomed.

The thought of Cole caused her heart to quake.

But she had her family to think of now. Her father and Fia and Vera to be strong for.

"Let's go over the maps once more," she suggested. Mercer nodded, and they pored over the maps for the millionth time, firming up their plan. Davis would escape, and when she did, she'd be prepared. She'd bring Dr. Hassman and the Durham scientists as much information about the disease as she could gather. She couldn't save Cole. But while there was hope of helping the others she loved, she'd never stop trying.

COLE

There was a loud explosion outside, and Cole startled, nearly dropping the portable radio he'd been holding. It came again—and this time it sounded like a series of guns firing. Were the Slants under attack? Cole's entire body tensed. When the third round of firing went off—this time much closer—he dashed out of his hideout before he could second-guess himself. Seeing a crowd amassing on the gravel path leading from Michelle's father's general store to the housing compounds, he ducked his head and stepped into a narrow alleyway between buildings. He felt suddenly terrified, exposed. The explosions fired again, and around him people gasped. There wasn't fear in their voices, though. No one screamed and ran as they might have if they really were under attack.

Finally, Cole got the courage to lift his head, exposing his face to the sky. There, above him, was a giant blimp. It was apparently the source of the sounds, which seemed designed to get their attention. But what got Cole's attention were the gigantic words emblazoned across the fluttering banner it heralded. FIFTIETH ANNUAL OLYMPIADS, it read in neon green lettering. FOR THE FIRST TIME IN HISTORY, GEN COMPETITORS WELCOME!

The crowd around him murmured, their voices rising in pitch. Gens had never been welcome in the Olympiads, and frankly, it seemed silly to think of Gens competing against Priors, who were engineered for peak performance.

Still. Hope bloomed inside of him. If he could compete in the Olympiads—and win—his world might open up again. Once again, a different future—far away from Columbus, maybe with Davis— would be possible.

Except it was impossible for a dead man to compete.

He waited for the blimp to recede and the crowds to disperse before moving out of the alley and ducking back into his hideout. His thoughts were swirling. He was so distracted that he nearly missed the rattling sound of the door opening a few minutes later.

He whirled, panic-stricken, certain he'd been caught. But it was only Worsley, holding a bag of something delicious-smelling. Cole had been famished a few hours ago, but now there was only one thing on his mind.

"What do you know about the Olympiads?" he asked.

"You saw." Disapproval flashed through Worsley's eyes. "You risked getting caught."

"I wasn't thinking," Cole said. "I thought we were under attack. What was I supposed to do, stay here and die? But, Tom, is it true?"

Worsley leaned toward Cole, his face serious. "It's true. The city is reinstating the Olympiads. But this time, Gens can compete. It's some publicity stunt," Worsley added, but Cole was already sitting straighter.

"Compete? Compete how? In which events?"

"It's just their way of boosting morale after the Narxis outbreak," Worsley told him. "You choose your individual event. If you win, you compete in the triathlon. The winner of the triathlon wins the whole thing. The prizes are huge."

"Money?"

Thomas nodded. "More money than FEUDS. More than you can imagine."

Cole was at his feet before he realized what had happened. He fought a wave of dizziness that overcame him briefly. He'd been inside for too long. He should have been outside, training. Worsley saw him falter.

"You'll have to train again," he said.

"I'll be able to travel," Cole whispered. "I'll be able to go to the Everglades."

"Cole," Worsley cautioned. "We don't even know if she's still alive."

"I need to see for myself," Cole said. "And my mother . . ."

"I saw her yesterday," Worsley said. "She's okay."

They both knew "okay" was a stretch. No longer able to pay for her tiny house, she'd been living in a home for destitutes along the far reaches of the Slants, not far from where dead bodies were still being discarded daily by Priors. Setting his mom up somewhere comfortable—where she'd never have to work or worry again—had been Cole's dream for as long as he could remember.

"It won't take me long to get back in shape," Cole told Worsley confidently. "Boxing has a lot to do with muscle memory. When's the competition? A couple of weeks at the gym, yeah—and food.

Protein, if you can get it. It won't take me long to get strong again, like I was."

Worsley was shaking his head. "Boxing isn't one of the events," he said. "You'll have to pick something new. I wasn't even going to tell you. I didn't want to get your hopes up. You'll have to train in a new sport, disguise your DNA . . . disguise your appearance somehow. You're notorious, even if everyone thinks you're dead. Once they see you, they'll know we faked the whole thing at the morgue. It's next to impossible to pull off, you sneaking into the competition."

"We've got to try," Cole told him. "I'll try anything. What can we do? Can we alter my DNA somehow? Is there some way to—"

"Cole. I can't do much. I need to finish my work on Narxis. I can't put that in jeopardy."

Cole took a breath, nodding. Anything he could accomplish by winning the Olympiads would be undermined if Worsley's work on developing the vaccine were interrupted.

"We'll think of some way to get you in," Worsley assured him, getting to his feet. "I need to get back to the lab. But there's this guy, Braddock. You should talk to him."

"Braddock. Why does that sound familiar?"

"He won FEUDS a long time ago. Maybe forty years. But then he went on to coach seven FEUDS champions and even two Olympiads champions before he disappeared. People say something happened with one of the Prior families—one of the kids he was coaching. It was amazing, being hired to train Priors. But after the second Olympiads champion, he was gone."

Cole raised an eyebrow.

"Not actually disappeared," Worsley corrected. "He's just off the circuit. He's kind of a hermit now. Keeps to himself. Lives in the woods. He's the only guy I can think of who would know exactly how to train you. He's seen both competitions, knows the drill. He's the best of the best. But if you go to him, you have to make sure no one sees you. No one can know you're alive, Cole. If somebody sees you sneaking out to Braddock, they'll know exactly what you're thinking of doing. Even if they're on your side, rumors get around."

"Where is he?" Cole asked.

"Past the Slants. In the Open Country. Beyond the old stone house. At least, that's where he was last. I have no idea if he's still there."

"I'll leave tonight," Cole said.

"You'll have to be careful," Worsley warned him. "There's radiation everywhere. It's a wasteland; the reason it's never been developed is because it's not suitable for human life. The soil and water have been tested a million times by Prior developers who want to expand, and it's never been possible. They say the radiation content in the soil would wipe out a population in a matter of months."

"So how does Braddock survive?"

Worsley shrugged. "That, I don't know. Maybe he hasn't. He may not even be there anymore, Cole. Don't get your hopes too high."

Cole opened the paper sack Worsley handed him, as Worsley settled himself atop the cracked blue bucket that Cole used as a makeshift stool. It had been nearly two weeks between Worsley's last visit and now. Cole's supplies—some tins of food along with a case of water—had been diminishing. He'd been about to panic when Worsley showed up that morning. It was a reminder that he couldn't hide forever, and it made him even more eager to cling to what Worsley told him about Braddock.

The smell of meat—chicken, maybe—wafted from the bag. Cole couldn't help himself; he pried open the food from its plastic confines and shoveled as much as he could into his mouth with his bare hands. The flavors of cumin and coriander and orange peel overwhelmed him. After days on end of canned soup and tuna fish, he almost cried at the taste of it.

"Vera's been very cooperative," Worsley commented as Cole ate.

Cole flushed. He couldn't believe he'd neglected to ask about Vera. He'd been so excited over the news about the Olympiads that he hadn't thought of her at all. He felt awful.

"How is she?" he asked. "Is she healthy? Is she in good spirits?"

Worsley unscrewed the top of a bottle of water, his face brightening. "She's nearly five and a half months along, now. The baby will be here before we know it. It's all going well. The fetus is developing just as it should at this stage. I'm hopeful."

"I asked about *Vera*," Cole reminded him sharply. He was shocked by Worsley's callous discussion of the fetus as if it were nothing other than an experiment—though he couldn't deny that the development of the Narxis vaccine was just as important to him as to Worsley, if not more so. Still, Cole felt guilty for thinking first of the cure, and not Vera herself. If Davis were there, she'd only be wondering how her friend was.

"Vera's good," Thomas said, ignoring Cole's tone. "She's strong, healthy. I'm making sure she gets all the right nutrients. She's a little pale from lack of sun exposure. But that can't be helped. She needs to be concealed. If anything—" Worsley cut himself off. "Well. You know how important this baby is."

Cole nodded. "I'm still not exactly sure how the baby is going to help with the vaccine's development," he told him. Now that he was satiated, he felt drowsy, foggy. Stronger, but less sharp.

"The baby needs to be born a Neither," Worsley explained. "Like Davis. It needs a natural resistance to Narxis, because I plan to give it Narxis once it's born."

Cole leapt to his feet. "What?" he said. "Why would you—"

"Relax." Worsley held up a hand. "I'm going to inject the baby with a diluted strain. My hope—no, I'm sure of it—is that the baby will develop a natural immunity, and I'll be able to develop a cure from there. I still have some of Davis's blood," he said, avoiding Cole's eyes. "I took samples when she was in my lab. I'm planning to use her exact strain of Narxis on the baby. I just need to perform a few more tests to figure out whether it needs to be weakened further for the infant's immune system to tolerate it."

"You're sure you know what you're doing?" Cole's voice was quiet. He gripped the sides of the cot where he sat. Something about this didn't sit well with him—the involvement of Davis, the ongoing experiments. . . . He couldn't tell how much of his discomfort was related to mistrust of Worsley's abilities and how much of it came from his need to protect Davis. It was a need that was powerful and innate—it had struck him almost immediately after meeting her and had yet to fade in its intensity. He wondered if it ever would.

Three months had passed since she'd been thrown into quarantine. Cole had felt less helpless when he was in jail. Here, he fought the urge to run every day. Where would he run to? He didn't know how he could possibly get to her at TOR-N, or whether she'd still be alive when he arrived. But sitting here, doing nothing . . . it had been torture.

He'd tried to recall everything he'd learned about New Atlantic geography—train lines, how to get from the Slants to the Everglades, where TOR-N was located. In the end he'd given up, shredding most of his makeshift maps in frustration.

"I should go," Worsley said. "I've been away from Vera for too long already. Cole . . . ," he trailed off, then took a breath. "I don't want to worry that I shouldn't have told you about Braddock. Be careful out there, if you look for him. Don't lose your wits."

Cole nodded, and Worsley stood to leave. Before Worsley could shut the door behind him, though, Cole reached out and pulled him into a hug. "Thank you," he said, clasping Worsley tightly for a brief second, his heart about to explode with hope.

Four hours later, night began to fall. It was dim enough for Cole to pass through the shadows with his head bent low and still look like any other guy, but not so dim that he wouldn't see where he was going as he ventured through the ancient tunnel system below the Slants, once used to store discarded Prior trash.

The tunnels were ventilated, and streaks of white moonlight filtered through gaps in their iron surfaces, illuminating Cole's path. Without the tiny gaps, allowing bursts of fresh air, Cole might have passed out from the odors he was breathing in. He took careful steps around heaps of discarded technology—old handheld computers and dated household appliances. He tried not to think about the toxic substances that had been down there for decades. He would never have taken the tunnels if the trip weren't short—only a quarter mile underground. They were widely known across Columbus for being lethal due to the mixing of various chemicals and wastes. Cole remembered Davis saying it had been a major part of her dad's platform to resolve the issue of toxicity beneath the city.

This is what he was thinking as his ankle caught on something sharp and metal, twisting just enough to cause him to lose balance. His foot landed in several inches of wet sludge, and something shuffled out of it, causing him to jump. Cole wasn't usually skittish. He'd become accustomed to the dark, from his months as a stowaway. But this was a worse, more sinister darkness than anything he'd experienced. He tried not to consider what might have been in that sludge, which oozed into his shoe and slopped under the arch of his foot.

Ten minutes later, he faced the tunnel exit, but it was mostly obstructed by large heaps of glass and rusted metal—old, broken machinery that had been shoved in there as an afterthought and apparently had gotten stuck, fusing to the tunnel walls. Cole swore under his breath. The gap remaining was way too slim for him to squeeze through, and its edges looked more treacherous than barbed wire. There was no way.

He kicked at the pile in frustration, and something in it shifted, sending glass raining down over his shin. Still, it was a hopeful sign—the pile wasn't as heavy as he initially thought. He kicked again and realized his mistake too late: a piece of metal punctured the bottom of his shoe, wedging itself firmly in its sole like a knife. The pile shuddered but didn't give. He tried to grip the scrap in his shoe and pull, but it was no use—it was so sharp that to tug at it would risk slicing his hand. Cole racked his brain, then pulled off his sweatshirt and wrapped it around his palm, tugging the metal. When he finally removed the embedded shard, his sweatshirt was in tatters and the sole of his shoe was so mangled that he could see his sock through the bottom. It wouldn't offer much in the way of protection.

Cole took a breath, delivering a sharp kick to a different portion of the mess. This time a metal rod tumbled from it and everything in the pile shifted a few inches lower. Cole seized the rod and jammed it against the pile repeatedly, until he was breathless and sweating and his muscles ached.

Finally, the gap was wide enough for him to push through, if he was careful.

He wrapped his sweatshirt around his palms again, lifting his body gingerly through in an awkward dance. He felt his shorts catch and tear, and he gritted his teeth against the pain of glass against his rib cage. Finally, he was out. He examined himself. He was covered in scratches—none very deep, but any exposure to the filthy metal presented a risk of infection. Still, he was out, free, and breathing crystal clear air with the beautiful night sky opening over him in the way he'd always loved . . . it reminded him of Davis.

Worsley had told him to walk toward a large vaulted campaign ad touting the Olympiads. The ad had been left up from the last election, when Parson Abel was still running for reelection. It was no longer illuminated, and some of the megawatt bulbs, designed to rise high over the city, were cracked, making the whole thing look like a relic from a ghost town. Still, Cole walked more than two miles until he reached the base of the sign, then followed a narrow gravel path downhill toward the tree line.

He walked for an hour, maybe more, following the landmarks Worsley had given him—some so vague they could easily have been misinterpreted: a junkyard here, a broken footbridge there. He was just becoming certain he'd made a wrong turn, when he saw the barn. It was unmistakably the barn Worsley had described: two stories high with five large windows, flanked by willow trees. To the right of the barn was a tiny shack, much like the one Cole used to share with his brother.

Cole took a deep breath and approached the shack. By then it was late, probably after ten, but Cole couldn't afford to wait until morning. He didn't have that kind of time to lose. He banged twice on the front door and waited. He banged again, harder, to no avail. Finally, Cole walked along the perimeter of the shack until he reached a window that was only partially concealed by a curtain; beyond it shone the faint but unmistakable glow of a lamp.

"Hey!" Cole shouted, banging on the window again. A figure moved inside. Cole squinted and could see that it was an old man, hunched but powerful looking. The man turned halfway around, looking toward Cole, but made no attempt to move. "Let me in," Cole called out, banging again on the window. The old man turned back toward the table, ignoring him entirely.

Cole tried the base of the window frame. It was loose—unlocked. Before he could think about what he was doing, he slipped his fingers beneath the frame and pushed it upward. Cole slid inside, standing to face Braddock, whose lined face was quivering with rage.

"What the hell do you think you're doing, barging into my

home?" Braddock yelled. His face was red and furious, but his eyes were tired. His shoulders were tense, but he didn't rise from behind the table. Cole saw immediately why he didn't rise to fight: the old man was wheelchair-bound. A fighter, unable to defend himself against an intruder. It was a horrible irony, and something in Cole stirred.

"I need your help," Cole said. "I'm not here to cause trouble. I just need to talk to you about the Olympiads."

"Go to hell," Braddock said. "All you Priors come sniffing around here, looking for more ways to win. You already have everything you want. Why can't you just leave me in peace?"

"I'm not a Prior," Cole told him, surprised Braddock wouldn't have seen it right away. At this, Braddock frowned and squinted.

"Then what do you want with the Olympiads?" he wanted to know.

"I need someone to train me," Cole said, struggling to keep the urgency out of his voice. "They're letting Gens in this year. I need a coach who knows the competition."

"I can't help you," Braddock said. "I'm out of the business. You're best off getting out of here. I don't want no trouble. If you're a smart kid, you won't compete. It's all about money. Everyone wants money, money, money. But it only causes problems."

"I'm not in it for money," Cole said, even though it was only half true. "It's a little about money," he corrected. "Just so I can get to someone I care about and help her. It matters so much," he said, breathless, feeling his face heat up.

Braddock twisted his mouth, thinking about something.

Cole held his breath, trying to hold his gaze steady.

Then Braddock's eyes changed again, hardening. "Love," he growled. "You love this girl you're trying to help? Listen to me, kid. Take a look at that." He pointed toward a black vase sitting on the mantel on the opposite end of the tiny room. "That's where love got me. That's what happened to my wife. So beautiful, so kind. And they killed her. Didn't even care we had a kid together. Those bastard Priors killed my wife anyway. I don't want shit to do with those Priors. You're smart you'll get the hell out of here and stay away from their corrupt, rigged contest." He practically spit the last words, shaking a little as he gripped the arms of his seat. "Go," he said again, yelling now.

"I won't go," Cole said. He stood, staring at Braddock, who blinked back at him, his jaw clenched. Cole felt a flutter of breeze against his neck; he'd forgotten about the open window, and he hoped their yelling hadn't drawn attention. But the breeze came from behind him, and the window curtain blew backward. Had the door swung open, or—

Cole turned fast, but not fast enough to prevent the intruder from knocking his feet out from under him and grabbing him in a stranglehold. Cole struggled, choking, his vision blurred. He blinked and it cleared slightly to reveal the face of his attacker . . . a pretty, delicate face. A girl's face.

Cole struggled free and leapt to his feet again, only to find himself facing a tiny girl about his own age, wielding a kitchen knife. She jumped up onto the table, seeming to defy gravity. Her dark hair was long and hung in dreadlocks almost to her waist—it was frizzy, wild, as though she'd never tried to tame it. The girl was fierce. Dark brown eyes seemed to take up half of her face, overshadowing a slender nose and delicate jawline. Her shoulders were narrow but muscular. Cole could see she wasn't a stranger to battle.

"What the hell?" Cole shouted, but instead of an answer, he was met with several plates hurtling through the air. Cole ducked to the side, narrowly dodging them. Next, the girl threw the knife. Cole barely registered it hurtling through the air but he somehow managed to avoid it by an inch. Her aim was impressive—her fury was monstrous.

"Get *out*," she demanded, letting out a bloodcurdling scream.

"Stop," Cole heard from Braddock, as Cole dodged two more plates. A shard of glass scraped his forearm, leaving a sharp sting and a line of blood in its wake. The girl was crazy, a monster. He didn't want to fight her—she was just a girl—but he'd be killed if he didn't do something to defend himself. Cole moved toward her and kicked a table leg, hard, until it broke in half—causing the entire table to collapse. The girl did a backflip off the edge of the table, landing steadily on her feet as silverware and debris crashed around them. She grabbed another knife from a rack on the wall before he could stop her, and turned toward him, wielding it impressively.

"Who are you?" he demanded as she moved closer, backing him toward the wall with her knife. She'd obviously been trained well; could Braddock have trained her himself? He'd never encountered a girl who was any kind of match for him, let alone one who was a real threat.

"She's my daughter," Braddock said, just as the girl uttered her name.

"Damaris. If you don't leave us alone of your own accord," she continued, "I'll *make* you leave." She moved closer, as if to strike—but Cole reached for the mantel, grabbing the black vase that he now knew was an urn. He held it aloft. He knew what the urn contained. He knew she wouldn't dare hurt him while he held it.

"Stop!" she shouted. "What is it you want?"

"I want your father to teach me what he knows," Cole told her.

"No," Braddock broke in. "If you want instruction, Damaris can decide whether *she* wants to take you on. And that's a hell of an offer."

Cole felt his jaw drop open. In his peripheral vision he could see

Braddock waiting, gauging his daughter's response. Braddock didn't speak for her, and she only glared. Damaris whirled, stabbing the knife into the door frame with all the force she seemed to possess; only the handle protruded. In an instant she was next to Cole, claiming the urn from his grasp before he could process what she was doing.

"What's in it for me?" she asked calmly, replacing the urn on the mantel.

"If you're going to train the boy," Braddock said, a hint of a smile forming on his lips, "his first order of business is to make us a new kitchen table."

Cole stared at Braddock, willing him to change his mind. Braddock stared back, unmoved. Cole felt himself relent. If Braddock had trained Damaris, maybe there was something there. And maybe he could eventually change Braddock's mind about training him himself.

"I can do better," Cole told them. "If you train me and I win the Olympiads, I'll split the winnings."

A long silence filled the room. Cole could tell Braddock didn't care about the winnings. But he could also tell that somehow, in the last five minutes, he'd earned at least a little of the man's respect. Damaris looked at her father and he looked back, but he gave no indication of what he was thinking.

"Okay," Damaris said begrudgingly, her teeth gritted. She was obviously just deferring to her father. "I'll train you. But if you're going to be hanging around, you can't call me Damaris. That name belonged to my mother. Just call me Mari."

"Shake on it," Braddock ordered.

Cole wondered if this all amused Braddock. He nodded anyway, and reached forward to take Mari's hand, which, despite her stature, felt calloused and strong. "Done," he said. They shook on it, and

Cole tried not to fear that being trained by second best could doom not only himself but also Davis. *No*, no matter how non-ideal the situation, no matter how frustrating, he had to believe it was getting him closer to Davis every day, closer to raising the money he needed to go and save her.

I'm coming for you, Davis, he thought.

DAVIS

Davis had only one simple task. Mercer was doing the heavy lifting determining the schedule on which the barges left the island, plotting their route to Durham, and stockpiling supplies for the journey. Davis only had to steal some chloroform.

Easy.

"We're ready," Mercer told her, adding a tin containing only a few hard, tasteless biscuits—the kind they were fed with their tea every day—to the pile in the corner of the abandoned lab. "We have enough food to last us a week. The barges leave the island every other Friday to bring supplies and take away the bodies." Davis tried not to flinch at this; she still hadn't gotten used to the smell of decay or the sight of the dead, their purpled limbs splaying from under tarps as they were wheeled away each week. The bodies were taken to a smaller island to be burned—they all knew that. They all wondered which one of them would be next, obsessively watched the column of smoke that rose from its distant green landscape each week. "It's leaving again in just a few hours," Mercer reminded her. "All we need is the chloroform. We can do it today, or we can wait another two weeks."

"I have an appointment with Dr. Grady," Davis said, trying to look confident. "In a half hour." She'd scheduled it for nine a.m. so they'd have ample time to carry out their plans. She'd been afraid to tell Mercer about the appointment, though. She wasn't sure she was ready, and she didn't want to get his hopes up.

"So today we leave," he said, his eyes glittering. Davis knew he was right—they had to leave right away. Waiting any longer would be torture, and once they set the plan in motion they couldn't afford to linger and risk arousing suspicion.

"Are you sure this is going to work?" she asked, and he nodded.

"It'll work if you pull through." Of course it would. They'd been over it a million times. The only thing they were missing was the chloroform.

Two hours and twenty minutes later, Dr. Grady smiled at Davis and waved her into his office, looking genial. He had a great smile, clear and dazzling, but something in his eyes seemed wolfish. Maybe it was the way he never failed to let them drift over her from head to toe, Davis realized. He was also a little too manicured. She wasn't sure why he needed to wear alligator-skin shoes and a heavy gold watch to treat patients who barely had enough to eat each day. Was he trying to subtly exert control? Did his luxurious accessories make him feel more empowered? Maybe he was the kind of guy who took pleasure from seeing other people suffer. Davis tried hard to stay calm, even though her blood was boiling. She couldn't betray her emotions. Anyway, if she played her cards right, he'd soon be exposed for what he really was. She drew a breath, steeling herself against what she was about to do. If she focused on the outcome— escape—she could get past anything.

"Welcome, Davis," Dr. Grady greeted her. He waved a tanned, meaty hand, ushering her into the room. His workplace was stainless steel and uninviting. It had a peculiar, sterile odor that made Davis's stomach roll from the discomfort it heralded. "Please slip on this gown in place of your shirt," he told her, handing over a thin, gauzy paper strip with ties in the back. "I'll be right back."

Davis slipped off her shirt quickly after he left. More than once he'd come back unannounced before she'd resituated herself, and she had the feeling it was never unintentional. Sure enough, she'd just begun to tie the paper gown together when he knocked twice and popped back in without waiting to hear her reply.

"Oh!" he said. "Did I surprise you?"

Davis forced herself to smile and shake her head. "I'm all set."

He moved into the examination, leaning over her as he listened to her heartbeat through her back. His bare hands pressed against the skin of her back, and his face was so close as he squinted over his digital reader that Davis could feel his breath along her neck. "Breathe in," he instructed, and she drew a breath. "Wonderful, Davis." He moved to another spot, allowing the fingers of his nonworking hand to linger along her spine. Davis shuddered, unable to mask her disgust as she spotted another expensive accessory—a hefty leather notebook embossed with his initials—in his jacket pocket.

"Your heart rate is accelerating," Dr. Grady informed her. "Are you anxious?"

"I'm always a little nervous here," she told him. *Escape. Escape.*

Escape. She repeated the words internally, focusing on the task ahead of her.

"Why is that?" Dr. Grady shifted around in front of her so he was facing her. His lab coat hung open, draping toward her. Davis could see the digital keychain he always kept in the left-hand pocket. She knew it would give the holder access to the medical supply room. She couldn't reach it, not yet. He seemed merely amused, not completely distracted.

He pressed the digital pulse reader against her neck. Then he brought it low on her chest, just above her rib cage, and examined its small black monitor. Davis looked down at his hand, at the line graph on the little device, which was beeping in red as it measured her vitals.

"I just hope I'm improving," she began, willing the words past the tightness in her throat. "I'm always afraid of having a relapse. And I've never really been around doctors before," she told him. "Not very often, back in Columbus. There was never any reason to be. I find it so . . ." She paused. She wasn't sure how far she could go without seeming suspicious. "Impressive," she finished, "that you're devoting your whole life to helping other people. You must be so brilliant."

Dr. Grady smiled, looking pleased. He was ridiculously susceptible to flattery, Davis realized. His ego was completely overblown. She racked her brain for other ways to flatter him, focusing on his jacket, which hung open and within easy reach. She merely had to slip her hand in without him noticing. She had to do it. It was her only chance. He wouldn't even see her; he was too busy focusing on her face.

"I admire a person so dedicated to his work," Davis said, aware that she was grasping. "You should win an award. A Nobel, maybe. Not many people can do what you do." Her words sounded saccharine, but he smiled down at her, soaking in her praise. Davis leaned in just a fraction of an inch, just enough to ensure that he wouldn't look away from her face, to what she was doing below. She tugged on his jacket playfully with one hand to mask the motion of the other in his pocket.

"Oh, I only do what I can," he said with false modesty. "I'm only a cog in the machine."

"You keep everything running here," she said as she closed her fingers around the digital key and folded it into her sweating palm. Dr. Grady grinned. She was searching her brain for something else to say, or some way to get out of there, when the digital reader beeped loudly. Davis seized the moment, jumping as though she'd been startled and kicking Dr. Grady hard in the shin.

"Shit," Dr. Grady gasped, moving backward.

"I'm so sorry!" she said. "I didn't mean to. The beep, it—"

"It's fine." But the look he gave her was suspicious.

"Can I . . ."

"Just sit there," he said. "Don't move. I'm going to get some ice." He exited the room fast, muttering under his breath, and Davis took the opportunity to bury the keychain in the pocket of her loose-fitting regulation green pants. Dr. Grady was back a second later, his tone frosty.

The rest of the examination was far less personal. Davis had taken advantage of his contact the way she'd intended, and her heart rate slowed to normal as she went through a series of vitals tests that involved standing in front of a laser reader and placing her hands on two LED sensors designed to test her reflexes. Finally, she gave a saliva sample, and then she was done.

"You can put on your clothes and see yourself out," he told her, not bothering to mask his displeasure.

When Davis left the room, Dr. Grady was nowhere in sight. She wended her way around the back of the building, taking the route she'd normally take to head back to the main sanatorium where she shared a room with Seraphina and several other women who were far sicker than she. At the last minute, when she was certain she was nowhere in sight of the medical clinic, she ducked left and moved to a path that led through a thicket of trees to a small, outlying building that was used to store medical supplies. She used the digital keychain to trigger the lock, and when the door swung open, she was relieved to find the place dark. She darted in, securing the door behind her, and tried not to think about what would happen if an orderly came in while she was there.

The bottles of chloroform only took a second to spot; everything in the supply room was clearly marked. She grabbed three, just in case, and fled the building before she could second-guess herself. Then she headed toward the water's edge, where Mercer was waiting. They'd agreed on the spot because it was obscured from the rest of the island by thick vegetation. None of the patients ever ventured out there, despite the tropical atmosphere and idyllic view. Anywhere else, the water lapping against the sides of the shore—with dense clusters of trees rising in the background—would have been tranquil. Here it was overshadowed by the low-lying industrial structure where the bodies were kept.

They were meant to be frozen until they were shipped elsewhere. It was the sanitary way. But upkeep on the island tended to falter, as Davis knew from her months there. Things that were meant to be attended to were neglected. So she wasn't surprised that the smell of decay wafted just under the fresh ocean breeze.

"Let me," she said, squaring her shoulders and pushing past Mercer toward the warehouse.

"You have it?" he asked, running after her in an effort to keep up.

She merely nodded. He knew she had it. Something about the island had made Davis tougher. She felt it, and she knew everyone around her felt it, too. Six months ago, she'd never have pushed ahead toward a massive freezer that housed dead bodies. She'd never have been able to imagine such a thing. Now, everything was different. She didn't want to rely on anyone anymore, not when she continued to find within herself reserves of strength she'd never known existed.

"How much time do we have?" she shouted over her shoulder as she used the digital keychain to open the freezer door. The keychain was universal, thankfully. That was one aspect of the plan that had been a wild card.

"Five minutes," Mercer told her. "Maybe ten. You really pushed it."

She looked over her shoulder to glare at him, but he was smiling in a teasing way. Trying to calm her down. "I'm joking," he told her. "You're amazing." She pushed through the door and they both gasped at the stench, much stronger within the confines of the building.

"Good lord." Mercer sounded stricken, and his face was frozen in an expression of horror. Davis looked around her, feeling faint. She'd known a few women from her quarters had passed away in the past two weeks, but this was different. Dozens of bodies were stacked neatly around them, all encased in body bags. More deaths had happened than she'd realized. She hadn't even known there were so many others at TOR-N. She felt Mercer's hand in hers. It was gentle, reassuring.

"We need to find an empty bag," he told her. "We can do this." When she failed to respond right away, he gave her a nudge. "I'll start over there, you start at that end." Davis nodded, willing her feet to move. She walked around the stacks of bodies until she found a locked door. She tried the keychain on it, but it still wouldn't slide open. She was about to panic, when Mercer called out.

"I found them!" He rushed over, holding a large, zippered navy bag. "They were over there." He gestured toward the far corner of the room, which was a little more shadowed than the rest. "Here, you climb in first and I'll climb in after you." She nodded, stepping into the bag. Their plan was risky—they didn't know how many workers would come to load the bodies. She was thinking this as she lay down in the bag, its scratchy vinyl fibers rough against her skin, allowing Mercer to climb in on top of her and zip it behind him.

The weight of his body shattered her.

Davis hadn't felt someone so close to her since Cole. Mercer was heavy on top of her, and present, and warm. His breath was hot on her neck. She felt a physical yearning that she'd thought had died, but it wasn't about Mercer, it was about Cole. She fought back a sob and Mercer grabbed her hand again, his hand rough in hers, mistaking the reason behind her emotion. He traced circles on her palm with this thumb, sending a shiver up her back. His soft hair tickled her forehead, and he rested his cheek against hers. His lips were close, so close to her own. Davis drew back, overcome by a rush of guilt. She thought of Cole: the first time they'd kissed, his palm gentle against her cheek. Cole would want her to fight. He'd want her to help Fia and Vera and everyone else she loved, because he'd never stopped fighting, not up to the minute he'd died.

Then she felt a surge of determination fill her—she had to fight for him, for his memory, the same way he'd sacrificed everything for her, never letting fear overcome him. She'd loved him so much. She still did.

Lying in this body bag was surreal. It was so quiet that all she could hear was their breathing. Lying there, alive and not dead like the others in the room, made her acutely aware of how lucky she was. It was all a matter of chance: if she hadn't been a Neither, she could have wound up in one of these bags under very different circumstances. Like Emilie. And Caitlyn.

And Cole.

She fought against the tears that threatened to overtake her, and Mercer pulled her close, comforting her. She shivered into him, wanting to reject his embrace but needing to accept it—they hadn't accounted for the sharp drop in temperature inside the storage facility, and goose bumps were forming on her exposed arms. They also hadn't thought about how long they'd have to wait. She burrowed closer to Mercer, his soft cotton shirt such a normal source of comfort that for a second she could imagine he was Cole and they were anywhere but here. She snuggled in, trying to generate body heat. Her teeth chattered. He drew her head toward his chest. She was about to say something to him, to explain why she was pulling herself close. Then they heard the footsteps.

Davis heard the door to the storage facility draw open. She reached into her pocket, withdrawing the chloroform and a scrap from an old pillowcase that she'd taken from her bed. She didn't open the chloroform yet. Timing was everything. If she acted too soon, she risked drugging the two of them.

Two sets of footsteps sounded against the cold stone floor: one heavier, and one much lighter and more rapid sounding. But the men weren't taking bodies and hauling them out like they were supposed to. Davis turned to Mercer, the question on her lips, but he silenced her with a finger.

"You got something good?" one of the workers asked, his voice muffled behind the air filtration mask all such workers were required to wear. Mercer knew from observation that the full-body suits and masks offered just enough coverage to guarantee anonymity.

"Gold watch. Could be better." The second man's voice was higher, his speech less languid.

"Shoulda seen the ring I drug off someone last week," the first guy bragged. "I'm hanging onto it awhile, getting a good value on it before I let it go." They moved on, zipping and unzipping the bags.

"They're stealing off the bodies," Davis whispered, horrified. "They're unzipping the bags."

"We'll have to be quick," Mercer told her.

"Did you hear something?" The guy with the deeper voice paused, his footsteps halting a few paces from the stack on which Davis and Mercer rested.

"Nah. Just nerves, man. You're always worried someone's gonna catch us. Like anyone wants to get near this shit." He spoke so fast that Davis had trouble making out his words.

"I've just got this last stack here. You better start hauling 'em out." The man was so close that Davis could catch a whiff of rank, musky body odor.

"Just don't pocket anything. Fifty-fifty split, like we agreed."

"Yeah, I know." Apparently satisfied, the second man bent, his knees creaking, and Davis could hear him beginning to push a cart away. The sound of his footsteps echoed loudly around the room as he retreated.

Davis felt the other man standing over their bag. He was so close she could hear him breathing. If he thought theirs looked lumpier or bigger than the rest, he wasn't giving any indication. Mercer dug his fingertips into her thigh, signaling for her to get ready. She slowly, carefully loosened the top of the bottle.

The man unzipped the bag.

Mercer reached out, grabbing him and knocking off his air filtration mask, as Davis doused the scrap of fabric in chloroform. Mercer and the worker struggled, and for a second, Davis couldn't get her bearings. The man let out a choking cough and his mask clattered to the floor. Then Davis reached for him, closing the rag around his nose and holding it there until his body fell limp to the floor.

"Hurry!" she hissed. Mercer stripped the guy of his uniform, and together they dragged him to the darkened side of the room where Mercer had found the stacks of unused body bags. They pulled him behind the stacks, and Mercer slipped on the man's uniform, zipping it all the way over his head and pulling the air filtration mask tightly over his face. He looked like a stranger. He motioned for her to step back inside the bag, and when she did, he bent low and picked her up, hauling her off to the barge.

A half hour or so later, Davis felt the boat beginning to bob slowly away from the shore. It was an eternity after that when she finally felt the zipper of her bag being pulled slowly down, felt a familiar hand reach for hers.

"I thought something had happened," she breathed.

"I had to wait until it was dark to come," he said, squatting beside her. "The other guys are eating below. We need to go now. There's a lifeboat just over there." He nodded toward the side of the boat, just a few feet from where Davis lay. "That's why I put you here."

"We're so close," she said, her heart accelerating. Mercer nodded, squeezing her palm. He pulled her closer to him. He looked like he wanted to say something; his lips parted, and his eyes glittered in the dark.

"We need to go now," she told him, getting to her feet. Whatever he wanted to say, she wasn't ready for it. Mercer lowered Davis into the lifeboat, grasping her firmly around the waist. She felt the boat rock steadily beneath her feet, felt freedom just inches away. Then Mercer untied the knot that held the lifeboat to the barge and leapt in after her, pushing off into the night.

They watched as the tinier boat separated from the larger vessel. The deck of the bigger boat, loaded with bodies, was otherwise quiet. Lights shone from the lower levels, but no one peered from the windows. If they had, they would have seen nothing, Davis imagined, other than what looked like a piece of bobbing driftwood. The night sky was cloudy, dark. And they were free.

"They'll hear of it soon," Mercer said into the still night air.

"I'm sure they know already," Davis echoed. "Dr. Grady would have looked for his key."

"We'll make it," he said. "We have a head start. They aren't prepared to handle this."

Davis hoped he was right. He had to be right—everyone's lives depended on it. This time, her fingers reached for his first and curled around them, holding tight.

8

COLE

Cole had been toiling for nearly an hour, and he suspected at this point that Mari was just toying with him. But he had no choice, if he wanted to get on Braddock's good side. The tree still barely trembled each time he swung the enormous ax Mari had given him. His muscles burned, and his arms and back ached so much he could hardly heave the ax through the air. Flies and gnats swarmed around him, attracted to his sweat. He'd long since given up on swatting them away. He was drenched, thirsty, and tired. All he wanted in the world was clean water, but water was scarce out here in Open

Country. Cole knew by now that Braddock paid a street kid to bring him an enormous case of water each month. Not many people were desperate enough to make the trek to Open Country, Braddock had told him. But he paid the kid well. Still, they had to be very careful to ration the drinking water. For bathing and cooking, they boiled the contaminated water from the nearby streams. Mari claimed her immune system was invincible, due to the toxins she'd probably absorbed as a kid.

Training, Mari had said. But what the hell kind of training was whacking at a tree all day long? It helped to funnel all his frustrations into that tree—to pretend *the tree* had separated him from Davis; *the tree* had caused the riots that had destroyed so much of the Slants. Instead of absorbing his anger, though, whaling on the tree made him hungry for a fight. He needed a human opponent. And not a girl half his size. The fact that Mari was training him—and not the other way around—was starting to feel like some sort of joke. There was no way he'd be prepared for the Olympiads with a girl in charge of his training.

"How's it coming?" she asked, emerging from the house with a bottle of water.

"Are you sure?" he asked. She raised her eyebrows and took a long swig before offering him some. Cole accepted it gratefully. He knew the water was scarce. Still, he wasn't going to play nice. Not when she was putting him through such pointless torture just because he came from a city she hated. In her mind, he realized, he was almost as bad as the Priors she clearly despised.

"Not going too well, I guess?" She eyed the tree critically. "So maybe you'll fell it by the time the contest happens. Awesome."

"I'm not really sure what this has to do with the Olympiads," Cole told her. "Should I be thinking about competing in the Paul Bunyan division?"

"Ha-ha," Mari said without humor. "But you're so right. This has pretty much nothing to do with the Olympiads."

"What the hell, Mari?" Cole threw the ax on the ground. "So you're wasting my time."

"Correction. It's *my* time *you're* wasting," Mari said. "It's not like I'm getting paid to do this. The tree is for the table you're building to replace the one you broke. Once you're done, we'll talk Olympiads."

"Right," Cole muttered, wiping sweat from his forehead. "Can't wait." His lower back was stiff, and it hurt to twist his torso. His arms felt like dead weights attached to his shoulders. He hadn't eaten in hours. He would have killed for one of his mom's egg salad and green olive sandwiches just then. For a second, he missed his dank, dirty hideout—which had never seemed like anything more than a glorified prison but now was taking on the properties of a sanctuary, in his mind. His tattered cot and the few novels Worsley had brought him beckoned invitingly. Besides, this entire endeavor was pissing him off. It felt like he was achieving nothing, frittering away time.

"What's with the attitude?" Mari wanted to know. "As I recall, you came to us for help."

"Not *you*, plural," Cole corrected. "Your dad. Personally, I don't think I should be taking instructions from someone half my size. Especially someone who's pretty much a hermit." Cole only sort of regretted saying it. Mostly, it felt like a relief.

"So that's what this is about. 'Someone half my size.' You're mad because you're taking orders from a girl. Is that right?"

Cole didn't answer. She'd pretty much hit the nail on the head. But she'd missed one thing: he was also mad because she hated him for no reason. Like he didn't have enough to deal with beyond the latent rage of some girl who barely factored into his life.

"Suit yourself, pawn," Mari said, her face furious. She stomped back into the house, slamming the door behind her.

Pawn? That could only mean one thing. She thought he was some sort of lemming because he lived in Columbus, aka Priorville. Forget the Slants; forget what he'd gone through. And if she knew he was in love with a Prior, well . . .

Cole kicked the tree and swore. Now his toe hurt. His back hurt. His arms were aching. And this whole stupid thing was pointless. He was better off going home, rethinking his strategy, training himself. Screw their table. If she hadn't attacked him, he wouldn't have broken it.

Cole was just past the front door when he heard a cough behind him. He turned to find Braddock on the front porch, sitting in his wheelchair, his arms crossed over his chest, a cigarette dangling from between his lips.

"You're making a mistake," the old man said gruffly.

"This whole thing was a mistake," Cole replied.

"No. With Mari. She might be small, but I trained her from the time she could walk. She knows more about athletics than you possibly could. She's seen the inside of the best training facilities in the country. Gyms were her playgrounds. The girl has lived and breathed FEUDS and Olympiads her whole life. She's seen all the best fighters, Prior and Gen. She's been with me from the beginning. She's sparred with the best. They all loved her, wanted to take her under their wings. She's the best and the smartest. You know why, kid?"

Cole didn't answer.

"I asked you a question. You know why? No? I'll tell you. It's because people like you underestimate her. *That.* That's her secret weapon. You think she's not fit to train you? You should be so lucky. Look around you." The old man stared at him, long and hard. Cole opened his mouth, feeling his neck burn. He'd never felt like more of an asshole. The front yard where he stood was littered with medals and ribbons hanging from tree branches to support the weight of dozens of tiny feeders for birds. Evidence of Braddock's brilliance was all over the place. Clearly, Braddock knew what he was talking about. Cole swallowed hard, wishing he hadn't offended Braddock. He realized he was still hoping that if he played Braddock's game—trained with his daughter—maybe Braddock himself would eventually step in. This wasn't the way to earn his trust.

"I'm sorry," he started, but Braddock waved him off and wheeled back inside, shaking his head.

Cole turned back around to find Mari standing on the lawn, her arms crossed. How long had she been watching?

"So?" She arched an eyebrow and Cole felt his face heat.

"Let's do this," he said. He'd do whatever it took to get on Braddock's good side. "I'll chop that tree into planks if it takes me all night."

She pursed her lips, waiting.

"I'm sorry," Cole told her reluctantly. He knew he had to say it, and if he was honest with himself, it was true. "I was an ass. A complete idiot. I'm really, really sorry. I'm just used to . . ."

"To being the best," she finished. "To not having a girl call all the shots."

Cole swallowed hard. "No. That's not it. Or at least, not all of it. I'm just . . . I have so much riding on this."

Mari was silent, and Cole hesitated, wondering how much he should say. "I'm not used to relinquishing control," he admitted. "I've overseen my own training pretty much my whole life. And now . . . this isn't just a competition to me. I *have* to win. I *have* to be the best."

"Why?"

"Because it's the only way to be with the girl I love," Cole told her. "Davis is sick. She's at a facility called TOR-N. If I have the money to get to her . . . we can finally be together again. She doesn't even know I'm alive right now. I don't know how she's doing. It's torture."

"You're in love with a Prior." Mari's face was expressionless, but Cole knew the significance the revelation held for her.

He rushed on, "And winning means I can maybe get my family away from the Slants—take them somewhere safe and peaceful. My mom's in a home for destitutes right now. She lost her job when the factory she worked at was destroyed in the riots. My brother has dedicated his whole future toward looking after her." At this, he saw a glimmer of understanding in her eyes. Mari had spent her life looking after her father. She understood what that was like.

"Where would you take them?" she asked.

"I don't know. One of the other territories, where conditions are better for Gens. I haven't thought that far ahead. I just know that money opens doors. And right now, we don't have any. We don't even have any hope for having any . . . except this. I'm the only one who can save my family. And it's the only way I can be with Davis again. But I *am* sorry, Mari. You're trying to help—you *are* helping," he said, realizing he meant it. Never had he subjected himself to such a tough workout. Mari knew things he didn't about survival; that was undeniable. He was never angry at Mari, he realized. The whole time he'd been hitting that tree, resenting training with second best, he'd been taking out his feelings of helplessness.

"What's it like?" Mari asked, avoiding his eyes.

"What?" he asked.

"Love," she said simply. "And what are *they* like in person? Priors." She shuddered, like the word was hard to spit out.

"Love is . . . difficult to describe," Cole said. He'd never tried to explain to anyone exactly how he felt about Davis. "It's tenderness and trust and knowing that this is your person, someone who's in your corner all the time and just gets you. And you want to take care of them, too. Protect them from everything bad. Make them happy. It's this feeling where you'd do anything to see them laugh," he told her. "Where their smile is enough to carry you through the day. Their happiness is your happiness. Their stress and fear are yours, too. It's like your soul expands so there's room to carry someone else's, too. It's like having a twin heart. And then there's the rest of it. . . ." He trailed off, embarrassed. He couldn't believe he'd opened up to someone he didn't even like. Someone who hated him for no good reason. Who saw the world in black and white.

"You asked about Priors," he said, changing the subject quickly. "How much have you interacted with them?" Maybe some of her hatred would dissipate if he explained that not all Priors were bad, that most were just products of bad influences. Many couldn't think for themselves beyond what they'd been taught all their lives. But some could. It was they who gave him hope.

Mari shrugged in response to his question. "Not much. When I was little, of course. There are photos of me with Priors, from when my dad trained them. They're so beautiful," she said. "But now I know they're monsters."

"They're not," Cole protested. "Not all of them. They're just people, like we are, and they're misinformed. We're all the same, inside. Sure, they're prettier. And they have genetic enhancements. And maybe some of them are a little shallow and cruel—but that's not innate, that's learned. All of this," he explained, telling her everything he'd learned from loving Davis, "comes from fear and misunderstanding."

Mari grunted, tossing her long, tangled hair over her shoulder. She looked angry. Cole guessed she wasn't used to anyone challenging her own beliefs—which was pretty ironic, given that that very concept factored into her hatred for Priors.

"Are we going to do this or what?" Cole asked, dropping the subject and gesturing toward the tree.

"Forget the tree. You can handle that on your own time. You wanna see what I've got? Let's get straight to the good stuff."

Now Cole let himself smile. Pissing off Mari wasn't going to make things any easier on him, that was for sure. "Challenge accepted," he replied, following her into the stretch of land that extended past the back of the house and on into the forest.

"Do you mind if I ask how you plan to enter the Olympiads? I mean, being 'dead' and all. . . ." Mari trailed off. Was she baiting him? "Training is kind of a waste of everyone's time if you're not able to compete." Cole felt his shoulders tense, but he couldn't deny that her question was valid. Mari had a direct, confident way about her that he wasn't used to, probably because she hadn't been exposed to social norms. Bluntness seemed to be her way of life.

"I haven't figured that part out yet," Cole said, his tone guarded. He wasn't sure she wouldn't use his personal life against him. "But I have someone helping me. It'll work out." He shut his mouth, unwilling to say more. Mari turned sharply at the tone of his voice, meeting his eyes. She nodded once, her expression somber.

"Well, then," she said. "Let's give you the hardest workout of your life."

She wasn't exaggerating. Over the course of two hours, Mari timed Cole with a stopwatch while he ran countless conditionals on a makeshift, roughly surfaced track. It was like she enjoyed watching him suffer. He figured she probably did, and it fueled him even more. After he finished each challenge—discus throwing, long jumps, leaping over makeshift hurdles nearly as high as his shoulders—she shook her head, frowning at the recorded time. Cole pushed himself harder than he'd ever pushed. But after several months in hiding, he was strong from lifting—something he could do within Michelle's hideout—but weak from lack of stamina, given that he hadn't been able to emerge in order to run. His reaction time was also a little slower than it had been when he was in peak physical condition. Finally, Mari motioned him over to a patch of grass and told him to sit down, handing him a water bottle.

"You can't enter with these times," Mari told him. "You're not even close to a Prior median in most of these challenges. You may not even qualify, let alone win."

Cole let the news sink in, fighting back frustration. His entire body was spent. He'd pushed himself as far as he could go. And still he wasn't even close. "I'll keep training," he insisted. "I'll get my speed back, and then—"

Mari shook her head. "Even then, I don't think we have enough time to put you in an advantageous position," she argued. "Priors have the genetic advantage, *and* a lot of them have spent their whole lives training."

"There's got to be another event."

"The rest of the events require equipment. We can't compete with Prior technology. You'd be facing a huge disadvantage, even more so than with gymnastics or track-and-field events."

"So what am I supposed to do?" Cole asked, running a hand through his hair. His shoulders were tense, and it was all he could do not to punch something—anything—to blow off some steam. "You don't understand. This is my only hope. I don't have any other options. Literally everything rides on this." He stopped, flushing. He'd let down his guard. He couldn't stand the brief flash of sympathy that crossed Mari's thin features.

"I'll try to think of something," she told him. "Let's just take a break for a little while, go cool off."

"Right," Cole said. "Where are we going to cool off? It's gotta be ninety degrees out."

"This way." Mari hopped up from the grass. "I haven't shown you all my spots yet." She led Cole into the forest. They stumbled over rocks and underbrush for about a quarter mile, until Cole started to wonder what the hell she had up her sleeve. Then the dense thicket of trees broke and opened to a beautiful, sparkling pond. "Let's do it," Mari said, grinning back at him. Cole hesitated, and Mari rolled her eyes.

"It's fine," she said. "I mean, there's some algae, and I wouldn't recommend drinking it. But it's a natural pond, totally disconnected from the city runoff."

Cole still wasn't sure whether to let down his guard, but the pond was tempting. And she was being almost . . . nice. It was kind of a welcome change after the morning he'd had. Besides, he hadn't been swimming in forever. You couldn't do it in the Slants—swimming in the streams polluted by runoff was strictly forbidden. There were gruesome tales of kids dying or developing disturbing physical symptoms just from touching some of that water.

He watched as Mari stripped down to her tank top and underwear and ran out onto the narrow wooden pier that stretched out onto the pond.

Cole raised his eyebrows. He couldn't imagine anyone else he knew just stripping down like that. For a second he was embarrassed for her. Then he realized: modesty was all a construct, just like everything else. Mari didn't have any social decorum, because she'd probably never had to. In that sense, she was free.

Mari dove in and resurfaced, laughing. "You have to come," she shouted to him. "It feels amazing!" He hesitated. Was it weird to strip down in front of a girl?

It did look amazing. The water sparkled under the sun-filled sky, and he realized he was thinking too much. The promise of icy water washing over his skin was enough to squash any remaining doubts. Cole pulled off his T-shirt, leaving his shorts on, and dove in after her.

The water felt like heaven. It swept away the stress and frustrations of the afternoon. Cole swam deep, close to the reeds that rose up from the depths. He opened his eyes, enjoying the otherworldly, murky feeling of it. He felt anonymous. He felt free. He swam farther. He stayed down, swimming farther still, letting the water drown all his worries.

When he rose to the surface, shaking water out of his hair, the sun was like a spotlight. Outdoor noises—birds chirping, the rush of the water, and the splashing of Mari several feet away—replaced the quiet he'd felt only a second ago. He turned to her, expecting her to yell at him for freaking her out. Instead, her face wore a look of quiet approval.

"I think we've found your event," she yelled across the pond at him. "You have the lungs of a blue whale and you crossed the expanse of the pond in, like, five seconds."

Cole couldn't help grinning, and his heart soared. Under the water, he'd felt more himself—more *alive*—than he had in many months. He suddenly wanted nothing more than to soak up life, relax in the blaze of the afternoon sun. These little pleasures were what gave him hope. He climbed ashore, and Mari followed a few minutes later, bending over and shaking her dreads out like a dog might shake its fur. She plopped down next to him on the banks of the pond. For a moment, he couldn't suppress his longing—not for Mari, but for Davis. Why couldn't it be Davis there with him, enjoying this moment? It was the closest he'd felt to being at peace in a long time, and his heart ached that the wrong girl was there to share it.

"I'd missed that feeling," he said to Mari a moment later, when they were lying on their backs, letting the sun warm them after the chill of the water.

"Which?"

"Just being alive," he told her. "You probably don't know what it's like not to feel free. You have all this land. But I miss my old life. My mom, my brother . . . my best friend, Brent."

"And her," she finished for him. "The girl you miss. The Prior."

"I miss Davis more than anything," he admitted quietly. "But she was different."

Mari's eyes darkened, and Cole knew he'd made a mistake. Her loathing for Priors was too deep-rooted. She'd never understand the depth of his relationship with Davis. How they'd just understood one another, without even having to explain. Mari didn't see Davis as human, though. Cole sort of understood why, but he wished it weren't so easy for her to separate good from bad, Gen from Prior, as if nothing existed in between.

"We should get back," Mari said, her voice bitter. She jutted her chin toward the setting sun, which illuminated the smattering of freckles across her cheeks.

"I'm going to head back into the Slants tonight," Cole mentioned as they stood up. "I need to see Thomas about getting me into the Olympiads. I'll be back in the morning." Truthfully, he thought it was probably better to be away. Maybe it would diminish the tension between them.

"We'll see you tomorrow, then," she told him.

As they walked back along the bank of the pond, Cole caught a familiar, minty smell.

"Peppermint," he realized aloud.

"It's all over the place," Mari told him. "Here." She squatted down near the bank and picked a bunch of the pointed, rough-textured leaves. "It makes great tea."

Cole pocketed it, surprised. An olive branch. He thought immediately of Vera; she'd like it. His mom had made peppermint tea when he was a kid. She'd poured it into a thermos for herself but had always given him a sip first—she said it kept her alert all day at work. The smell cleared his head, giving him energy for the half-hour journey awaiting him.

The trek back to the Slants was much easier this time around, because Mari had shown him a new route.

"You took the *tunnels?*" she'd scoffed when he'd detailed his treacherous journey out there. "Why not just dive into raw sewage next time?" Then she went on to outline a far more direct—and somewhat less treacherous—route, through a mile of woods and over a rickety twenty-foot bridge cobbled together from wooden beams that were half rotted. In ancient times the bridge had functioned as an overpass for horses and buggies. Now, Mari warned him, it was falling apart. He'd have to tread carefully, but she'd done it dozens of times—and worst-case scenario, he'd fall into the water below. Her directions were great; he knew exactly where he was headed, and sort of looked forward to trying a new route.

Once he'd crossed the bridge—which held his weight but looked like it shouldn't have—he traversed an abandoned plot of land that Mari had told him was meant to be a site for a new high-rise, back when Priors thought the land was safe to develop. Now there was just a huge pit in the ground. Cole walked around it cautiously; Mari had said that the dirt near the pit's lip was loose—and if he fell in, he'd have little chance of pulling himself out. He was nearly past it when he tripped over a mound of trash, tearing the skin just above his ankle.

The scratch was superficial, but when Cole touched it he felt the unmistakable wetness of blood. He fumbled for the offending object. From the look of it, he'd come across what had once been a squatters' lair, and he shuddered to think what had happened to the people who'd camped out there. He stepped around an abandoned, collapsed tent and held the object up to the thin ray of moonlight that partially illuminated his path. He saw that it was an old-fashioned instrument—maybe a ukulele? It looked like it had all its strings intact. He plucked one, and its melody rang out clear and sharp, echoing around the tunnel. Its rough edge—where the wood had chipped—could be easily sanded down. It was no cello, but he figured Vera would appreciate any access to a musical instrument.

Buoyed by the tea and the gift, he quickened his pace, and the rest of the journey was unremarkable. He reached Thomas's new lab—housed in an abandoned parking garage in order to avoid attracting attention from the Prior guards that now patrolled the Slants—in record time.

Vera's face lit up in a genuine smile when he walked in. Her blond hair was clean and shining, and she wore a long worker's tunic—the kind his mother had once worn at the factories—rather than the pink silk dress he'd seen her in last. The tunic was shapeless and drab, but it hugged Vera's growing belly and set off her rosy cheeks and light brown eyes. Her sterile, plain surroundings offered a stark contrast to her beauty and had the effect of magnifying it.

"Brought you something," he told her, withdrawing the ukulele from behind his back. At first she wrinkled her brow in confusion. "Is that . . ."

"Are all stringed instruments not the same?"

Vera laughed. "It's perfect," she told him. "God, I've only seen one of these in my music theory textbook."

"It can't be that old," Cole told her. "Still in pretty great condition, right?"

"It's just what I needed," she reassured him. "Seriously. Was it that obvious how bored I've been?"

"Hmm. Judging by the array of friendship bracelets on that table yonder, I'd almost believe you were crying for help," he teased.

"There's a lot of extra yarn lying around," Vera told him. "I think it's my calling. By the way," she added in a faux whisper, "think Worsley knits in his down time? I wouldn't have pegged him for the type...."

Cole laughed. He liked Vera. They'd started to develop an easy rapport, and he genuinely looked forward to seeing her. At first it had been about doing what Davis would have wanted; now he just enjoyed it.

"Hang on a second," Worsley said, rolling his eyes and confiscating the ukulele. "I'm not going to dignify that last comment with an answer, by the way." Vera and Cole smirked. "Just let me wipe this down...." He produced sterilized cloths from a set of chrome drawers set up in one corner of the small space. Cole took a second to examine the room; he'd never seen the new iteration of Thomas's lab, and this one was even nicer than the last. Even the cement floors somehow glowed with a sterile-looking sheen.

"Nice space," he commented. "Wanted to be discreet, my ass."

"They were catching wind of the last place, I swear," Thomas said. "You know I can't jeopardize my research. What'd you bring me, Casanova?"

Cole produced the peppermint leaves from his pocket.

"No!" Thomas said. "Amazing. You can't find those anywhere around here. So you got to Braddock's okay?"

Cole nodded, taking everything in. Thomas's equipment looked state of the art; more imports from one of his old mentors, Cole guessed. "Found it," he told him. "Interesting guy."

"Think he'll be able to help you?"

Cole paused, reluctant to mention Mari in front of Vera, for some reason.

"Yeah. So, you sleeping here or what?" He was eager to change the subject. Worsley nodded, acknowledging the old sleeping bag that was balled up in one corner.

"It isn't ideal," he said. "But I want to make sure I'm here in case something happens with the baby. If Vera goes into premature labor . . . I want to make sure I'm around to help."

"Still. It's cramped quarters. You guys must be dying to get out."

"Remember how it was when we were kids?" Worsley laughed. "We could run all over the place. There weren't any guards, no one to stop us."

"We were troublemakers," Cole agreed. "Remember that time you, me, and Hamilton glassed that old haunted house?"

"Glassed? What does that mean?" Vera broke in.

"Just literally threw a bunch of old glass bottles at this abandoned house that was near the Slants. We did it in the middle of the night on a dare. Obviously we made a huge mess."

Vera smiled, and Cole was relieved she wasn't totally horrified by their behavior.

"Yes! The house just north of the outskirts of the woods," broke in Worsley. "Man, those were the days."

"I really thought it was haunted," Cole said. "It was so creepy looking. I was certain we were going to wake the ghosts with those bottles, and they were going to come after us. Hamilton ran screaming like a baby after he threw his first one. But the bet was three each, so we lost."

"What were the stakes?" Vera wanted to know.

Cole shrugged. "I don't know. An ice cream bar or something."

"Well you could have gotten that easily on your own!" She laughed.

Cole and Worsley exchanged glances. That hadn't exactly been the case. They'd had to save up for months for treats like that, doing odd jobs. Instead they'd had to buy Dylan Church, the guy who'd dared them in the first place, a double-scoop cone.

"Wiped out my savings, losing that one," Cole said, and Worsley nodded.

Vera gave them a funny look, like she thought they might be joking. "It sounds like you guys had fun," she finally said, strumming gently on the ukulele. "It sounds almost . . . idyllic. Not like our highrises and constant pressure to excel in whatever it was we showed promise in. Even our playdates were structured. I can't remember ever running free."

"Yeah, fun . . . but I wouldn't say idyllic." Cole was trying not to bristle at her naïveté. It wasn't her fault. "Living in the Slants was filthy," Cole told her. "That abandoned house was a disaster waiting to happen. When I look back . . . it's a miracle none of us got sick and died. We were always running around in garbage heaps, cutting ourselves and not worrying about infection—until the Priors figured out the disposal system, which you've seen. It's just that lot near the Swings, where I used to work out. They crush it and dispose of it about once a month with their machinery. It starts to smell pretty bad toward the end of the month, but at least it's fenced off. When we were kids, there were open piles that we treated like mountains, and half the time when I went home to bathe I did it in the lake with no soap."

"Why don't you dispose of the garbage yourselves, instead of letting it build up for a month?" Vera wondered aloud.

"We don't have the machinery," Cole told her. "The Priors have offered to 'sell' it to us, but at a price we could never afford. So we have to wait for them—you—to do it on your own terms."

"It was pretty dangerous, when we were kids," Worsley agreed. "But to us it was just normal. It's partly why I wanted to go into medicine. To think of alternatives to the insanely costly medical care you guys have in downtown Columbus. That just wasn't an option for us."

Vera turned away, blinking back tears.

"Hey. It's okay. We didn't mean to upset you," Cole told her.

"I'm just . . . it's so hard to hear about," she said. "I can't believe this was all going on right next to me all my life, and I had no idea. That it's still going on. That Priors have so much power over Gens. Part of me feels so bad for you. And part of me is . . ."

"Disgusted?" Worsley finished, his tone neutral. Vera nodded, looking guilty.

"It was a different way of life," Worsley agreed. Cole was glad he stopped there. He knew he had stronger opinions than just that. But it seemed to calm Vera. She looked back toward the ukulele and began to strum a light tune Cole couldn't place—some sort of lullaby.

"I'm a little scared," she said as she played, her eyes focused on the instrument. "Will my baby be a Prior if it's not given in utero treatments? Can you do that here?"

There was a long pause. Cole looked hard at Worsley, willing him to tell her the truth. Of course the baby wouldn't be a Prior. It wouldn't be an Imp, either, with Prior parentage. It would be a Neither. Something about the way Worsley was conducting experiments and working on the vaccine without bothering to explain to Vera the implications felt very wrong.

"When your baby is born, she'll be a hero. She'll be acknowledged as a savior of mankind," Worsley said. He reached out for Vera's hand, and she clutched it. She trusted him—Cole could see it in the way she held his eyes with her own. "She'll be known as the one who got rid of the deadly Prior disease. She'll be a hero. Your family will be proud."

"Maybe they'll take me back," Vera said hopefully. "Maybe Oscar will have me."

Cole looked away, but Worsley nodded.

"I think so," Worsley told her. "This baby represents salvation. Yours, yes. But also everyone else's. One way or another, the lives of everyone in Columbus are at stake."

On that point, Cole had to agree.

DAVIS

Mercer hummed under his breath, absentmindedly drumming a beat on the side of the narrow motorized lifeboat. It was a small boat—built for a handful of people—with a little cushioned perch on one end. It was actually much nicer than Davis would have expected of a lifeboat. Mercer had waited to turn the motor on—it was risky, given their close proximity to the larger craft—but he was steering it as best he could with the help of the tide. His blond hair was flopped over his forehead and his muscular calves flexed as he kept rhythm with his foot. For about an hour, they'd paddled softly together, not wanting to turn on the motor and arouse any suspicion with its noise. But now the motor was humming along and Mercer was steering with one hand as he gazed out into the darkness. He seemed unaware of Davis's presence, and she watched him quietly from her perch at the opposite end of the craft. She'd heard him humming before, but when he began to sing, she was transfixed.

"You and me, baby," he sang. "We'll be quite all right, if only we're together tonight. . . ."

Mercer's voice was luminous. It captured warmth, emotion, and a sense of longing that Davis didn't know was possible to translate into words. Part of her wondered if he was singing it for her, about her. She caught herself hoping he was, and flushed. She liked Mercer. They were friends. It was nothing like what she'd had with Cole—not even close. But still, sometimes when she saw Mercer like this, and found herself drawn to him, she wondered: would she ever feel love like that again? Even wondering it felt like a betrayal.

"What is that?" she asked.

He shrugged. "Nothing much. Just something I made up."

"I didn't even know you were into music."

"Oh yeah," he said. "Big time. I always wanted to start a band in high school, actually."

"Why didn't you?"

"I guess I realized I wasn't good enough. Starting a band takes a lot of work. This is fun for me, not some sort of distant career path."

"Well, you're great at it. Your voice . . ." She trailed off, blushing. The truth was, his voice had sent shivers down her spine. It had awoken her from within. It was even better that he hadn't seemed to know she was listening—he'd been raw, unguarded. He'd projected the kind of confidence Davis had only ever had while dancing.

"What's wrong?" He looked at her with concern. He glanced back at the larger craft, now nearly half a mile away thanks to the wind and tide. She adjusted herself on the cushion, watching him from where she sat. There was a bench in between them, but she felt a little bit of distance wasn't necessarily a bad thing.

"Nothing," she said. "You just reminded me of a friend."

"Yeah? Don't tell me he's as talented as me."

"*She* is extremely talented," Davis said, thinking of Vera. "She's amazing." Davis laughed. "God, the things we used to put Fia through," she added. "We'd wait until she was asleep at night and stuff playing cards in her underwear and write messages on her forehead. We tortured her. Poor Fia. But she always wanted to be around us anyway."

"It sounds like you have a lot of great people in your life."

"I do. I miss them." Davis blinked back the tears that had begun to form behind her eyelids.

"You'll see them again," Mercer reassured her, his voice gentle. "We're already past the hardest part. Now it's just about being patient."

"You're right," she agreed, pushing away her fears. "This is so good." She gestured at the boat. "I'm feeling like I'm actually *doing* something, for the first time in so long. If these Durham doctors are as amazing as you say, maybe I can help Fia and Vera and everybody else."

"That's the idea," Mercer said, smiling at her. "The doctors in the research triangle are the best. Dr. Hassman is practically a legend. If all he needs is our blood samples, then I know we'll be in great hands."

"How long until we hit land?"

"We're hugging the coast relatively close while still staying out of sight," Mercer replied. "I'd give it about five days. But it looks like we have plenty of fuel. Hopefully we can avoid hitting land, though. That'll be more dangerous."

"Five days." Davis's brow knitted. She'd known so many parts of their plan were a gamble, but now she was concerned about food and supplies. "We're really going to have to ration our water and the supplies we took from the other boat," she said. "I think we only have three days' worth at best." *Not to mention the inability to shower for that long,* she thought.

"I know," Mercer said, his voice grim. "Believe me. It's just that I didn't know what kind of a lifeboat we'd be using, and this motor isn't strong. We can stop at a port if we absolutely have to."

"And risk getting caught," said Davis. Instinctively, she moved closer to him.

"We're already constantly risking that," he told her.

"I don't know if I can wait five days, with or without supplies. I just want to get there, get the cure, and get home."

He was quiet for so long that she worried she'd offended him somehow.

"I want those things, too," he told her, his voice low. "But I'll miss you when you're home."

Davis bit her lip, suddenly acutely aware of the water lapping against the side of the boat and Mercer breathing beside her, only an inch of space between them. She'd loved getting to know Mercer these past few months. In many ways, he'd been her only support. It would be impossible not to miss him. But that didn't imply anything bigger about their relationship. It was situational, she told herself.

"You should be counting your lucky stars," Mercer told her, breaking the silence. He wrapped an arm around her shoulders and pulled her close. "Who else do you know who can serenade you *and* navigate a boat *and* doesn't care that you spent the evening inside a morgue sack? Huh? These next five days could be a heck of a lot worse."

Davis smiled and rested her head on his shoulder. He always knew just what to say to lift her spirits. And he was right—as impatient as she was to bring a cure back to Columbus, there wasn't anything she could do until they reached Durham, except make the best of her time with her friend.

She inhaled deeply, trying to calm her nerves and focus on the tranquility of the night. Even Mercer's humming sounded more melodic than other people's. She tried to do what her father had taught her when she was young: put herself in a good, peaceful place when she was anxious. Because if she didn't, in this case, all her anxieties would drive her crazy—anxieties over getting caught, getting thrown back into TOR-N. . . . She couldn't think like that. She closed her eyes, only to open them a second later when she felt raindrops.

"Hmm," Mercer said. "We aren't exactly equipped for this."

"What are we going to do?" she asked, looking up at him as rain trickled down their foreheads.

He gazed down at her, locking his eyes on hers. "What should we do?" he asked softly. His hand tightened on her shoulder, and Davis felt a pang shoot through her chest, realizing for the first time just how close he was. She looked up at him, her face inches from his. She could feel his warm breath through the cold, sleeting rain. It would take nothing to close the gap between their lips. She could feel him wanting it.

Davis drew back suddenly, reaching for her jacket. "I'm cold," she said unnecessarily, looking away.

Mercer reached around her and helped her pull on her coat. She couldn't believe how close she'd come to kissing him. It felt wrong, bad somehow. Cole was dead, but she wasn't over him. He was in every animal-shaped cloud formation they'd once speculated over, every word or phrase that reminded her of him—even being on the water, which he'd loved. She almost laughed at that, because *that* she couldn't understand. The water beneath the boat was choppy, and all she could see around her was black. And yet, above her there was the night sky . . . and he'd adored that, too. She gazed up at it; it was mostly hazy from cloud coverage, but here and there she could pick up the clusters of stars he'd always admired. Her love for him was as strong as ever, and kissing Mercer would be like . . . It just wouldn't feel right. Her heart thudded with the nearness of him. Until tonight, they'd just been friends. She loved their banter, how easy and comfortable they were together. So what was this? A breeze rustled her hair, and she realized for the first time that the wind had picked up significantly. She hugged her arms to her chest, and Mercer frowned as he fought to steer the boat. Large droplets of rain began falling faster. Davis hoped against hope they'd abate. They had a tarp for coverage—she'd seen it on the floor near where she sat—but would it be enough?

They jolted sideways as the waves tossed the boat more roughly. The rain was really coming down now, and the vessel felt completely at the mercy of the storm. "What are we going to do?" Davis shouted to Mercer, who was looking as worried as she felt. "I don't know how to sail through this kind of storm."

"Neither do I," he said. "I guess we just ride it out."

They pitched from side to side until Davis clutched her stomach, feeling nauseated. She gripped the side of the lifeboat, which suddenly felt like a child's toy, as another wave pitched them forward. This time, though, they didn't simply ride it through to the next—they slammed into something hard, which spun the boat counterclockwise. When the boat righted itself it felt oddly weighted on the left side, which caused it to pitch down toward the water unevenly.

"Shit," Mercer muttered. "There's a hole in the side of the boat. We must have hit a rock!"

"A rock? How flimsy is this thing?" She was genuinely concerned. The boat had seemed sturdy; it was made of metal or chrome or *something*, after all—not wood.

"It's a lifeboat, Davis! It's not meant for violent storms. It looks like the rock punctured all the way through."

"What can we do?" Davis's voice was shrill, and she moved even closer to Mercer as the boat tossed in either direction.

"We need to patch it. Just a second." Mercer stood, but Davis held out a hand to stop him.

"You navigate. I'll look." She pulled herself unsteadily toward the plastic safe that rested near the bow. She dug around in the box until she found something in a plastic bag labeled *Waterproof Caulking Material*. "I'm not totally sure," she told him, "but I think we can plug it with this. At least temporarily." She scanned the directions on the bag, which indicated that the material was for patching minor holes. She handed the bag to Mercer, and he nodded, moving toward the side of the vessel where the hole was.

"It looks like it's just meant to be a temporary fix, but hopefully it'll hold us over until we hit land." He leaned toward the hole, but again Davis pulled him back. "Let me get it! You need to keep us steady."

He shook his head. "It's not an easy one," he told her, motioning toward the hole. It was far down the side of the boat, almost kissing the surface of the water.

"It'll work better if I do it," Davis told him. "You're too big to reach down there. You might tip the boat."

"No way! It's too dangerous."

"What choice do we have?" She plucked the caulking from his hands and shimmied over the side of the boat, bending in half and stretching her torso as far as she could go. The instructions on the packaging said it would adhere to the outer surface of the boat only—something about the way it welded to the external siding. She was just glad the hole was above water level. She felt Mercer's hands on her waist behind her, steadying her. "I need to move onto the side of the boat," she told him, starting to climb over.

"No!" he shouted. "Are you crazy? You'll fall in."

"Just let me do it," she said, using her upper body strength to propel herself over the side to the thin ledge that encircled the exterior of the boat, unprotected. She balanced there, grateful for years of ballet training that enabled her to exert expert control over her muscles. She pushed the caulking into the gap made by the rock, all the while aware that at any second, they could hurtle into another sharp object.

She was just cementing the rim of the hole when she felt another jolt; this time it was the wind. There was nothing she could do; her fingers were ripped from their grip on the side of the boat and she was hurled into the air, her foot snagging on something as she went down. Then she was in the water, thrashing, unable to fight her way to the surface. She kicked her legs hard but found they were tangled up in something—reeds, or a rope?—and the more she kicked, the more she seemed to push her body further into the murky water. She gasped for air and inhaled water instead.

She panicked, fear coursing through her body and water filling her lungs. She felt herself choking, and for a minute she was certain she was going to die. Images of Vera and Cole and Fia and her father flashed through her mind, making her panic all the more. She reached out to the boat like she would have reached out to them, because they were the only reason she had to survive. Everything she'd done—all that she'd risked to find a cure and save the people she loved—was wasted. The realization gutted her. She couldn't accept it. She fought harder, scrambling to reach the surface, to no avail. Then she felt a set of arms around her, stabilizing her, and a voice yelled at her over the pounding of the waves, urging her to keep calm. *Mercer.*

She relaxed into his grip, feeling him free her feet from whatever it was that was binding her. He wrapped her arms around his neck and swam the few feet back to their boat, hauling her body up to the rope ladder that hung from the back of the boat. He helped push her up and over the side before pulling himself up, and they dropped onto the deck, gasping for breath.

Davis coughed, hacking up water. She felt tears burn in the backs of her eyes, but she struggled to stay calm and breathe deeply. The rain was abating a little, but she was freezing. Freezing and terrified. She'd been certain she was about to die. She'd swum before—they all had, in basic athletics programs at school growing up—but this was so much more. So unpredictable, the way the waves had moved her body and she'd lost control. She gasped, realizing just how close she'd come to never seeing her friends and family again. She'd thought she knew how to swim, but nothing had prepared her for the volatility of the sea. It was like it had been a living, breathing monster with its own mind. She trembled, feeling her feet and hands begin to warm up enough to move again. Still, she was bone cold and having a hard time moving her body after the shock of it. She was alive. She sobbed at the realization of it. She rolled toward Mercer and welcomed his embrace as he pulled her toward him. His touch sent her back into a tailspin of emotions. He made her feel real, alive, human. All the things she'd nearly lost.

"I told you not to go," he whispered into her hair, kissing her forehead and cheeks and ear.

"I did it, didn't I?" she asked. He looked around and laughed—sure enough, the boat had righted itself and didn't seem to be drawing in any water.

"You did," he agreed. "Davis," he whispered, pulling her closer. "I don't know what I'd have done if . . . if . . . ." He sighed, and then said even more quietly, "I can't do this alone."

She tilted her face toward his so she could see the expression in his eyes—it was one of fear and passion and relief. She felt all those same sensations. And it was true—she couldn't do this alone, either. They needed each other.

This time, when their eyes locked, she didn't resist. His lips on hers were gentle and searching, but strong. His kiss was warm and tender, and she almost gasped from the emotion of it. Surprised to realize how long it had been building up inside her, too. How badly she wanted it. She leaned into it more. He was confident and firm but not fierce, like Cole had been. *Cole.*

She pulled away, gasping.

"I'm sorry," he said, worry in his eyes. "Was that too much?"

"No." She shook her head. "At least . . . I don't know. I don't know," she said again. "You're my friend." She knew her answer wasn't adequate, but she didn't have anything better. She didn't know what any of this meant. But the kiss had been very real and powerful. She couldn't process what she was feeling just then, or what she wanted, and Mercer nodded, seeming to understand. But he couldn't. He couldn't understand how her heart still felt toward Cole. Maybe she'd always love him. Maybe even though he was gone, that part of her, that part that loved him, was unbreakable.

The cushioned portion of the back end of the lifeboat was tiny and cramped, and the floor below it was filled with supplies, but they found space for both of them among the stacks of life jackets and fuel. Mercer unfolded the tarp to spread over them for warmth. The rain had abated to a slow drizzle, but it was enough to chill her all the way through. Exhausted and shivering, she collapsed next to him, allowing him to encircle her in his arms. There was barely space for the two of them down there; it was intimate and familiar. It felt like they were two parts of the same person. The thought that their friendship would inevitably be altered was terrifying.

That's why, Davis thought as she began to fall asleep, her chin tucked against his shoulder. It was why she felt so deeply connected to him—they were similar people. They both understood what it was like not to fit in. It wasn't anything more than that. Even though she couldn't be with Cole, her heart was his. She knew it. Being with someone else felt like a betrayal. Lying with Cole on the hospital rooftop had been so charged; their love had been apparent in every kiss, every soft touch to each other's faces. It had been manifest in the way he held her, like she was a delicate thing.

Mercer liked her. But she couldn't make the mistake of blurring their friendship again. She wasn't ready, and she wasn't sure she'd ever be ready. It wasn't fair to him. Even as she thought it, Mercer's arms encircled her tighter, and she couldn't ignore the comfort in his embrace. But she couldn't worry about it; there wasn't time. All she could think about was getting safely to Durham and finding doctors who could figure out how to help her family and friends. The rest would fall into place.

Davis awoke cold and alone, the morning sunlight streaming through the sides of the trapdoor that led to the lower deck. Groggy and aching, she pushed into a sitting position. *They'd hit land.* A beautiful, hilly farmland stretched out in the distance, still too far to reach without swimming but there nonetheless. It gave her a slight surge of hope. They'd seemed to have reached a kind of inlet or river, surrounded on three sides by low-hanging trees. It was lovely; she'd never seen natural beauty in such abundance. It was like nothing she'd ever seen before.

But Mercer was gone. *Oh, God.* They had kissed. They had held each other all night. Their relationship before . . . it had been clearly defined; now everything was called into question. Davis didn't know what she wanted. She'd tried so long to reassure herself that her attraction to Mercer was just a normal result of being close to someone in a strange situation. She didn't feel for Mercer the same kind of passion she'd felt for Cole. She thought back to the night *Cole* had lain next to her, holding her until dawn on the roof of the hospital. That had been magical; it had made her happier than she'd believed possible. Last night with Mercer was different. It was comforting and safe, but it lacked that same magic.

She was attracted to him, though. And sometimes, their easy affection felt like something more. But at TOR-N, everything was bound to be a little blurry. They'd *had* to be close—neither of them had had anyone else. But now . . . she didn't know how she felt. Did he? Had he wanted this all along? And if so, how much? Davis wasn't sure she was ready for anything. Cole's death was too fresh; she loved him still. She didn't want to hurt Mercer.

The boat felt eerily still, like they'd dropped the anchor. The whole situation was odd, because Mercer had specifically said they should avoid land at all costs—it was too dangerous. The air was muggy and stifling, and suddenly it was all she could do not to scream from the claustrophobia of it all, being in this tiny ship with no way out. She struggled to compose herself, rising from the bench and looking over the side of the boat.

Where *was* he? Maybe he'd jumped off the side to "bathe" as well as he could, or maybe he was making sure the anchor was secure so they could find more supplies on land. But the water around her was still. Sunlight flooded the deck. She blinked against its rays, waiting for her eyes to adjust.

Davis pulled herself upright and moved toward the opposite end of the deck. She started to call for Mercer.

Then she froze.

The sound of a long howl broke the tranquility of the peaceful setting.

It was followed by a cacophony of barking, followed by the rattling of chains and the sound of deep male voices.

Dogs. *Police dogs.* She knew it instinctively. She'd heard those same chains rattling before, and men didn't keep dogs as pets, not since fifty years ago. Dogs were trained for service, generally in the military or police force.

She was paralyzed by fear—every limb felt weighted down by bricks, or sluggish, the way they felt in her nightmares when she tried to run and couldn't, as if she were mired in quicksand. She heard the thudding of what sounded like a pack of dogs in the distance, drawing closer, patrolmen likely on their heels.

And then she clambered down from the boat and began to run.

❧ 10 ❧

COLE

Cole had mentioned the old stone house—the one he and Worsley and Hamilton had played in as kids—when he returned from Worsley's lab. But he hadn't expected Mari to weave it into his training. He'd merely wondered if she'd played in it too as a kid—if they'd had any shared experiences. Now, though, they drew closer and closer to the edge of the Slants, north of where Cole's community was located, and he was growing suspicious.

"Where are we headed?" he asked for what felt like the millionth time, shouting to be heard over the pelting rain.

"You'll see," she told him again. Sure enough, they came to the top of a gentle hill and the decrepit building rose out atop a smaller hill ahead of them. It was alone and abandoned against the backdrop of the wilderness. Stretching out beyond the mansion's crumbling facade was nothing but wild, undeveloped parts of the territory. It felt peaceful out there . . . but Cole was exhilarated by the untamed aspect of the land. He wondered what lurked in the woods past the house; it was an area he'd never ventured into. He hadn't had reason to—he didn't even know what exactly lay beyond it.

"I'd been wondering what challenge would bring you back to your past," Mari told him, watching his face. "Then you mentioned the old Blackwell house. It's perfect."

"Why do I need to go back to my past to train for the Olympiads?"

"You'll see. So much of winning is mental."

Cole scoffed. He knew that well. He'd known that when he'd entered, and won, the final rounds of FEUDS. He wondered what Mari thought she could teach him about it, but he fought to keep his face neutral and his mind open. When they crossed the foyer into the house—which was musty and damp—Cole was thrust back into a torrent of memories from childhood.

The house reminded Cole of his days with Hamilton and Worsley, but also of the two or three old, crumbling chapels that remained in the Slants. This, though, was in better condition. The chapels in the Slants had mostly fallen apart beyond their facades; he and Hamilton had used to pretend the buildings were castles, as children, and they were knights. They'd loved buildings like these.

The structure of this house was still intact, but its tall ceilings and damp stone walls had a similar archaic feel. Cole remembered a conversation he'd had with Davis about his escapades in the old churches as well as in the Blackwell house, and she'd remarked that they sounded simpler and more atmospheric somehow, unencumbered by advancements. She'd seemed to like knowing that relics from the past still existed in Columbus. Cole had always wondered if it was because she was hanging on to the past in her own way, in order to connect with her mom.

Now he squinted into the dank and musty space, breathing deeply to minimize the bittersweet feeling that threatened to overwhelm him. As his eyes adjusted, he saw that the space wasn't empty and barren as he remembered it. In addition to cobwebs and dust, the room was strung with ropes and appeared to be set up to resemble some sort of obstacle course.

He turned to Mari. "What is it?"

"Some homemade challenges, à la Mari Braddock." Mari puffed her chest theatrically, showing off. "They're meant to test you physically and psychologically. Because that's what the Olympiads will do. When you're out there, you have to be prepared for anything. So. Challenge number one is an obstacle course. Go."

Cole rolled his eyes. If an obstacle course was all she had in her, this would be easy. Still, she seemed cockier than he would have liked—her arms were crossed over her chest, and her shoulders were thrust back. She stood with her feet planted hip-width apart, and with her head held high like that, her long dreadlocks resembled a lion's mane. Her mouth turned up just slightly, as though she was amused by his reaction. It didn't sit well.

He moved forward, easily ducking beneath a web of ropes until he entered a narrow corridor blocked on all sides by a puffy plastic tarp that appeared to be filled with air. The tarp-lined walls narrowed until Cole was forced to crawl on his hands and knees through a space no more than a few inches wider than his body in all directions. He couldn't see an end to the tunnel; it was pitch black. He began to back out, but he hit a wall.

"Hey!" He banged on the wall, certain it hadn't been there before. Had Mari blocked him off? What kind of twisted game was she playing? For not the first time, he felt angry that someone he didn't trust was in control of him.

"Keep moving forward, Cole. Once you're in the Olympiads, you can't turn back, no matter what happens."

The space was so tiny he could barely breathe. Cole felt the walls closing in on him as he moved along, crawling lower as the walls and ceiling began to press down on him and converge. Finally he was moving forward on his belly, using his arm strength to pull his torso forward inch by inch. He was drenched in sweat and near panic. But he had to keep moving.

It was then that he heard it. A faint but familiar moan. He moved forward, straining to hear. It became clearer as he inched forward. But what was it? Cole pushed against the air-filled tarps. He worried that he'd just hit another wall if he kept going. Had he missed a turn? He felt panic beginning to overtake him, and he thrashed around, hoisting his body forward with as much strength as he could muster.

Then he broke free, tumbling over a ledge into another dimly lit room. The noise was all around him now, and there was no mistaking what it was: the sound of his mother's voice, guttural and bereft.

"Help!" Her voice echoed all around him, followed by the pounding of fists against a wall.

"Mom? Where are you?" Cole looked around him, panicked, but couldn't see an exit.

"Won't somebody help, please!" She broke into sobs, and Cole's chest wrenched at the sound of it.

"Where is she?" he shouted. "What did you do to her?" He was overcome by fury and confusion. Had Mari and Braddock done something to his mother? He'd been a fool to trust them! Was this all some sort of trap designed to exploit him? But why? He ran the length of the room, feeling the walls until he located a crack. He followed the crack vertically until he came across a metal latch, which he flicked. It led to a long hallway—thankfully lit this time. Mari stood at the other end of the hall, watching him.

"Stay calm, Cole," she told him.

"What have you done?" he shrieked, hearing his mother scream for help, her fists echoing on a distant wall. "Where is she?"

"She's not here," Mari told him.

"What?" He looked around him, confused. "I hear her. She's got to be nearby, then. We need to help her!"

"No, Cole. It's a recording. She isn't here."

"It sounds so real." He hesitated, unsure whether to believe Mari. She approached him, raising her fists.

"Fight with me, Cole. See if you can remain centered."

"My mom—"

"No." Her voice was sharp. "It's an illusion."

Cole clenched his fists. He couldn't tell whether to believe her; his mother's voice sounded immediate and desperate. He felt torn in every direction. Confused.

"Focus!" Her voice snapped him back to attention. "You think this is bad? They're going to throw you a lot worse in the Olympiads. They fight dirty, Cole."

"But how did you do this?" And *why*? It was cruel, what she'd done.

"Easy." She shrugged. "I'm tiny. I'm a girl. I have an innocent face. I can slip in and out of places without being seen. I got a clip of your mother's voice at that place where she's staying—that home. I copied it, used it as a template, and programmed in my own script."

"She was never screaming for help," Cole clarified. "Even the recording isn't accurate." His entire body burned with anger.

"It's not. But if it were, you'd need to be able to fight through it.

You need to fight through it right now. Fighting isn't technically legal in the Olympiads . . . but believe me, Cole, there will be rules broken all over the place. So spar with me."

She raised her fists and came at him, swinging for his face. Cole blocked it but found himself stumbling backward from the force of it. He wasn't prepared to fight a girl, didn't know how to handle it. He was angry, but too angry. Angry enough to do real damage. He didn't want to do anything he'd regret. And his mother's voice was still all around him, pouring into his ears, distracting him.

"Concentrate!" Mari shouted. He moved after her, swinging as she ducked away. She was startlingly nimble, darting through small doorways and under mezzanines in a way that made him feel clumsy and his fists bumbling. If only he could concentrate. His mother was everywhere. It was oppressive. Every movement he made that wasn't a movement toward his mother felt like a betrayal. He didn't know what to do or where to swing—his anger and confusion about *how* to fight with Mari, especially when he was so furious, thrummed in his ears.

"It's okay to feel things, Cole," he heard Mari say. "Emotion is what makes us stronger. It's what gives Gens the advantage. Why do you think Priors came to my father for training?" She was panting, her eyes glittering, and when he paused, she laid him flat with a dirty kick to his shin. "It's because he understands suffering."

Cole lay on the floor in front of her, clutching his painful leg. He simply couldn't focus.

"Think. How are you going to get out of this? How can you beat me? Be smart, Cole. You have the edge. Priors don't know pain."

Cole thought. Mari had told him to recognize his advantage. To start fighting smarter. But he could barely focus with the recording on.

That was it. Cole needed to find and destroy the recording! With renewed purpose, he leapt to his feet. He avoided Mari's strikes, looking around him. In a stone house, the best acoustics would be . . . up top. Near the roof. Cole looked around him, seeing a balcony stretch high above him on the far south side of the massive room in which they were sparring. *Bingo.* It had to be there.

Cole darted away from Mari and moved toward a staircase that led to the balcony. Now that he was focused on the source of the noise, he could move faster, running with strength. He lost Mari when he vaulted over a wide railing. He looked behind him; she was moving toward the staircase still, but her deftness was no match for his shortcut. He pulled himself up and over, scaling the balcony railings until he was safely on a hovering platform. There it was. A small box. His mother's voice wailing from within it. Cole grabbed the box and tossed it over the railing. It crashed on the stone floor below, splintering into a dozen pieces. The room was filled with an eerie silence.

"Nice work," said Mari from beside him. "I think you're getting it. Finally. Heart and mind."

"Heart and mind," he repeated, ignoring the barb. "How is it that you're such an expert, tucked away from the rest of the world and all?" He was only teasing this time, but the light vanished from Mari's eyes and her mouth formed a grim line.

"Good point," she said. "What do I know? My best friend is my father."

Shit. He really hadn't meant to hit a nerve, but it was impossible to talk to this girl. He'd just opened his mouth to respond, when he heard the sound of crying rising up from the ground floor.

"Another illusion?" But Mari shook her head, looking as confused as he was. Still, he didn't quite believe her. If this was his chance to prove himself, he wasn't going to screw it up. The crying grew louder, and Cole darted down the stairs that led from the mezzanine to the ground floor, two steps at a time. As he descended, he identified Vera's voice, loud and anguished, coming from just beyond the front door. Jesus. How far had Mari dug into his personal life to discover Vera? How screwed up was she? He burst through to find Vera huddled on the front porch, filthy and sobbing. Mari followed close on his heels, gasping when she saw her.

"If this is a hologram, this is very messed up," Cole informed Mari, who just shook her head, her mouth agape.

"I can't take credit for this one," Mari said, shaking her head. Worry creased her forehead, and her eyebrows knit together. She brought a hand to her mouth, her eyes widening as she peered around Cole.

"How did you get here?" Cole knelt by Vera, who turned a dirt-and tear-streaked face to him. "Were you looking for me?"

Vera gasped, apparently unable to answer.

"Cole, who is this?" Mari whispered, swaying slightly.

"A friend," Cole said simply. Vera shifted toward him, and he noticed a crimson stain running down the front of her dress, where it was tucked tightly against her thigh. Mari saw it at the same time, and her face went white. Vera let out another long sob. Cole's heart stopped.

"What happened? Vera—did you lose the baby?" He grabbed her hand, squeezing it tightly. Vera shook her head, and Mari lifted the hem of Vera's skirt and wiped some of the blood away with the corner of her sleeve, revealing a long gash on Vera's thigh. So it wasn't the baby. Cole willed himself to stay calm.

"She'll be okay," Mari said. She was affecting confidence, but Cole heard the tremor under her breath. "I've been through this before. We didn't have doctors, you know. I broke a leg once, and cut myself in the woods. . . ." She was babbling.

"Then you can help," Cole told her firmly, and she nodded.

"It's okay," he soothed, turning back to Vera. He smoothed her hair from her forehead, which was sticky with sweat and dirt. "We're going to help you. Just catch your breath." Vera nodded slowly, and Mari knelt, gripping Vera's hand in her own. Vera's eyes widened as she took in Mari's appearance, but Mari didn't flinch. Cole eyed Mari, who was bravely squeezing Vera's hand. It was the likely first Prior she'd ever touched. He knew what it took for her to do it. He saw her as Vera probably did, taking in her disheveled appearance, matted hair, and sun-darkened skin. But to Mari, Vera was equally monstrous, merely for being a Prior. Still, Mari rubbed Vera's wrist with her other palm, and Vera seemed to relax. Soon, her sobs quieted. After a few minutes, her breathing returned to normal. Cole was quiet.

"Thank you," he said finally, meeting Mari's eyes. Hers were unreadable, but something was different. She nodded in return, and he realized what it was: her face looked vulnerable for the first time since he'd met her. Maybe she'd finally seen the shades between black and white.

"I've been hurting everywhere," Vera said, shifting so she leaned against Cole rather than the step. He cradled her, staring down at her stomach, which was still rounding out. It was hard to tell, even five months in, that she was pregnant. He hoped Worsley was taking good care of the baby. Something about Worsley had worried Cole lately—it was as if Worsley cared more about his experiments than about the people around him. Pushing this troubling thought aside, Cole focused on Vera's words.

"I get long flashes of pain all over my body," she continued. "And Thomas can't give me pain medication. He says it's bad for the baby. But I hurt *so much*, all over. That can't be good for my baby, either, right? I can't sleep, Cole," she said, her eyes welling. "Half the time it's so awful. And then the other half, I feel fine. Normal." She stopped, her voice catching. Cole eyed her with concern. "I was going to run away all along," Vera said, her voice heavy. Cole reeled as if he'd been slapped. He could feel Mari looking at him, waiting for his response. Mari smoothed Vera's hair back from her sweaty forehead with her palm. None of this sounded good to Cole.

"I didn't trust you; I didn't know you. Don't you see that? I thought if I returned to Columbus with the cure, I'd be a hero. I thought Worsley might be able to do it, give me the cure, and then I'd run. He told me he was getting close. But now I'm so . . ." Her voice shook as she trailed off. She didn't have to say it. Cole could plainly see she was falling apart—weak, tired, sick, confused.

"It's okay," Cole said. "You're panicking." He thought hard. Did Worsley have any idea how bad it was for Vera? But still—for her to have planned to run away—things were far different than he'd imagined them to be. He'd thought he'd gained her trust.

"I can't even tell what's real anymore." Vera's voice was now almost a whisper, frantic. "The pain feels like a nightmare. It makes me light-headed. Sometimes, in the mirror, I look the same as always. Then sometimes I look like a different person—gaunt and pale, with sallow skin and bags under my eyes. I don't know if the pain is even real. I cut myself, just to see—"

"You did this to yourself?" Cole interrupted, recoiling.

"I couldn't tell if I was awake or not." She wept now, her tears washing some of the dirt from her cheeks. "I had to know if it was real. I don't know what to do. Thomas is out, and I took one of the cars from the parking garage. It still had its keys in the ignition. I remembered what he told you about finding Braddock. I followed you two here." She looked up at Mari, then, her brown eyes bright. "Who are you?" she asked. "Cole, what's going on here? Why are you even at this house?"

Mari looked to Cole.

"She's just training me," Cole told Vera. "This is Mari, Braddock's daughter. Can I trust you, Vera?" Sometimes, the best way to gain someone's trust was to show you trusted them back. He met Mari's eyes to find her looking hurt. *She's just training me*, he'd said. He wished he could take it back now. Mari was trying to help, despite years of hating Priors—despite all the feelings and beliefs that had stemmed from her mother's death at their hands. As misguided as she'd been, what she was doing now took bravery. He had to respect that. "Mari's helped me a lot," he amended, watching Mari's eyes flicker in surprise. "I'm going to be competing in the Olympiads. If I win, I'll have enough money to go to Davis at TOR-N." He watched Vera, waiting for her reaction, knowing how much he was risking.

"You're competing in the Olympiads. For Davis," she repeated, her eyes wide. "You'd do all that for Davis?"

Cole nodded. "And for my family," he said. "I just want a better life for us. But Vera, I'm glad you found us. Thomas is the only one who can help you. You need to trust us."

"I can't go back," she moaned, burying her face in Cole's shoulder. "You should see him, Cole. He wanted to inject the baby with some sort of solution today—he wouldn't even tell me what it was—to see how she'd react. I screamed and threatened to reveal the location of his lab if he went along with it, and finally he backed out. But I don't know how long I can do this."

"He'll keep her safe," Cole assured her. "I promise you. He's doing the best he can for both of you." But even as he said it, he felt a niggling qualm. *Was* Worsley doing all he could do? Vera looked less healthy than when he'd seen her last—and less cared for. Beyond her dirt- and tear-streaked face, her hair was lank and her nails had grown long. She looked thinner, too; her cheekbones protruded in a way he hadn't noticed before. He hoped desperately that he was reading too much into it, that the physical changes were happenstance.

Anyway, there was no choice. He had to get her back to the lab. "You can't go to a Prior hospital," he told her. "Not after your parents threw you out. They'll just send you away to one of those research facilities, maybe wherever Davis is. Who knows what they do over there." He winced at his own words, hoping to God Davis was safe. "You might not even make the journey. You need help now. We'll take you back." Vera nodded, looking defeated.

"I'll stay with you for a while," Cole told her. "I'll make sure Worsley's doing everything in his power to keep you and your baby safe. Here, help me," he said to Mari, lifting Vera gently. Vera wrapped slender arms around his shoulders and rested her face against his neck. He felt her warm breath on his skin. She felt human. Healthy. Alive. Not like someone with Narxis. He prayed she would stay strong.

Cole carried her to the car, Mari running ahead to open the door to the backseat. Once there, he placed Vera gently inside.

"I'm sorry, Cole," she said to him, her voice faint. "I'm sorry for not trusting you from the beginning."

"Don't be," he said, trying his best to smile at her, to hide his worry. "Just stay strong." Mari slid in afterward, and shifted Vera's head so it lay in her lap. Cole looked at Mari gratefully—she hadn't needed any explanation. "Thank you," he mouthed at her.

She smiled in return.

He only hoped that, by telling Vera the truth, he'd done the right thing.

"Oh thank God," Thomas said, rushing to greet them when Cole slid the car into a spot near the lab and killed the engine. Cole breathed a sigh of relief. He hadn't wanted to drive; it was too easy for him to be spotted. But Mari didn't know how, and even though Vera did, she was in no condition. He'd taken one-way back roads and put his hood up to conceal his identity, but every time another car passed, his blood had run cold.

Worsley flung the back door open and reached for Vera, ignoring Mari entirely. "Vera! Where did you run off to? You could have been hurt! Oh, God," he continued. "You are hurt. Is it the baby?"

"It's her leg, Tom," said Cole. "It's just a deep scratch. You'll need to disinfect it. This is Mari, Braddock's daughter," he said, motioning to Mari. Worsley nodded distractedly in her direction but didn't say hello. Cole gritted his teeth. It was as though Worsley didn't care anything about the baby—only the testing, Cole realized.

"Wait," he told Worsley, after they'd carried Vera inside and Tom reached for his medical supplies. "First I need to talk to you." He settled Vera on her cot, and Mari rushed to the sink to pour her water. Cole felt another unexpected flash of warmth toward the girl.

"I'll take care of her," she told him. "You go."

Nodding, Cole grabbed Worsley's arm and pulled him back outside.

"She's having a hell of a time," he hissed. "Hallucinations or something. She's out of her mind. What are you doing to her? It's time to end this, Tom. It's not worth it. Something's obviously not right!"

Worsley ran a hand over his face, his eyebrows furrowing. "I'd end it if I could," he whispered. "I expected this. But not to this extent. Believe me, there's nothing I want more than for this baby to be born in peace. But it's too late for that."

"What do you mean?" Cole's heart sank. If Davis came back and found that Cole had let her down—had let something awful happen to her best friend, when it could have been prevented—he'd never forgive himself.

"It's not too late for her," Worsley corrected. "She could be— she *will* be—fine, if I monitor her closely. It's just too late to go back. She's already entered phase two. I've injected the baby with Narxis."

Cole stepped back, stunned.

"What?" he uttered. "You didn't even run it by me."

"And why should I?" Worsley argued, his eyes hard. "I know what I'm doing, Cole. You'd only get in the way."

"So is that what shipping me off to Braddock was all about?" Cole raised his voice, and Worsley placed a hand on his shoulder. Cole shrugged it off, stepping back. "No," he said, furious. "This isn't okay. What's happened to you?"

"Cole! Stop shouting. You're only going to scare her."

Cole gritted his teeth, fighting to stay calm.

"You need to trust me. Or if not me, trust science. I'm on the cusp of a breakthrough! If we just stick this out, think of all the lives we'll save."

Cole stared at Worsley. His last sentence had seemed canned, as if uttered from a script. Worsley's eyes glittered as he spoke. He believed in what he was saying, Cole realized. But was his excitement for the cure, or for some sort of fame he was hoping to achieve?

"You're not who you used to be," Cole said, moving back toward the lab. "I just hope you're right."

Worsley wasn't the same kind, meek doctor he'd been only months back. His eyes darkened at Cole's words. For a second—a second in which Cole fervently hoped he was wrong—they seemed crossed by a shadow of doubt.

11

DAVIS

Her lungs burned and her muscles felt weak. She stumbled over rocks and sticks, exhausted, hearing the panting of the dogs not far in her wake. When her foot hit a root, she flew forward, landing face-first in the dirt ahead of her. She fought to catch her breath. Her right arm burned, and when she pushed herself up to a kneeling position and wiped the dirt from her face, her fingers brought back blood. She coughed, and it was long and racking. She heard the dogs drawing closer, but it was muted, as if in a dream. A ringing noise filled her eardrums. She wasn't used to feeling weak, but the disease and weeks away from supplements and exercise had turned her into a shell of her former self. She wondered if this was what it felt like to be a Gen.

When rough hands wrapped around her waist from behind, she tried to resist. But the man—she could tell without turning it was a man, by the breadth of his palms—wasn't even forced to shift his grasp. She turned and caught sight of the trademark navy uniform of TOR-N security. They must have tracked them somehow, or anticipated the direction they'd be heading.

"This is a mistake! You've got the wrong girl!" she shouted as they hauled her toward a cluster of waiting quarantine vehicles. Her words sounded hollow, even to her. The vehicles' chrome exteriors shone so brightly she was forced to squint; for a second, the ludicrous thought crossed her mind that they were taunting her. Davis relaxed into the security guard's grip, resigning herself. After all this, she was going to be thrown back into quarantine.

Then, just as suddenly, the security guard lost his grip, dropping her into the mud. He uttered a loud groan and stumbled backward, losing his footing.

"What the—" Davis turned to see him clutch his head, then crumple to the ground. Before she could process what was going on she saw several figures spring from the brush around the vehicles. And *Mercer*. He threw a punch at one of the other three guards, incapacitating him. From behind him, two other guys wielding long metal rods ran at them. The guards drew their Tasers, but not in time; their faces registered fear and confusion. These men hadn't expected to be met with resistance.

Within seconds, all four TOR-N guards were lying on the ground in a crumpled heap, and Mercer and his friends had seized their weapons.

His friends. Who were these guys?

"Come on!" Mercer grabbed Davis's arm, pulling her after them. Two of the guys—a blond one and a dark-skinned one with longer hair, were already making decent ground.

"Wait." Davis stopped, pulling her hand from Mercer's. "Are they okay? Mercer, what did you do?"

"They're fine. Just knocked out. We need to get out of here, now, before they wake up."

She nodded uncertainly. If the guards were seriously injured, the manhunt for both of them would grow to epic proportions.

"Come on," he said again, urging her forward into the woods. She realized as she ran that she could be running after anyone. Despite her questions, Davis charged after him into the forest.

She ran until her lungs burned. Mercer reached for her, offering to hold her up, but she pulled away each time. He'd left her—left her vulnerable to getting caught. He'd saved her, too, though. Beneath the terror of getting caught, she was shaken and frustrated. They'd touched land too soon; they'd almost been caught—*she* might have been caught—because Mercer had left her alone.

And he had said on many occasions that he'd never been outside of Durham before TOR-N, yet suddenly he'd made allies here. Which could mean nothing, but it still bothered her.

So she stumbled along, refusing assistance, until she could barely breathe, for what seemed like hours. And then the trees broke, and before her lay a valley with tents pitched at intervals and people walking throughout. It was some sort of settlement or camp. Davis wondered if all Gens in this territory lived like this, on the fringes, or if this was something she was seeing that was entirely unique.

"Come on," Mercer said, waving for her to follow him down the hill.

She slowed to a walk as Mercer and the other two guys bounded downhill toward the other people, who were milling about the camp. People were scattered everywhere, gathering firewood, sewing cloth-

ing, mixing stews, planting flowers. Some of them had built a bon-
fire and were hovering near it. Mercer entered a tent and let it flap
shut behind him without even waiting for her.

She shivered, even though she was sweating. Who were these
people? She'd been uprooted so many times that the feeling of being a stranger had ceased to feel strange. But among the community were people who were clearly Priors—taller, stronger, more
lovely than she—and she didn't know what to make of it. They
walked among Imps without reservation, without maintaining the
distance that was customary in downtown Columbus. Children
held Priors' hands and toddled about happily; they were more flawed
than their parents, Davis realized. Some had gap teeth or a bit of
baby pudge—even blotchy coloring—but all were smiling, as though
these physical imperfections weren't an issue at all. Prior babies were
more beautiful: uniformly pudgy, with symmetrical features and full
heads of hair from day one. But other than the children of her father
and Terri's friends, she hadn't been around many—out of doors,
they were concealed, tucked into strollers that contained bacteria-
resistant shields. These Gen babies interacted with their environment
freely, laughing and pointing at the crickets that hopped above the
grass.

Mercer popped back out of a tent, holding a canteen, which
turned out to be full of water. It was warm but still a relief as it
washed down her throat. He led her to a part of the hill that was
slightly secluded from the camp and she sat down, not wanting to
look at him, not wanting to remember how they'd kissed and then
he'd disappeared just when the TOR-N officers were nearby. It was
midafternoon, but it was a little chilly in this shaded part of the
woods, and she realized she was shaking.

"Why did you leave me this morning?" she asked finally, her voice
hoarse.

"I didn't," he told her. "Not for long, anyway. I'd heard about this commune and I wanted to be sure things were safe before I led you in here. I didn't want to bring you anywhere risky. Here," he told her, handing her a warm mug. "You need to rest."

"But you said we weren't going to stop."

"We needed supplies, Davis."

She knew that. She couldn't pinpoint why she felt so thrown off. Maybe it was just the heat, the adrenaline, the stress. "But," she persisted anyway, "you said you'd never been outside of Durham before. And now you seem so confident, so . . ."

He wrapped his arms around her and she took in the smell of his sweat, and something else, too—a little smoky. She liked his smell. "Davis, I'm just trying to get us safely to Durham like we've talked about."

She pulled back and stared at him, conflicted. "I want to believe you," she said finally. "But I can't shake this feeling that there's something you're not telling me."

Mercer paused, and Davis saw a flash of guilt cross his eyes.

Her pulse leapt. "There *is* something," she whispered.

He looked away, avoiding her gaze. "There is."

"What is it?" She felt light-headed. The whole experience on the commune was surreal, and now, without anyone she could trust, it felt as though she weren't tethered to reality.

"I never told you how I got Narxis," Mercer reminded her. Davis wrinkled her brow in confusion. "Didn't you wonder how I could be a Neither and live in Durham?"

"Not really." Davis shook her head. "I just assumed your story was something like mine. It was an accident. Some sort of mistake at birth."

Mercer laughed hollowly. "I wish it were that simple," he told her. "When I was eighteen and applying to universities, my dad told me I couldn't. He said it was impossible. That was the first time he told me I was a Neither. He'd been keeping it secret my whole life."

Davis's eyes widened. "I'm sorry," she whispered, even though the same thing had happened to her. Hearing someone else talk about it only brought back her own horror and shock.

Mercer shook his head to himself. "He thought he was being kind—thought it would be worse for me if I knew. We—my parents—have enough money. They were going to independently support me, but spin some sort of story for their friends. Say I was an entrepreneur. Basically force me to live a lie. He had a whole faux business model set up for my fake company. The company that would cover my identity."

"It sounds like they love you," Davis said carefully.

"The thing is, my dad's a Neither, but he'd been passing as a Prior for my whole life and for most of his. My mom's a Prior. My dad knew firsthand how hard it was to be a Neither. They tried to get me the operations necessary to be a Prior, but they couldn't. I know he thought he was doing the right thing, but he could have talked to me about it. It would have helped if he'd been honest. It could have been something we shared. I know my dad loves me, but I can't help hating him for this. He ruined my life. He left me with no options but the path he'd chosen for me. When he told me, I thought my life was over. So I ran away."

So that was it. He *had* been outside of Durham before. "You left on purpose," Davis confirmed. Her heart went out to him. He must have been distraught to leave the only home he'd ever known. In exchange for what? Where had he thought he was going? "Oh, Mercer." She leaned into him, feeling his body vibrating with emotion. He focused on a spot behind her, his eyes fixated on nothing.

"I was furious. I ran outside of Durham, where it wasn't as safe. There weren't the same security or sanitization measures on the outskirts. And I got Narxis there. From Suen—a woman who . . . who took me in. Nothing romantic, I swear. Just horribly bad luck." He shook his head. "That's pretty much it. But it's embarrassing, and I was too ashamed to tell you before. If I hadn't been so stubborn and so angry, maybe I wouldn't have left, and maybe this never would have happened." He stopped and looked at her. "But then, I never would have met you."

Davis furrowed her brow, wanting to ask more questions. She understood what Mercer was saying. She knew how it felt to have everything you thought you were turned on its head. "The woman—Suen—did she . . . make it? Did she end up quarantined, too?"

He sighed heavily and shook his head. "We got separated. All I know is I want to go back. I miss Durham. I miss everyone there. And when you came along . . . and you needed answers . . . well, the best doctors are there. I thought we could go together, to help you. We both want to be with the people we love," he continued. "This is the best way to get us there. I just need you to trust me." Suddenly, his face changed. "Oh my God, Davis—you're bleeding." He touched her arm gently, his mouth turned down in concern. His care for her was written all over his eyes. They were the same, she and Mercer. They understood each other, and that was the kind of bond that would never break. The realization moved her so much that she gasped. He misinterpreted it as pain.

"Let me help you," he said. He retreated to the tent where he'd found the canteen and returned with a sponge and a couple of jars. He helped Davis carefully roll her sleeve up to her shoulder, and then tenderly touched the wounds on her arm with the sponge. He was gentle, his eyes bearing true concern. He dipped his hand into a jar of sticky, green paste—aloe, it looked like—and massaged it into her forearm. His head was bent, so she couldn't read the expression in his eyes, but each of his movements was deliberate, as if each conveyed meaning. She didn't want it to end.

Almost immediately, the burning she felt from her wounds subsided, only to be replaced by a feeling equally intense but more pleasurable. His fingers felt gentle and comforting, and it was tempting to relax into his touch. Her skin tingled under his fingers, and Davis felt her body responding to him in a way that went beyond relief from pain. Their intimacy was born not just of genetics but of history, and of a shared longing.

"How do I know I can trust you?" she whispered. "I don't even know where we are—where you've brought me." Even though she already knew she could trust him, she needed to hear it from him.

Mercer leaned toward her in the small tent until his face was just inches from her own. Davis's heart pounded and every part of her body felt alert to his presence, but she didn't duck away. When his lips met hers, gentle and soft, she responded. She could feel through his touch how much he cared.

He lifted a hand to her cheek. "You can always trust me," he said. "This place we're at now—it's a commune that welcomes strangers. They'll help us. They'll give us supplies and show us the safest path back. I will do anything to keep you from danger. I promise."

Davis took in his words, her mind reeling. She had to trust him; she had no choice. But his intentions were clear now. He wanted her. And for her part, she wasn't sure what she wanted. She wasn't sure she could give up on Cole, put Mercer's emotions at risk while she tested herself that way. She wasn't sure romance was something she should even be thinking about just then, even though she felt close to him.

Mercer pulled her to him once again, and this time when she separated, both of them were breathless. The kiss had said it all. She had to trust him; she had to see how things would unravel on their own—but also, she had feelings for him. And with that came the responsibility to discern what she wanted. It was up to her to decide.

12

COLE

He thrashed in his sleep, feverish and sweating. Images of Davis's frightened face flashed through his mind: the hopelessness in her eyes as she struggled to break the straps that held her to a narrow hospital bed. He reached for her, but every time he did, the straps held her tighter, until they were pressing into her skin, cutting off her blood flow. Cole tried to break the heavy, leather straps, and then he was in the Olympiads arena, tugging at them with Davis on stage in front of hundreds of people, and through it all Mari shouted, "Pull yourself together! Cole, be strong! Cole!" Her face was loud, real-

seeming, and he fought to free Davis, but the voice was too immediate and distracting.

"Wake up, Cole!" Mari shouted, and Cole jolted awake, nailing
his head on the top of the bunk he'd made himself in their old barn.
"Must've been a doozy," she commented, eyeing him with concern.
Cole nodded, breathing heavily. It had been two nights since he
started staying in the barn rather than returning to the Slants, but
he was still disoriented.

Since the incident with Vera, he and Mari had been treating each
other with tentative kindness. It was as if they'd reached some sort of
understanding—a mutual respect. They'd seen each other naked,
with their guards down, when they were helping Vera—and both
of them had approved. Part of him was glad Worsley had told him
to stay away, stating it would be safer for both him and Vera that
way—the anxiety of the trip home each night had taken its toll. Even
though he felt less on guard in the Open Country, his dreams were
more troubled than ever. Probably, he thought, because he felt inef-
fectual so far away. He grimaced, pushing the thought from his
mind. He was here to train. To get stronger. So he could make a
difference. He had to remember that.

He reached for the thin handkerchief Mari extended, and wiped
the sweat from his upper back and brow. "Pull yourself together,"
she told him, an echo from his dream. "We're going out for testing.
You need to challenge your senses in the dark. It's the only way for
them to develop. And Cole . . . put a shirt on."

Cole cleared his throat, feeling his face heat. He was glad it was
too dark for her to see too much . . . except, apparently, his shirtless
torso.

"Okay. Just give me a minute," he told her.

After Mari left, Cole struggled to do exactly what she'd asked—
pull himself together—but he was still shaken from the nightmare.

It had felt so *real*. Davis had needed him, and he wasn't able to get to her quickly enough.

When he pulled on his sweatpants and stumbled outside, feeling around in the dark to get his bearings, Mari was already waiting for him. It wasn't a clear night; there was barely even any moonlight to illuminate the landscape. The cold night breeze caused goose bumps to rise on his skin, and Cole shivered. The darkness was oppressive. He wondered if hell was as dark and barren as this.

"You're wearing these," Mari told him, securing two small pouches to the sides of his sneakers.

"What for?"

"We're going to race through the forest. And every time you fall, you're going to put stones in those sacks. There are stones all over the forest; it won't be hard for us to find them."

Cole felt his mouth lifting in a wry smile. This was the kind of training he liked.

"What makes you think I'll be putting any weight in those sacks?" he asked, his question a challenge.

"What makes you think you'll be the one adding the weight?"

Cole grinned, but Mari had already spun away from him and begun to move toward the woods.

"Hey! Wait up," he called after her, taking off toward the sound of her movements. If he'd thought it was dark before, the woods catapulted him into a black abyss. For the first several steps, Cole merely stumbled toward the crunching noise Mari's shoes made against the piles of leaves on the ground. That was the trick, he realized. There was no way he could get ahead as long as he followed her, and he had to follow her in order not to get them both lost. His eyes began to adjust to the dim lighting, and he began to enjoy himself as he darted after Mari—who was as swift as she was tiny. Then his foot caught a branch and he fell, skidding across rocks and twigs and rolling right into a tree.

"Here." Mari was on him almost instantly—what was she, magic?—and extended her hand, offering him four rocks the size of Ping-Pong balls, which she'd apparently scooped up without him noticing in the darkness.

"How am I supposed to run with those?"

She shrugged. "That's your problem. Hurry up." Then she was off again and Cole muttered in frustration as he tried to stuff the stones into the pouches connected to his shoes. When he stood up, he was technically about four pounds heavier. But he hadn't felt so light in a while. The thrill of competition mixed with the clear, brisk night air was exhilarating. He took off after Mari; she was insanely fast, so he'd have to really work to catch up.

Running after her, Cole felt primal, as if part of a pack. After that first fall, he'd begun lifting his feet higher and taking longer strides, and although his muscles were burning, he was flying. The more sure-footed he became, the faster he moved. The darkness worked its way around them until it was just him and Mari and the impact of their feet against the ground and their breathing. Cole surged ahead, gaining momentum as adrenaline kicked in. He felt anonymous—not Gen, not Prior—just like any other wild creature, running to survive and fueled by passion.

When the woods broke to reveal the pond behind Mari's home, Cole could sense that the murky black water was the finish line. He picked up his pace, moving past her inch by inch. Just when he thought he'd left her in the dust, her hands gripped his waist and she vaulted her body weight into him, knocking him down.

"It's not over yet," she told him, locking her legs in his and rolling him into the water. When they hit the surface of the pond, Cole gasped. The water momentarily paralyzed him, and Mari released her grip. She pushed away, bracing her arms against his chest. Then she swam toward the bank and pulled herself from the water. "I think we know who won," she called out in a playful tone. But Cole bristled. She *had* won. He still wasn't good enough. He followed her to the shore, where she knelt, picking sprigs of peppermint in the dark.

"Here," she said, noticing him next to her. "For Vera." She handed him a bunch of peppermint.

"No," he told her. "No. Don't act like it's okay. You won. I'm still not good enough for the Olympiads. Don't act like this whole thing isn't a waste, despite everything you've done. I'm horrible." The words were causing him to unravel—everything he'd been holding in, tightly controlled, for months. Trying to stay strong, trying to keep it together, to focus on the plan. The plan was horseshit. "I'm helpless," he blurted, "and horrible. I'm going to lose this thing and let down everyone I care about. My time's not good enough for the Olympiads. It's just not. I've pushed myself so hard. It's all for nothing. And Davis—" Here his voice cracked. He couldn't look at Mari. Could hardly face himself. "She would never even have been taken away if it wasn't for me."

He sank to the ground, resting his forehead on his knees, trying to force the emotion down—all the regret and the impossibility and the walls, always walls, rising up higher than before to keep him from ever getting to the other side, until he almost stopped believing there *was* another side. But the tide within him refused to be held down. It writhed through him, becoming one choking sob, and then another. He hadn't even known these tears were in him, but they had been, welling in his chest, for weeks, maybe months. He felt Mari's hand on his back but he couldn't look up.

"I can't fix this," he choked out into his knees. Finally, he pulled his head up, harshly wiping the wet from his face. He let out a breath. "No one can, Mari. I can't win the Olympiads. I can't find Davis. I just can't do this."

"Cole—"

He shook his head, cutting her off. "I ruin everything—everyone who gets close to me. My mom has suffered. Michelle. If you know anything about survival, you should know to get the hell away while you can."

"That's not true," Mari began.

He looked at her then—at her strong, stubborn jaw and innocent eyes. He half smiled. "Maybe I'm not meant for love. Maybe I'm just meant for fighting."

Mari punched him in the arm. "Snap out of it, Cole. I know you've been through a lot. But none of that is true." She crossed her arms. "It's normal to grieve. You're putting so much pressure on yourself to fix everything. You're right—you're fucking up along the way. But so does everybody. The people you hurt will forgive you, because they love you. I forgive you for being such an ass to me for so long." She smiled gently. "All you can do is try your best. And . . ." she hesitated, as if gathering her thoughts. "We've had our bumps. But you've shown me what it is to commit everything to someone else, even without any promises, without knowing whether you'll see that person again. That takes incredible courage. You have no idea how much I . . . admire that. How much I wish I had something like that to fight for."

Mari's words cut deep into him, releasing some of the pressure he'd felt for months. She knelt beside him, pulling him into an awkward hug. "It's okay," she told him. "It seems like it isn't, right now, but everything will be okay. Sometimes things are too broken to fix. But you're not there yet—especially not with me."

"Thank you," he said, roughly wiping his eyes again with his T-shirt. "I'm so lucky to have you." He meant it. Beyond the training, she'd become a friend. He saw it now; it was so obvious.

"I'm lucky to have you, too," she told him, pulling back. "You need to realize it. Now," she said, her voice brusque, "pull yourself together, buddy. You have another friend to visit. Maybe you should take these peppermint leaves over to Vera before the sun comes up. I think she'd probably like them. It'll give you some alone time. To clear your head."

Cole looked up at her, his eyes searching. He'd never done that before—broken down in front of anyone. He wasn't sure he'd ever gone there at all. But Mari's eyes were kind and forgiving, and a feeling of tenderness built within him. She wanted him to be strong, and believed he could be. He *could*.

"Sure," he said to her.

"Better get going," she said, nodding in the direction of the Slants. "Stay safe. We'll finish training tomorrow. I'm going to get some shut-eye." She hugged him again, then turned back toward the house without looking back.

"Cole!" Vera's face lit up in delight when he arrived forty minutes later. He'd shown up early on purpose, to avoid Worsley, and hadn't expected her to be awake at only six a.m. From the look of it, though, she'd been awake for hours. She was propped up on the bed she used in the back of the clinic—a curtained-off space formerly used for Worsley's occasional patient. Her lap was covered with the brightly striped afghan she'd knitted, and the ukulele Cole had given her was propped in the corner of the room, along with a cello. Some marigolds rested on the table next to her bed. Her face was freshly washed, though her eyes were hooded and rimmed with dark circles and it looked like it had been a while since she'd brushed her hair. Still, she looked alert, and he was happy to see it.

"I'm so glad you came," she told him. "But why so early? Not that I'm complaining! I get so *bored* around here. It's nice to have a gentleman caller." She winked, smiling up at him. "I'm feeling so much better, Cole. I can't tell you how much. Worsley brought me a cello, a real cello! But I'm so glad to see you. Sometimes I still have nightmares . . . and I'm so lonely . . . anyway, I'm babbling." Her bright look had a hint of sadness around her eyes, but her gratitude was palpable. "What did you bring me? I'm so sorry about last time," she rushed on. "I just . . . I was scared. I lost it. I was afraid I'd alienated you. Come sit." She patted the side of the bed eagerly.

Under strict instructions from Worsley, Vera was supposed to lie prone as much as possible. Cole knew she must be suffering more than she made out to be. He felt a pang when he realized that he and Worsley were her only friends right now . . . and soon he'd need to taper off his visits.

"Number one, you'll never alienate me," Cole said. "And number two, I brought more of your favorite." She smiled, and he smiled in return.

"More peppermint?" She clapped her hands, and the sleeves of her shirt shifted back to reveal fresh cuts.

Cole recoiled. Had she been hurting herself again? "Vera," he said, reaching for her arm. "Let me see."

She yanked it back. "Those are old," she said. "I'm not doing that anymore. I'm so much better now!"

He wasn't sure whether to believe her. "Where's Thomas?"

"He slept at his house tonight," she told him. "I was feeling so much better and he wanted to pick up some supplies. He should be back in a few hours."

"I hope I didn't wake you."

"No, no." She waved off the suggestion. "The baby makes it uncomfortable to sleep, and I get up so early anyway. I used to practice my cello at five every day anyway. And now I can again! I'm so excited, Cole. My turnaround has been wonderful. Everything is going to be wonderful. When you win the Olympiads and the baby is born and you bring Davis back, I'm going to throw us all a huge rooftop party at my parents' place." She beamed at Cole, waiting for his reaction.

He managed to force a smile. "Okay," he said. "That sounds nice."

"Nice? It'll be perfect. We'll even play Spins." She winked at him, and he again tried to smile. Something was off about her. She was disconnecting, separating herself from the reality of the situation. She might never return to Columbus, not after disgracing her family. She was so clearly in denial.

"So what brought you out here?" Vera asked. "I wasn't expecting you again for a while."

"No reason." Cole shrugged, avoiding her gaze. Something about Vera's concern tugged at his heart.

"You miss her," she said quietly. Cole nodded, tensing up. He did miss her. Every day, all the time. Not being able to talk to Davis was one of the great disappointments of his life just then. Not being able to see her, hear her voice, make her laugh. There was so much he wanted to say to her. "I miss her, too," Vera said. Her face was no longer manic, as it had been only moments before. Now she seemed to be herself again. "Part of me . . . I feel like there was so much time we wasted."

"What do you mean?"

"You know." She waved a hand. "We were so preoccupied with the Olympiads, and parties, and how we looked, and just . . . *winning*. But I'm more than that. And she definitely was. Is," she corrected. "Looking back, I'm seeing all the things I never saw before. She was so *open* about things. Really accepting, in ways the rest of us weren't. I remember some of the conversations we had about Priors and Gens. She would speculate, ask why the segregation was necessary. What purpose it was achieving. And we all thought that kind of thing was so weird. And now I see the rest of us were just afraid, and she was the only one thinking for herself."

"She's special," Cole said softly, his throat tight. Vera reached out and put a hand on his.

"Yeah, she is," she agreed. "She's lucky to have you. And we'll all be together again soon!" Cole blinked twice, trying not to let tears well in his eyes. Vera had no idea what he was feeling. She was trying to make the best of it by existing in a fantasyland.

"Vera," he started, half afraid of what he was about to say. "It's been over three months now. I don't feel like I *do* have her." He stopped, drawing in a breath, his throat tightening. "She thinks I'm dead. She'd have known that if I died, I'd want her to move on." He looked away, swallowing hard. Vera pushed herself forward to touch his elbow.

"You're right," she told him. "She'd have known that. But she wouldn't have been able to do it. Listen to me, Cole." She put a hand to his face, forcing him to look at her. Her own chocolate-brown eyes were wide and earnest. "Davis never had a love like you. None of us did. When you came along, you changed her. Everything is different now. Davis is a good person, a loyal one. She's not someone who forgets. She's yours, Cole. She always was."

Vera's words pushed him to tears. He pulled her close to him. Vera's words reminded him that what he and Davis had shared was bigger than anything time or distance could break. It was just what he'd needed to hear in his most vulnerable moment.

"Thank you," he said, giving her a kiss on the cheek. He didn't even care anymore whether she saw him cry.

"Let's get you some tea," she suggested, pushing back her blanket and standing up before he could stop her.

He moved to help her, but she shook him off. Still, she swayed a little on her feet. Cole frowned, worried.

She moved to a tiny pantry mounted on the wall, each step slow and deliberate.

"Vera," he said. "Just let me get it." He moved to help her, but she was already reaching for the jar of honey. She'd just closed her palm around it when she stumbled. Cole saw her eyes roll back in her head, and she fainted. Cole caught her just in time, but the jar crashed to the floor and shattered into a dozen sticky shards.

Cole lifted her back into bed with some effort, his heart racing. He wet a cloth and dabbed at her forehead, wondering where the hell Worsley was and why he wasn't there watching her, when clearly she needed it. What was really going on here? He wiped up the mess, careful to get every minute shard of glass off the floor, as she lay there.

Three or four minutes later, Vera's eyes fluttered open. Cole fed her sips of cold water, allowing her to get her bearings.

"How often does this happen?" he asked, his voice serious.

"It's nothing," she said, her voice a little curt. "I told you, I'm a million times better. This is the first time I ever fainted. It's probably just because I'm lying down so much; I'm not used to standing. Is everything okay? Did I fall on my back or my stomach? The baby is kicking, but . . ."

"I caught you," Cole assured her. "There was no impact." Still. What if he *hadn't* caught her? What if she'd gotten up to go to the bathroom or make her own tea—or anything, really—and no one was there to catch her? His blood boiled, and he was near panic. He'd never forgive himself if Davis's best friend was injured, and it was entirely preventable. But why wasn't she improving? She didn't seem better at all. All of a sudden, the feeling that had come over him at the pond—the one that had caused him to break down in front of Mari—was returning full throttle.

"Worsley should be back soon," Vera told him, once again shifting, becoming more urgent, more manic. Her eyes wouldn't stay still. "Would you like to eat breakfast with us?" she asked. "He makes me eggs or pancakes every morning. It's so generous. He says eggs are difficult to get, but the baby needs protein."

"Vera—" Cole started, but Vera cut him off.

"I'm so glad she found you," she told him. "She's always deserved the best. And now she's found it."

He leaned toward her, wrapping her in another quick hug.

As he pulled away, Vera broke into a series of hacking coughs.

"Good God," Cole said.

She coughed harder, phlegmy and loud, and Cole went to get a rag from Worsley's supply of sterile equipment to wipe her mouth. When he returned, she was trembling all over, and there was blood covering the front of her tunic and splattered on her chin.

"Vera!" he gasped.

"I'm fine," she insisted. "Really, Cole. It barely ever happens. You should just go." But her eyes were rolled slightly back in her head and her words were slurred. She coughed again into the rag he held against her mouth, and sure enough, when he pulled it back it was dotted with blood.

"I'm just going to sleep, Cole," she said, leaning her head back on the pillow. "I'm so tired. But I can't wait for everything. The party, the fun. We'll give it just a few more weeks. Just a few more weeks and it'll all be over."

Cole didn't know what to say to that. He wasn't sure what she was anticipating—whether it was delirium or some foresight on her part that she had just a few more weeks left in her. When she fell asleep, he took her pulse. It was strong, but her breathing was shallow. He sat by her bedside, waiting for Worsley to return.

He tried to swallow back the terror in his throat, but found that it was impossible.

13

DAVIS

Davis beat at a rug with a large wooden broom, watching clouds of dust pour out of it. These were the rugs the people of the commune used in their homes—a far cry from the designer area rugs they'd had steam cleaned each week back in Columbus. Davis didn't mind the physical act of beating dust from the rugs, though. It was unfamiliar, and her arms ached, but it felt good to take out all her frustrations that way.

"Must be thinking of someone you wanna give it to pretty good," said May, one of the older women at the commune. Davis smiled, wishing May knew even half the truth: how the feeling of power-lessness was eating away at her. They were still waiting to hear back from one of Mercer's contacts in Durham, and every hour that passed with no word was an hour lost, one that brought even greater uncertainty.

"You could say that," was all she said. She was trying her hard-est, but she was still lagging behind Kira, a girl of about fourteen.

"This is what you do," Kira told her, repositioning the broom so the handled side—not the side with the bristles—made contact with the rug. "I know it seems weird, because you cover less space, but actually you get more oomph this way."

"Thanks," Davis told her gratefully. They had to get through a dozen rugs before the end of the day, because there was more work to be done tomorrow. Lots of it, Kira had informed her. Davis had never had to work hard in her life—at least at manual labor—and she knew it showed. Still, she knew how to work hard generally, like in ballet, and she could tell the others sensed it. Because of that, they were kind and patient. Or maybe they were just kind and patient overall, she realized.

Davis glanced over at Mercer, who had just finished building a fire and was now strumming a song on one of the Neithers' guitars. She smiled as a little girl with blond pigtails, Madeleine, sidled up to him and nudged her way under his arm, his rich voice filling the space between them. He plucked a few chords, then guided the little girl's fingers on top of his own, allowing her to control the melody. She giggled loudly, tossing her head back. The gesture reminded Davis of Fia, and her chest tightened. Mercer looked down at the girl, laughing a little at her enthusiasm.

Seeing him with her ignited a wave of emotions that Davis had been fighting to suppress. She still felt tingly and light from their kiss. Over the course of the past day, it had wormed its way into her brain at random times; and now, as he sang to the little girl, rasping just a little and gently moving her smaller fingers along with his, Davis couldn't ignore the familiar fluttering in her heart. The kiss had been intense; gentle and somehow endless. It had taken her by surprise—Mercer was her *friend*, and all of a sudden, he was something more.

But he wasn't Cole. When she thought of Cole, the tenderness she felt for Mercer dissipated, giving way to guilt and confusion. Cole was dead, and she still hadn't found a way to tell his family how much he had meant to her. As far as they knew, Cole and Davis had never met, had never fallen in love. He was fading in her memories, and she felt wholly disconnected from everything they had shared.

Every time she looked Mercer's way and thought about their kiss, she felt an overwhelming sense of betrayal to Cole's memory. Davis resolved to push any romantic feelings aside—she needed to focus on their mission. Still, she couldn't help but take one quick glance at Mercer and the little girl. The little girl titled her head back, singing at full volume in duet with Mercer. It was a song Davis knew well, an old folk tune her father had sung to her as a child.

"Every day with you," Davis sang, moving toward them. Mercer met her eyes and smiled. "Every day with you is like a freight train without its brakes."

Three hours later, Davis heard a knock on the door to the laundry room, where she was working with two other women and a friendly man who painted watercolors. "I'd love to make you a miniature," he was saying when Mercer walked in. Mercer had told the others at the commune that he and Davis were just passing by, hoping to relocate from Columbus to Durham. It was a lie, but a necessary one, and one the people hadn't questioned. They seemed comfortable with ambiguity here. Had Mercer and Davis admitted they'd escaped from TOR-N, however, it could have been a different story. They might have been afraid.

The painter smiled at Davis as he folded a stack of T-shirts. Mercer strode into the room, his face alight with excitement, and said a quick hello to the man before breaking into their conversation.

"What is it?" Davis asked.

"Come outside," he whispered. He grabbed her hands, pulling her into the shadows of the commune. Davis glanced back at Hugh, the painter, who gave her a small wave good-bye.

It was past midnight, and most of the commune was already in bed. Just a few lights shone from within the modest cabin walls. "I sent a message out with Jefferson late yesterday," he told her, keeping his voice low. "He's one of the most reliable sympathizers. He was heading to the border of Durham under the guise of meeting up with a guy who was passing him some supplies for the commune. His guy went to school with me, knows my friend Jan. Anyway, he went back again today, and Jan sent a message back." Mercer was so excited, she could barely understand him. "I told you coming here would work. I told you they could get a message across."

"What did she say? What did your message say?" Davis had to stop herself from biting her nails.

"Jan's dad has connections in Durham," Mercer explained. "He's the most powerful person I can think of to help us. I just wanted to run it by Jan rather than showing up and expecting it. But she just sent over the okay. We can leave tonight and be there by morning." He seemed charged; he was pacing back and forth. It was infectious. Davis felt an overwhelming contradiction of emotions—the eager anticipation she used to feel the night before her birthday as a kid, mixed with the dread she'd felt while lining up for the Physical Aptitudes.

"Okay," she said, taking a huge breath. "Let's do it."

Five minutes later they were gathering their things and saying their good-byes. Davis stooped to hug Madeleine, who handed Mercer a picture she'd drawn of him playing his guitar, with her in stick-figure form next to him. Mercer smiled and gave her a kiss on the cheek. "Stay in touch," said Madeleine's father. "This one's become awfully fond of you."

"We'll be back," Davis promised, belatedly surprised at her own use of *we*. She and Mercer weren't a "we." Were they? Every little admission to her feelings for Mercer shook her up. His voice. The way he kissed little Madeleine. His way of soothing Davis when she felt panicked, simply by placing a hand on her forearm, as he did now.

By the time they reached the outskirts of Durham—walking much of the way and hopping aboard a train illegally for a full day, stowing away with the luggage—Davis's legs burned with exertion and her hair was stringy and filthy. She barely felt it, though, when Mercer reached down for her from the top of a craggy drop-off, hoisting her over its jagged edge to the top of a hill overlooking a valley city. Before them spread Durham, startling Davis with its beauty.

She couldn't help sounding awestruck. "It looks a little like Columbus from the monorail . . . except bigger." Skyscrapers rose toward the sky and stretched in seemingly endless rows before them. In the fog of the night, their lines were blurred, and their windows resembled a sea of glittering eyes. Davis's pulse accelerated. It wasn't home, but it felt close enough to Columbus to move her.

Light projections crisscrossed above the buildings, heralding theater productions and broadcasting the faces of movie stars. It was a cluster of beautiful chaos. Davis felt more alive than she had in months.

"There are the primary research facilities," Mercer told her, pointing out three behemoth buildings with tall, red-lit spires. They were too far away to see people, but in a city like this, Davis imagined the streets would be teeming. "That's where our answers are."

"It's stunning," Davis breathed.

"It's the best city on earth," Mercer said quietly.

"Only 'cause you haven't seen Columbus," Davis teased.

She reached for his hand, squeezing it gently. She knew what it was like to miss home. "So what are we waiting for?"

Neither of them talked about what would happen when they found Dr. Hassman and delivered to him the samples he needed. Neither of them mentioned the kiss, or what it meant, or what it would mean to be separated again. But the way Mercer looked at her just then, his eyes full of feeling, she knew it meant a lot. It would be painful for them both.

As they drew closer, Davis felt her anxiety steadily increasing. Mercer, on the other hand, was walking several paces ahead of her, more eager than ever.

The sight of a big city triggered flashbacks of the last time she was in Columbus, fleeing from patrolmen. This situation—sneaking into another heavily patrolled city—was no safer. "Are you sure Jan's going to help us?" she asked, suddenly doubtful. The thought of getting thrown back in quarantine—or worse—put her nerves on edge. She fought against her anxiety, taking a deep breath and standing tall. She had to fake confidence, even if she didn't feel any. This was happening, and she needed to be strong.

Mercer casually slung an arm around her shoulders, rubbing them to keep her warm. "I'm positive," he said. "She's getting us IDs. Once we're past the checkpoint, we're fine. I spent my whole life here as a Neither; both of us still pass for Priors. Getting in is the hardest part, and we've got that covered." Davis nodded, but his words didn't entirely vanquish the heady doubt she felt. "We're picking them up just south of Checkpoint A. They're going to be inside an old outhouse just outside the city border. If they're not there, we'll know something happened. We just turn around. If they're there, we're clear. It's less than a mile from here," he told her, lifting her chin with a finger. "Hang in there for a little while longer."

They approached the outhouse quietly. Davis's heart was in her throat as Mercer reached into its rusted exterior, withdrawing a thin white envelope and a change of clothes for each of them. He wrinkled his nose as he did. Davis grimaced. She didn't want to know what the inside of an ancient outhouse looked like, but she gratefully accepted the blue sundress and sandals Mercer extended toward her. Mercer opened the envelope and grinned, waving them in the air.

"Told you," he whispered, pushing his thumb against the digitized plastic to activate it, and nodding for Davis to do the same. "Nothing to worry about."

They pocketed their activated cards and retreated the way they'd come, stopping behind some trees to quickly change before approaching the security checkpoint from the mining side of the outskirts. Davis swept her hair up in a ponytail; it was the best she could do. But looking at Mercer and seeing his appreciative glance, she thought they could pass for normal again. They'd already planned to say they'd gone to the mines outside of Durham for research for a school project, if the patrols asked why two teenagers were wandering outside the city limits.

"IDs," the officer said in a gruff tone as they approached. He held out a meaty palm, eyeing Davis from head to toe without reservation. She found herself tensing as he examined her photo. For the first time, she wondered how far the news of her episode with Cole had traveled. She'd assumed it would stay in Columbus—it was rare that they were privy to the goings-on in other territories—

but watching the man's eyes narrow as he took in her information ignited fresh panic. She breathed audibly when he nodded and handed the small digitized card back to her.

He accepted Mercer's next, his eyes narrowed. "Just a minute." The officer stood and approached his colleague, muttering something low as he showed the other man Mercer's ID. Mercer and Davis exchanged anxious looks. Of the two of them, Mercer looked the most similar to his identification picture. Davis had dropped at least ten pounds from her illness, and her hair wasn't as lustrous as it had been in the photo used for her own ID. Hers was the risky one. His had been the safe bet.

The two officers returned to the checkpoint. The one wielding Mercer's ID was frowning. "You'll need to move through the DNA reader," he said, gesturing toward a short line that was forming to their left, in front of an elaborate metal gateway. "Standard procedure." Davis watched as lasers scanned the figure of a slim, middle-aged Prior. The machine beeped green and a patrolman waved her through to Durham.

"Is that really necessary?" Mercer asked, drawing up to his full height.

"'Fraid so," said the officer. "Random screening. We can't have non-Priors entering Durham."

"I'm a personal friend of Chris Thurber's," Mercer said in an authority-laden tone. Davis drew back, surprised. Her own palms were sweating from fear—if he stepped through the machine, it would definitely give them away—but Mercer's body language conveyed confidence, authority, and irritation.

"Is that so?"

"It is," Mercer told him. "And we have an appointment scheduled. I can't wait in a line. I don't have time for this. And frankly, I'm insulted by the implications of this testing."

"No one's saying you're not a Prior," the guy said, rolling his eyes. "Like I said. It's standard."

"Then I'm sure you can make an exception for a close friend of the Thurbers," Mercer pressed, his face adopting a look of determination. He stared at the patrolmen directly, his gaze unfaltering. His stance was wide, his shoulders squared. He was the picture of confidence and authority.

"Look," the patrolman said, his face turning a little red. "You don't have time for that line, but I don't have time for this conversation. Save us all a little trouble and just go through the checkpoint. Unless there's something you're trying to hide?"

"Merkin." The patrolman, still clutching Mercer's ID, swiveled at the sound of his name. His colleague was squinting over the ID. "Hold up a second." The second patrolman motioned to Davis to hand over her own ID, and her heart seized.

"They're special clearance," he said to Merkin. "Let 'em through."

Merkin looked at the light blue indicator that flashed in the corner of the IDs. Davis hadn't even known what it meant, and she sensed from the look of relief that passed over Mercer's face just briefly that he hadn't either. Merkin gritted his teeth and motioned them through, glaring, without another word.

"Thank you, sir," Mercer said as they passed, without a hint of condescension.

They were through.

"How did you do that?" Davis asked as they crossed the narrow path that led from the gateway into the city proper. "You were so . . . Prior snobby."

"I lived among Priors, as a Prior, my whole life," Mercer reminded her. "Did you forget so quickly what it was like?"

She had forgotten, a little. Even though her whole life she had believed she was a Prior, she'd always felt a little removed, as though no one fully understood her. Still, she'd been able to function easily in that world because it was all she'd known. But now, entering the city, she saw it as more than just a different city. It was a different *life.*

Tall, Nordic-looking Priors milled around her, mixing with dark beauties and muscular redheads. All were different, but all possessed the same level of physical perfection: whether built for athleticism or delicate enough for the runway, they were perfect specimens, designed for what they excelled at. Davis had known it would be like this. But she was unprepared for her shocking feeling of inadequacy.

"Are we going to your family's place?" she asked Mercer, drawing her shoulders back in an effort to mimic his confident stride.

"First to Jan's," he told her. "Jan Thurber's," he added.

"So that wasn't just a story?"

"'Friend' was a bit of an exaggeration," he admitted. "I'm close to Jan, but I've only met her father a couple of times. I'm glad she was able to pull this off."

"Is it far?"

Mercer shook his head. "Just around this next block." He gave her shoulder a comforting squeeze, seeming to sense her anxiety.

Durham stretched out around them in a grid of skyscrapers, much like Columbus, with the exception of the coast—which could be seen from nearly every angle. The beautiful water lapped at the sides of long boardwalks, reminding Davis how much of the land had eroded over the last one hundred years. It was breathtaking, almost like an island but rife with skyscrapers, which made her feel right at home. So Davis wasn't surprised when Mercer led her into a towering apartment building. They shot up fifty stories in a glass-bottomed elevator, and then the doors opened onto an elaborately decorated foyer.

"It's beautiful." Davis motioned to a watercolor she recognized by a prominent modern artist whose name she couldn't place.

"De Ville," Mercer told her. "The Thurbers are collectors." He pressed the doorbell and they waited as the security monitors read their faces. Less than a minute later, a pretty blond girl threw open the door and hurtled into Mercer's arms.

"I'm so happy to see you!" she said into his shoulder. "How are you? Are you okay? Are you sick?" She pulled back, looking Mercer over from head to toe. "I'd never know you were sick. What was it like there? I'm so glad you're back safe." Her voice was thick, as if she was trying not to cry.

"I'm better now," Mercer told her. "Davis and I both are. But it was a long road. TOR-N was . . ." He trailed off, averting his eyes. "Let's talk about it later, okay?" He reached back for Davis's hand, pulling her closer.

"If you're worried about my parents, they're away all week at a conference," she said, pulling him to her—and away from Davis—once again. Davis averted her eyes; she didn't know why she felt a pang at their closeness, but it was unmistakable.

"I just can't talk about it now," Mercer replied. "I can't believe I'm home. I want to soak it up," he murmured into Jan's neck. "We owe you big for the IDs. How are my parents?" he asked suddenly. "I thought they'd be here."

"They don't know you're back yet," Jan said, looking sad. "After the way you guys left it . . . they were deeply hurt, Mercer, when you ran away. I thought you'd want to handle it yourself."

He nodded. "Thank you. You've done so much."

"Don't think about it," she said, finally releasing him. "Of course I would do anything for you. Just like you would for me."

"I would."

"Exactly." She turned to Davis, fixing her with a bright smile, her thick eyebrows knitting together. She was an unorthodox beauty, with a gap in her teeth that only accentuated her good looks—Davis had to assume it was there on purpose. "You must be the friend! So good to meet you." She extended a palm and Davis took it, but Jan withdrew it almost immediately, turning back to Mercer. "Are you sure you're feeling all right? How did they treat you there?" she asked. "I'm guessing not well or you wouldn't have wanted to bust out of there."

"Let's talk about it later," said Mercer. "Tell me what's been happening in Durham. And Columbus, if you've heard anything. That's where Davis is from." Davis smiled at him gratefully. She'd been dying for news.

"We have *so* much to catch up on!" Jan exclaimed, grabbing his arm. "Come in, come in! You have no idea what's been happening since you've been away. Keith Sterns is dating Emory. *Emory.* Right?" She laughed at the expression on Mercer's face. The two walked ahead of Davis, arm in arm, leading the way through a modern living room decorated in more watercolors by the same artist as in the foyer, if Davis was right about the style. Davis trailed after them, impatient, although Mercer turned, shooting her an apologetic look. She knew Mercer was happy to be home, and she knew Jan had been dying to see him, but maybe Jan didn't realize the significance of why they were there. Maybe Mercer hadn't told her everything. For her part, Davis wanted to get right to the laboratories. She wanted to get answers as soon as possible. She couldn't help but feel a wave of irritation at Jan's small talk—Jan clearly didn't understand what was at stake.

"Davis, where did you say you were from?" Jan asked a few minutes later, when they were seated across from one another at the family's long dining table. Davis sipped the hot chocolate Jan had given her. It was the best thing she'd tasted in months; at TOR-N, they'd had very limited sustenance—some vitamin shakes and a bit of produce and biscuits here and there. Once, they'd had chicken. Nothing sweet or indulgent.

"Columbus," Davis reminded her. "It's a lot like this, from what I can tell."

"Oh no," Jan laughed, sharing a look with Mercer. "Durham is much better!"

Davis's fingers tightened around the mug. "You've been?" She didn't know why this girl was irritating her. It wasn't fair, given how kind Jan had been to help them out. Davis told herself she was being irrational. Still, to hear Jan so casually insult the city she loved and missed every single day was difficult.

"I have friends who have," Jan clarified. "Actually, my friend Peter is there right now. You remember Peter Sloan?" She turned to Mercer again, dismissing Davis. Davis flushed, fighting the urge to stand up and move on without Mercer. She needed his connections to make this work—she couldn't do it alone.

"I've been gone for a few months, not years," Mercer reminded her. "My short-term memory is a little better than you give me credit for. And anyway, from what Davis has told me, Columbus sounds great. They have these competitions every year called the Olympiads—"

"Peter's cousin is competing in the Olympiads in a few days! I guess the city is making a huge recovery after the riots and . . . well. The disease." Jan paused awkwardly. "Anyway. They're supposed to be the best Olympiads in years. They're going to be covered all over the New Atlantic."

"The Olympiads are happening?" Davis's body was stock-still. She couldn't believe the city was moving forward with the events. What else had happened in her absence? Every part of her longed to be back with her family, a cure in hand, Narxis obliterated.

Jan nodded with enthusiasm.

"Is there any other news from Columbus? Have any deaths been reported?" Davis knew it was a stretch, given that the city had always fought to conceal the disease's existence. Still, anything—any little crumb of news—would be something to go on.

Jan shrugged. "Nope. Just the Olympiads. That's pretty much dominating inter-Atlantic news right now. Oh!" she said, her voice bubbling over with enthusiasm. "That reminds me, though! There's a party tonight. In Raleigh. It's a huge gala thrown by the Research Triangle Institute. A bunch of research kids will be there."

"That's what we call the kids we know whose parents are scientists," Mercer clarified.

"Mercer," Davis reminded him quietly, "we have to find Dr. Hassman. Remember?"

"Dr. Hassman? Why do you need him? He'll be there," Jan said.

"That's great!" Mercer exclaimed. "Can you get us in, though?"

"Already taken care of," she said with a grin, producing three tickets from her bag. "It's a huge event. But we'll know people there. And you guys can ask questions if you want. It won't seem weird— the whole event is centered around young donors. We're 'the next generation of research,' and all that," she said, rolling her eyes and using air quotes around the phrase. "Basically they just want to take our inheritances."

Davis tried not to cringe at the reference to Prior wealth. She'd been just like Jan only a few months ago. But now this all felt foreign to her. She looked at Mercer, trying to gauge what he was really thinking behind the cloak of his enthusiasm for being home.

"We need to find Dr. Hassman as soon as we can," he told Jan, reading Davis's expression. "Like Davis said. It's super important."

"He'll be at the gala for sure," Jan assured him. "He's so rarely in town lately. He's coming back from a conference in China just for this. It's your chance. Care to explain?" She raised her eyebrows.

"Nah," Mercer said. "Long story. We'll tell you everything later."

Whether or not he meant it, Davis wasn't sure. But Mercer looked relieved, making Davis wonder just how confident he'd actually been about their plan from the start. "Give it just a couple of days," he told Davis, when Jan excused herself to the bathroom. "We're almost there."

"I can wait," she told him. "It'll be hard, though. This mission— Dr. Hassman, getting the cure—it's all we have. It's all *I* have. I need to get back to Columbus with an answer."

"And you will. But you need to be patient, play it cool until the gala." His expression was earnest. In the look they shared, Davis's worries about Jan fell away, as did her anxieties and her impatience. He was right. The stakes were too high; she had to wait just a little while longer. In order to enter Columbus safely again, she had to find a cure. And the gala was her only chance.

14

COLE

It was a full four hours before Worsley returned. And in that four hours, Cole's blood had run from hot to boiling. When he heard the key in the latch, he leapt up, palms clenched. Vera was still asleep—deep asleep. She didn't even move when Worsley walked in. She was sleeping far more than was normal, and her face was sweaty and pale.

"What the fuck kind of operation are you running, here?" Cole demanded of Worsley, who looked startled to find him there, and then slightly ashamed.

"I'm not usually gone this long, I—"

"I don't care what your bullshit reason is," Cole said, crossing the room toward Worsley. He knew Thomas was intimidated by his physicality, so he drew himself to his full height and squared his shoulders, flexing his forearms as he clenched his fists. If he was made to fight, he'd fight.

Thomas didn't back down, as Cole had expected.

"You'd better stop whatever it is you're doing here," Cole told him, his voice low. The last thing he wanted to do was wake Vera and frighten her. "She's worse, not better. She *fainted* today. She was coughing up blood. How often has that been happening?"

"*Back off*, Cole." Worsley folded his arms. "Maybe you weren't aware of how bad she was when she came in here. She's improved dramatically. All the tests are coming out positive. The experiments are working. I'm close. So close."

"But is she close, too?" Cole hissed. "Close to death?"

"Maybe you've just been a little too distracted to notice her progress," Worsley snapped. "Out there in the woods with . . . what's her name? Braddock's daughter. Mari? Maybe your vision's been a little cloudy lately. And maybe that's understandable. You're sparring with a pretty girl all day long, isn't that right?"

That was all it took. Cole swung at him, knocking him to the floor. Worsley had no right to accuse him of those things. No right to imply anything about him and Mari.

"Hypocrite," Worsley muttered from where he lay on the floor, nursing his face. "You act like you care. You're nothing but a common hypocrite."

Cole resisted the urge to kick him, punch him again, anything—because he knew his next punch could kill Worsley. Instead, he moved for the door before he could do anything else he would regret.

"You can forget my help with the Olympiads," Worsley called after him. "That was a stupid idea from the start. Go ahead and get yourself killed. Just don't bring me down with you."

Cole slammed the door on his way out. He was fucked, truly fucked. Now he had no chance of entering the Olympiads and no control over what happened with Vera. He'd never be able to go visit her, to check on her progress, unless he staked out the lab and snuck in while Worsley was away. There were no more options.

By the time he got to his hideaway, he was panting from exertion. He'd jogged from Worsley's lab, but he was still feeling furious and keyed up about Worsley's accusations about Mari and about the state of Vera's health—not to mention his own total loss of control. Worsley's words had struck a nerve. But he should have been able to keep his temper in check.

The second he entered the shoe box of a room, he instinctively knew someone had been there. It was as if the air were different—heavier somehow, and carrying the scent of someone else. What else could go wrong? He wasn't normally so skittish, but each time he'd been caught in the past—up to the day he and Davis were torn apart—he'd felt this same sense of dread in his gut. It wasn't something he could ignore. Now Cole leaned against the door, calculating his next move. He needed a clear head.

The room was small enough that he'd have seen someone already, if they were still there. As he took a quick survey, though, his suspicions were confirmed. Distinct footprints—at least a size bigger than his own—made slight impressions in the dust that had collected on the floor in his absence. The books he kept stacked in a neat pile next to his bed were scattered about. He didn't have anything in the room that would reveal his identity. But the thought of someone invading his space—and potentially returning—made his whole body stiffen in fear.

He dragged a bag of rice from the opposite corner—stored provisions, just in case—and moved it in front of the door. The rice weighed about twenty pounds but clearly wouldn't be enough. There were some old cans of paint thinner, long expired, lining another wall, and he hefted these over, one by one, creating a strong barricade. When he was done, he jiggled the knob and gave the door a hard wrench toward himself. It didn't budge. Still, there was the matter of the back window.

Its shade hung open from a loose latch, exposing an empty, gaping hole where there should have been a windowpane. Cole swore under his breath—he'd thought about fixing it since Michelle had led him to the abandoned hideaway a few months ago, but he'd figured fixing it might draw attention to the hideaway. Now he saw it was practically an invitation for unwelcomed visitors. He might not be able to completely block off the window, but he could at least set a trap to alert him of any intruders and slow them down.

Cole filled a plastic tub with flour from his makeshift pantry and strung a long rope through the handle of the tub, hanging it from an electrical cord that snaked across the ceiling. Then he tied the free end of the cord to the dangling shutter, pulling it tight so the shutter was partially closed. Just to be sure, he tested it, tugging the shutter open. The cord pulled the tub's handle and the tub tipped over altogether, spilling flour all over the floor. Cole smiled. *Success.* If someone was after him, at least the sound of the trap being activated would give him time to react.

Now for some sleep.

Cole lay in bed, tossing and turning, unable to drift off. He wanted to be back in the barn behind Mari's house, where he felt safe and comfortable. He wanted to curse Worsley, throw another punch, knock him down cold this time.

Cole sprang out of bed, grabbing his boxing gloves. He was just keyed up. His fight with Worsley had messed with his head. Cole threw a few air punches, moving in a circle as he did so. Then he dropped to the ground for push-ups, pushing his fury further away each time he lifted his body off the ground. He took more of the flour and rice and filled a burlap sack with it, then strung it from the ceiling with a cord. His makeshift punching bag was lumpy and uneven, but it was good enough. With each punch he took he found himself relaxing a little. As much as he resented the FEUDS and his role in them, he had to admit he missed fighting. He missed the power of it, the opportunity for emotional release. He missed his old life.

Then a long scraping sound emanated from the other side of the room, followed by a big poof of flour, far denser than the soft tufts spraying out of his punching bag with each hit.

Cole leapt back, heart pounding. The shutter swung open. Some-one *had* been following him! Cole let out a low, guttural growl and lunged toward the trespasser, pulling his right elbow up and back for a punch. The guy was covered in flour, hacking. He seemed to be trying to say something.

"Wait!" the intruder's voice called, just as Cole was about to swing. There was something about the voice that was familiar, and Cole paused. He couldn't make out any defining physical features beneath the flour . . .

"Cole! It's me, Brent."

Brent. Cole gasped in relief.

"What the hell, man? What are you doing here?" He moved toward Brent, drawing him into a one-armed hug.

"It *is* you," Brent said, his voice filled with awe.

"It's me," Cole whispered. "But lower your voice and get in here. Man, is it good to see you." He pulled Brent in and partially closed the shutter, looking out before he did so to make sure no one had seen them. It was great to see Brent—really to see anyone from his life before he went into hiding. The fact that most of his friends and family thought he was dead was weird, unsettling. There were so many times he'd wanted to sneak over to Brent's and tell him the truth, but it had been too risky—he didn't want to implicate anyone. With Brent standing in front of him now, he felt a surge of elation coupled with terror.

"You can't tell anyone." His voice was urgent. Brent gaped around him at Cole's hideaway, and Cole saw it for the first time from someone else's eyes: the sink that didn't even have working water, the stockpiles of provisions, the filthy mattress. It was worse than even the poorest parts of the Slants. It was a hovel.

"Cole. Are you okay? Jesus. I'm so glad you're alive. But what are you—"

"How did you find out?" Cole interrupted him, his pulse hammering. "Who else knows?"

"Relax," Brent said. "Just me. Michelle told me. She tried to play it off at first . . . but I know her well enough to know when she's lying. She explained everything. She told me not to tell, and I haven't."

"God." Cole ran a hand through his hair. If Michelle had told Brent, who knew who else she'd told? "Why is Michelle randomly telling people? I thought I could trust her." He began to pace the room, but he didn't miss Brent visibly bristling.

"It's not like that," he started. "Like I said, I could just tell. I know Michelle. She can't lie to me."

Cole paused, turning to him. The way Brent had said it . . . and now he was avoiding his eyes.

"Why is that?" Cole asked, his tone guarded.

"Michelle and I have been spending a lot of time together." Brent paused, tugging on the neck of his gray T-shirt, as he allowed Cole to absorb the full significance of his words.

"A lot of time," Cole repeated. "Are you guys . . ."

"We're together," Brent confirmed. "She didn't tell anyone else. She wouldn't. I needed to see it for myself, though. Listen, I know you two have history. But I didn't think—"

"Are you kidding? I'm happy for you," Cole told his friend, who gave him a slight smile, his hazel eyes brightening. Cole really was happy for him. Brent hadn't been crazy about a girl in forever, and Cole could tell by the way he was blushing that he was into Michelle in a big way.

Brent broke into a full-on grin, causing his dimples to deepen. "It's just so good to see you," he said. "When I thought you were dead . . . God. I'm so glad you're okay. It's hard keeping the secret from the rest, though. But don't worry," he said, as Cole's eyes widened. "I know how to keep a secret. And I've got Michelle. We talk about you a lot. It's just so messed up, man. You didn't do anything wrong."

"A little wrong," Cole said, grinning. "But I have a plan to fix it. I'm going to compete in the Olympiads."

"You're joking."

"Nope." Cole grinned wide. "Dead serious."

Brent laughed, picking up on the joke. "Well how do you plan to pull it off?"

"Details are still being ironed out," Cole said, slipping easily back into their old dynamic. Then he paused. He could be honest with Brent. He sighed, sinking to the edge of his cot with his head in his hands. "Worsley was supposed to help. But we had a huge fall out just now, and time's running out. I'm not sure what to do, at this point. But I need to figure something out. I'm freaking out, Brent. I have no options left."

"Actually," Brent said, "I might have something that could help."

"Yeah?"

"There's this party tonight," Brent started. "You should come. I'll hook you up."

"I'm not looking for performance boosters; I'm looking for a new identity," Cole told him.

"I'm on it," Brent said. "Be there around eleven. It's dark down in the mines and everyone'll be so toasted at that point they'll assume they imagined you."

"All right," Cole said. "You've really got something for me?"

"No promises," said Brent. "I mean, I've got something. I found a laser, an old tool from the mines that might work to . . ." He paused, as if realizing that what he was about to say would be difficult to hear. "I was just thinking, maybe it could burn off your fingerprint," he finished. "No idea if it'll work. And it's way too big for me to haul out on my own. I'd ask someone else, but—"

"No," Cole interrupted. "You're definitely not asking someone else. That would be way too risky." It would be risky to go to the party, too. But he'd think of a way to pull it off. It was better than trusting his life—and the plan—to someone else.

Brent nodded. "It's gotta be painful," he said, frowning. "But it's your best option, am I right? Unless Worsley comes out of hiding. But frankly, I don't think you're his first priority these days." Brent's face darkened, and Cole went on high alert.

"What's up?" he asked. "What do you mean about Worsley?"

"Just . . . dude has an ego," Brent said. "He acts like he's cooking up some amazing cure for the disease, but he's changed. I can't explain it. You had to have noticed if you've seen him."

"I guess so." Cole shrugged uncomfortably. It was true that Worsley's motives were questionable lately. He seemed to get such a high out of the research, but it was unclear what the research was doing to help anyone else. And Worsley didn't seem to care. Cole felt a pang of worry for Vera. The baby was due in just a few months.

Cole wondered if he should get her out of there—if what Brent was saying was true, could Worsley be trusted to take good care of her? But if he got her away from Worsley, where would he take her? It wasn't like he could care for her himself. No, she'd be fine there, Cole assured himself. Maybe Worsley had an ego problem lately, but he was a good guy. He always had been. He couldn't have changed that much at his core, no matter how cocky he was getting.

Brent, however, had always been down to earth. He was a true friend—but maybe his own lack of pretension had made Worsley's seem worse than it was. Brent cared, Cole knew. He wanted to help. Brent and Michelle were good people; he was glad they'd found something worthwhile in each other. Most of all, Cole was glad Michelle had gotten over him.

As Cole and Brent neared the mines, Cole felt the familiar pull of exhilaration. Music pulsed through the ground, and although the parties were illegal, he knew there would be no patrolmen there tonight. When it came to the mines, everyone looked the other way; it was how it had always been. Still, there was something charged and illicit about mine parties. It had been so long. He'd almost forgotten how much fun it could be. Cole quickened his pace, easily slipping down the mine shaft after Brent, like he'd never been away at all.

If he thought the music was pulsing from the outside, it was consuming from within. Bodies swarmed around him—the space was packed even tighter than usual, and everyone was gyrating on rhythm and oblivious to the space around them. People pushed into Cole, picking him up in their movements, and he felt a flash of panic. If *anyone* recognized him—anyone at all—his entire plan would unravel. Cole ducked his head, grateful for the dim lighting and the fact that lots of the people there weren't sober. As he began to relax slightly, he let himself ease into the familiarity of everything. He wasn't on anything—and most of the others were—but the feeling of being back in a familiar space, doing what he'd done for years, had him hyped up. It had been so long since he'd felt at home anywhere.

He followed Brent through the cavernous space, staying on the alert for anyone else he knew, just in case.

"Where is the laser?" Cole asked, keeping his head down as he spoke. "You're sure no one knows I'm here?"

"No one but Michelle. It's right here. Come on." Brent grabbed his shoulder and tugged him into a smaller space adjacent to the main room. It was quieter back there, the music muffled by the dense stone walls. It was more of a sliver than anything else—a crack in the rock, not a room carved intentionally. It reminded Cole of the perilousness of the mines, how dangerous these parties really were. Back when he was a little kid one of the mines had caved in, killing a bunch of teenagers. Even when Cole was technically "alive," he'd never told his mom when he was partying down here.

His eyes adjusted to the dimmer cavern, and he saw Michelle waiting for him.

"Cole!" she squealed a little too loudly, moving toward him. "Sorry," she said. "Sorry, I didn't mean to blurt your name. I'm just so happy to see you." Cole was glad to see her too, and he wrapped his arms around her, holding her close. Her arms tightened around his neck as she pressed her body against his. Aware of Brent's presence beside them, Cole released her quickly.

"Great to see you, Michelle," he said, taking a step back. Brent was frowning. Cole caught his eye and Brent snapped out of it, giving him a tight smile.

"You shouldn't be here!" Michelle exclaimed, oblivious to the tension in Brent's face. Then she laughed. "I mean, I'm glad you are.

But I'm so worried about you. If I could lock you up in that hide-away until all this is past us, I would. But I know you. You'd break down the doors. My rebel." She reached up and ruffled his hair.

"You letting me use that space is the best thing," he told her. "I don't know how the heck you've managed to keep your dad out of it. Doesn't he ever need to come down there, to store supplies for the shop or something?"

Michelle shrugged. "I may or may not have deterred him with a tale of cockroaches," she told him with a wink. "My dad. So afraid of cockroaches. You'd never know it."

"Come on, Michelle," Cole said. "What's the real story?"

She looked reluctant. "It's just . . . the store hasn't been in use since the riots. Everything's in disarray, and my dad's a little afraid to leave the house, most days. Not to mention, we don't have the money to repair it."

"I'm sorry," Cole said simply.

"Everyone's going through it," Michelle replied. "Not just us. And anyway, we're making do."

"You're a fighter. Always have been," he told her.

"*You're* the fighter," Brent broke in, reminding them of his presence. "Speaking of which. Let's get this show on the road." He gestured toward the laser.

"I'll leave you two alone to do your thing," Michelle told them. "I just wanted to say hello." She gave Cole's arm one last squeeze and gave Brent a quick kiss on the cheek, and then she was off.

"So." Brent was silent.

"Let's do this," Cole said, leaning over to lift the laser.

Brent nudged him out of the way. "I've got it."

"Dude. It's heavy. I thought you needed my help. That's the whole reason I came down here in the first place. Here. I'll get the heavier end."

"I said I've got it!" Brent shouted, so loud and sharp that Cole tensed, sure someone would investigate.

"What is your problem?" he whispered after a beat, as his nerves began to quiet. "Why are you all of a sudden pissed off?"

"Because you act like you're so much better," Brent said. "You want to lift this thing because you think I can't. Because I'm the weak one, you're the strong one. You're always acting like you can do everything better and I'm just your sidekick."

Cole reeled, shocked. He'd always loved Brent like a brother. These comments . . . they were coming from somewhere deep. It pained him to know that he'd hurt Brent without even knowing it. "Where is this coming from? I don't think I'm better, man. I wanted to help you lift this thing because you *asked* me to."

Brent went silent. He sucked in several heavy breaths, looking shaken.

"Forget it," he said finally. "It's . . . Never mind. It's my bad."

"What's this really about?" Cole asked, his voice quiet. "We don't fight. That's not us. There's something else going on, isn't there?"

"Michelle's still in love with you," Brent said then, not making eye contact. "She always will be."

Cole flushed, looking down. He badly wanted for it not to be true, but they both knew it was. Cole didn't feel superior. Brent had to know that. But it wasn't fair that he was the one who could even have a prayer of competing in the Olympiads. And that he was the one who Michelle wanted most of all.

"What we have is amazing," Brent continued, his voice hard. "I love Michelle. I have for years. She loves me, too. And we work. It's not the same way she feels about you, but she knows you'll never love her back. The two of us, we fit. It's effortless, and she sees that, even if she doesn't feel the same way about me that she feels about you."

"Or that you feel about her." Cole felt a pang. Brent deserved something better. He hated that he was the one Michelle loved that way. If he could change it, he would, in a second.

"It works," Brent said again. "And helping you will make her happy. And it'll bring you closer to Davis," he said, meeting Cole's eyes for the first time since the outburst. "What happened with her?" he asked. Cole knew the situation with Michelle was painful for Brent; this was an olive branch.

"She's in quarantine," Cole told him. "She has Narxis. But there's hope. . . ."

"I'm sorry."

Cole shook his head. "She'll be okay. When I win the Olympiads, I'm going to go to her."

Brent's eyes were sympathetic. Like that, the roles had reversed. It felt good to open up to Brent this way. Maybe part of Brent's resentment was because Cole *hadn't* confided in him. He didn't like to betray his vulnerability. He knew his friend was hurt, deeply hurt, by years of living in Cole's shadow. If only Cole had known, he'd have kept further distance from Michelle in the past. And he would have confided in him about Davis—about how much he loved her and how much he stood to lose—much sooner. Brent deserved his trust. He'd been so worried about Davis's safety, as well as his own family's, that he'd kept it all a secret. But Brent *was* family.

"So what is this plan of yours?" he asked.

"You assume my identity for the Olympiads," Brent told him. Cole raised his eyebrows, waiting for Brent to continue. Brent reached behind him, pulling out an oblong metal machine with a glass panel and what looked like a laser positioned above. Brent illuminated the machine with his lighter.

Just then they heard a loud giggle, and a drunken girl, wearing only tiny frayed denim shorts and a bikini top, stumbled into the cavern.

"Shit." Cole scrambled to conceal the machine.

"Oopsie," the girl laughed. "Didn't know you two were in here *together.*" Her eyes were glazed—and she wasn't someone Cole had ever seen before.

"We were hoping for some privacy," he said, playing up the misunderstanding.

"I'll just be on my way, then," she said, feeling her way out and narrowly avoiding colliding with a sharp ridge that protruded from the entrance. "You boys have fun!"

Cole rolled his eyes. It was a miracle more people didn't get hurt during these parties. It was idiotic to get so drunk in such a treacherous environment. He moved away from the laser and raised his eyebrows at Brent, motioning for him to continue.

"Not the first time that's happened," Brent said wryly. It was true. Cole laughed, and just like that the tension between them dissipated. "I found it in the mines," Brent explained, turning back to the laser. "It was used for cutting away debris on the mine walls. We can use it to re-create my fingerprint. I've already tested it on rock. It still works."

"What makes you think it'll work on skin? That sounds insane." Cole was skeptical. It sounded like the machine could burn his finger off. Maybe Brent wasn't so gracious about Michelle's feelings. . . .

"It can work. If Worsley won't help, I'll do it myself, or you can do it. It'll be painful. We'll have to burn off your fingerprint, replicate mine, and carve it onto your finger with the lasers. But what it amounts to is minor surgery, if done right. And you'll want anesthetics. Maybe at the very least we can steal some from Worsley's lab." Cole raised his eyebrows. "It'll work," Brent repeated.

"Hey," Cole said, taking a breath, "it's worth a shot. It's all I've got. But . . ." He turned to Brent, his friend, who had always been his right-hand man in training for the FEUDS. "Don't you want to compete?" He thought he owed his friend the courtesy of asking.

Brent shook his head. "You know I'm no athlete. I'd never win," he said. "And anyway, like I said, this is for Michelle." He placed his index finger on the transparent plate that was angled just below the laser. "There. You have my print. Now let's get this thing out of here before someone sees you." Brent wrapped the laser in his jacket. It was heavy, but not so heavy that one person couldn't carry it—at least until they got to the ladder that connected the elevator shaft to the mine exit. When they got there, Cole pulled himself up first, then bent back over the gap and reached down for the laser, which Brent handed up to him.

"Careful," Brent called. "Don't drop it."

"Are you coming?" Cole asked, once he had deposited it firmly on the ground next to him, his biceps burning from the effort.

Brent shook his head. "I've got to get back in there," he said. "I'm going to find Michelle."

As Cole walked home, he thought about Brent and Michelle, and felt a pang of jealousy shoot through his heart. Not for Michelle, but for how easy Michelle and Brent's relationship was. They liked each other, and they could be together—it was that simple. There wasn't anything in their way. Things would never be that easy with Davis.

And yet, maybe they could be, if he won the Olympiads. He felt the weight of the machine in his hands; it felt like a physical manifestation of hope. This was the most momentum he'd had in months. He couldn't wait to get the machine safely back to Braddock's barn. He was desperate to share the news with Mari. He knew she'd be thrilled that there was a real shot at him putting their training to the test. He quickened his pace, struggling only a little under the weight of the laser.

When he arrived at Mari's house, she was already up to meet the rising sun. She was bent over the garden, carefully tending the herbs. She lifted her head as he approached, and he didn't wait for her to say hello. He grabbed her, spinning her around, his body filled with elation. She laughed, and the sound of her laughter lit him up.

"I did it," he gasped. "I've found a way to compete."

"Cole!" She laughed again, jumping up and down, then hurtled her small frame into his arms. "I'm so happy for you."

Alone in the barn a few minutes later, Cole felt himself coming down from his endorphin rush. For the first time, he found himself wondering what winning would mean, aside from being with Davis. It could mean freedom for him and his family, finally. It could mean a new life in a new territory—and winnings to share with Mari, who could improve her own life with her father. It occurred to him that even if he could relocate his family to a new, safer, more accepting territory, Davis might not want to join him. Joining him would mean abandoning the life she knew and loved in Columbus. And even if she *did* want to join him, he would still be taking her away from the family she adored. A life like that wouldn't be built on happiness. It could easily turn to anger, loneliness, and resentment. To see that happen to them would break his heart.

For the first time, Cole wondered if it would be better for both of them if he just let her go.

15

DAVIS

The gown Jan lent her was floor-length chiffon and fancier than anything Davis had worn since Terri and her father's wedding. It gathered at the waist with a jeweled belt that buckled in front in the shape of a butterfly, and the back was draped and almost fully exposed, a style Davis had always favored. Finally, the peach-colored silk swished in pleats against her ankles, and silver strappy shoes finished off the look. It was undeniably pretty, and there was once a time when Davis would have enjoyed this kind of attention. But as Jan's in-home stylists had blown Davis's hair out into long waves and applied subtle, natural-looking makeup, she'd felt increasing anxiety build. When they were done, Gina and Garth walked Davis over to a full-length mirror so she could admire herself. Davis forced a smile but focused on the reflection of the clock in the mirror. There were still roughly twenty minutes until the event started. Every minute that passed, in which she was being fussed over but couldn't just run straight to the gala and search for Dr. Hassman, felt like agony. Somehow, being in Durham and being inactive felt worse than when she was miles away, without the certainty of ever reaching the heralded city.

She hoped she could find the answers she needed that night. She couldn't while away time the way Mercer seemed inclined to do. *He* was home. He was the only person he knew, besides her, with Narxis. In Columbus, people were falling sick every day. The longer she had to wait, the surer she was that Fia or Vera or her father would be next. Durham was her one hope. The dress felt tight around her waist and chest, and she struggled to breathe steadily. A sheen of sweat appeared on her mirrored image.

"Gorgeous," said Gina, the far more effusive of the two stylists, into the mirror.

Garth nodded in agreement. "It's certainly a transformation," he allowed, mopping the sweat with a tissue, then applying power with a feather-soft makeup brush. "Is it hot in here? You're so wan, sweetheart," he told her, squinting his brows. "You need to beef up a little."

Davis saw the prominence of her cheekbones and rib cage in the mirror. Her months at TOR-N had not been good to her. Yet, despite her fragile look, she felt stronger than before. She'd been through hell and back. Knowing she'd survived made her less afraid of what was to come.

Gina and Garth had never seen anything close to the horror she had.

It felt wrong. All of it. The luxurious feel of the fabric against her skin. The smell of rose petals in the air. The soft, airy quality of Jan's bedroom, which boasted blue-tiled walls and white down comforters and white peonies in a tall vase at a window that overlooked a flowering courtyard.

At TOR-N, the courtyard had often held wagons full of the newly dead waiting to be carted off for refrigeration until the ferry could take them to the mainland. At TOR-N, there was no smell of roses in the air, only human decay. At TOR-N, Davis had been afraid to touch and be touched—except for Mercer, who steadily healed alongside her. She'd been too afraid of contracting the disease again. Thinking this, Davis shuddered, recoiling from the stylists' fingers.

"They're going to love you, sweetheart," Gina assured her, mistaking her reaction for run-of-the-mill social anxiety.

Davis walked down the winding staircase, a luxurious descent from the top story of the three-floor apartment building, to meet Jan and Mercer below.

"Wow." Mercer's eyes were huge, and he uttered the word involuntarily, his mouth agape. Davis blushed, her eyes trained on his.

"You clean up well," Jan said, her mouth set in a grim line. "Sure took you long enough."

"Easy," Mercer told her.

"I was only kidding!" She broke out in a wide grin that looked false to Davis. If Davis didn't know better, she'd say Jan felt threatened. But Jan herself was the picture of health and beauty. She was naturally tall and rose several inches over Davis in her metallic heels. Her skin glowed with a subtle artificial shimmer, and her blond hair cascaded in soft waves down her back. Her own dress of choice was lavender. It set off her creamy skin and dipped in a sweetheart neckline at her chest. She was curvaceous. Glamorous. Bombshell.

Everything Davis wasn't, in her thinner state. Everything she'd never been as a petite, slender, muscular ballerina.

"You look great, Davis," Mercer said, resting a palm against her back. He looked handsome himself in a black tux. His hair was newly cut, too. Davis couldn't help but notice how his checkered bow tie—his one nod to personal fashion—set off his eyes.

"Do you have . . ." she asked, speaking of the vials of blood and their thumb drive medical records.

"Yep," he broke in, patting his breast pocket.

"Then let's do it," she said, excited to get moving.

The party was elaborate, and more sophisticated than anything she was used to. "It's sponsored by some major science foundations," Jan whispered as they gave their names to a security guard and entered a vast foyer that lead to an even more expansive ballroom.

"This is amazing," Davis whispered, straightening her shoulders. Even though the party was fancier than she was used to, there was something familiar about it, too. This was Davis's sweet spot; she was in her element in situations like this, and it felt comfortable and right to be there.

Everywhere she looked, beautiful people milled around. "Let's get you two a drink," Jan said. "Sadie's parents don't care. Everyone looks the other way at these things. I think they figure the tipsier we are, the more likely we are to bid a portion of our trust funds."

Davis smiled, but it was forced. Jan said these things so casually, even knowing what Mercer had been through. She acted like this kind of extravagance was no big deal. But Davis had seen the other side of it, and this kind of luxury now felt both familiar and repulsive at once. Still, they didn't know any better, and she had to keep reminding herself of that. A waiter passed by with a tray of effervescent cocktails, and she couldn't help but thrill at the luxury of it all.

The crowd was dazzling. Everywhere she turned, clusters of stunning teenagers milled about. Davis hadn't been in the company of healthy Priors in so long. It, too, felt an odd mix of familiar and uncomfortable. After spending so much time among the diseased at TOR-N, it was especially seductive to be back around perfection. Davis had thought Jan was tall, when she met her—and she was, at around five feet eight, Davis guessed—but she realized that the population of Durham as a whole seemed taller on average than that of Columbus. There were tall, willowy types and tall, curvaceous types like Jan, but most of the girls were pushing five feet ten, and the men were all over six feet. Davis felt minute by comparison. She followed Jan and Mercer over to a relatively secluded corner of the room and plopped down on a long leather sofa.

"Over there," Jan said, sipping from her champagne flute. "That group. They're kind of a clique, but I'm close enough with Anais. They're all in the research scene, though—grew up together in that circuit, and I guess it's kind of a mafioso thing. Once you're in, you're in."

"What do you mean, the research circuit? Is this like, a group of people?"

"Their parents all work at Duke-UNC Research Facilities. If anyone knows anything about Narxis, it's them. Or at least they can maybe get info for you. And they'll definitely be able to hook you up with Dr. Hassman. He doesn't have any kids, but he's friends with half their parents. You should introduce yourself. Say you know me. We're a nerdy group in Durham," Jan added. "Intellect is prized over athleticism. That's how we differ from Columbus, I guess," she said, sounding superior.

It was all Davis could do not to roll her eyes. She bit back a retort and looked toward Mercer, intending to ask him to talk to the research group with her, but he had already wandered off to another cluster of people and looked deep in conversation with a handsome, bespectacled Clark Kent type. Good. Maybe he was already making headway. It was a little weird that Jan wasn't offering to introduce Davis herself, but she figured the two of them had a lot of catching up to do with the group, so she straightened her dress and approached the group herself.

". . . the high is incredible," one of the guys was saying as Davis approached. She wended her way just past the group, to the bar, as though she was just there to order a drink. She leaned against the bar, angling her body toward the group. She caught the eye of one of the guys and smiled in what she hoped was an open, casual way. He returned the smile, leaning toward her and away from the group. His friend watched them curiously for a minute, then turned back to the group, his broad shoulders blocking them off from the rest of the circle.

"I thought I knew everyone in Durham," the guy said, raising his glass to her. "I'm pleasantly surprised to find I was wrong." He was lean, and his face was striking—all sharp angles and a well-defined jaw. Blue eyes made for a stark contrast against deep brown skin, and thick eyebrows accentuated his confident manner. He had the kind of silky way of speaking that Davis used to be accustomed to, but which she now loathed. Still, she flashed him a wide smile.

"Just visiting," she told him. "I'm here with Jan."

"Ah, Janet. Solid girl." His forehead creased. "How do you guys know each other?"

"Mutual friends." The guy nodded and surveyed her face, his eyes narrowing. For a second, Davis's heart seized. What if he recognized her somehow? Just as quickly, she dismissed the paranoid thought. Still, the guy openly analyzed her.

"You look familiar," he remarked.

"People say that." Davis flashed him a broad grin. "Accessible face,

I guess." The guy pursed his lips but merely nodded, trailing a finger from Davis's elbow to her wrist. "So," she forged on, "Jan tells
me your parents are some of the leading research scientists on
Narxis. That's pretty awesome." The words sounded canned, even
to her.

He grinned, chucking her on the chin. "That's right," he agreed.
"I'm surprised Jan had to tell you. They're world-renowned. They
travel all around the world on their private yacht conducting research
at various ports," he added. *Yacht-dropping.* That was something she
hadn't missed from her old life. "Maybe you can join me sometime."
He gave Davis a long, simmering look. So he was a Grade A douchebag, but he was potentially a douchebag she could manipulate.

"The best part of having parents at the labs, though, is my access
to free shit," the guy continued. "Want some?" He opened a palm to
reveal a handful of performance-enhancing drugs. Davis recognized
a libido stimulant and fought to swallow her disgust.

"What about the disease?" she asked, shaking her head at the
palm of pills.

The guy—whose name she still didn't know, she realized—
popped an energy stimulant and smiled broadly. "We don't hear
much about that," he told her. "And besides, who really cares? It
hasn't hit Durham. A lot of people say it's just a myth."

"It's not a myth," Davis snapped, and he raised an eyebrow. "How
can you say that? People are dying every day. It's devastating." She
was breathing hard and felt close to tears. He frowned at her, narrowing his eyes. She realized belatedly that he'd already said she
looked familiar; she risked exposure by identifying with Columbus
in any way. "It's just . . . I have cousins who live out there. They know
people who passed away."

"Okay." The guy shrugged. "If you're really interested, I know
where all that stuff is stored. Kalil's parents own the place." He

nodded toward a curly-haired guy who commanded the attention of the group, talking animatedly. "They have a lot of the research stored in their library. Massive collections of medical studies from all over New Atlantic. I'd be happy to show you. . . ." He trailed off, raising his eyebrow seductively. Davis could tell his hidden agenda was to get her alone. But if she could somehow put him off, it would all be okay.

"I'd love to see them," she told him, taking his arm.

They wandered through a maze of hallways, looking for the library. "You know, you should get back to the party," Davis told the guy, whose hand was trailing against her lower back. "I've got it from here."

"I don't mind," he told her. "It's just up here."

"I'm sure you don't," Davis said, more firmly now. The guy's hand was snaking its way around her waist. "But really, I'd rather do it alone."

His expression hardened, and he moved his hand away. "Suit yourself." He held his hands up, palms facing outward, and backed away. Davis could have sworn she heard him mutter the word *frigid* under his breath as he retreated, and she shuddered involuntarily.

Ten minutes later, she *almost* regretted having sent the guy away. She couldn't find the library, and although she'd run into another group of well-to-do, attractive teenagers, any mention of Narxis yielded blank stares.

She turned down the only pathway she hadn't yet tried, and groaned in frustration when she saw that it led to a balcony rather than to the library. She moved to the stone fencing around the balcony, taking in the night. Durham spread out around her in all its shining glory. It looked much the same as Columbus, at its core—a sea of high-rises that blended together in the center and rose up at different heights into the clear night sky—but that's where the similarity stopped. Beyond the epicenter were vast plots of land with extravagant homes styled to resemble old-fashioned mansions, complete with gardens and porches. Davis couldn't see the detailing, but Mercer had described their vast ballrooms and even nostalgic touches like tennis courts. He'd waxed poetic about their beauty many times in the past. And Durham was beautiful, from what she could see—even Jan's apartment had a sprawling, sleepy beauty that she wasn't used to seeing in fast-paced, high-energy Columbus. Beauty was one thing; but if this was the research capital of New Atlantic, she wasn't seeing it. Her search wasn't yielding any results—and it was shocking to her that no one seemed at all aware of the disease, like it hadn't yet entered their realms of thought. She'd just have to dig deeper, try harder.

Just then she felt a hand on her shoulder. She turned, startled, to find Mercer standing behind her. He held out a palm, and she gave him hers. "May I have this dance?" he asked with faux formality, before gently pulling her body against his, humming along with the sounds of jazz emanating from the main ballroom, his hand circling her waist as he spun her around the balcony.

"Have you seen him yet? Dr. Hassman?" Davis asked as they danced.

"No," Mercer told her. "But I'm sure he'll show up. I saw his name on the confirmed guest list, and Jan pointed out his assistant earlier. We just need to give it time. It's early yet. Meanwhile, may as well enjoy ourselves, right? Or at least try to." Davis nodded and pressed her face against his neck, breathing in his salty smell. Mercer looked as perfect as the rest, and yet he felt more real, more accessible. She felt like he somehow knew her in a way no one else could. Not even Cole. She felt a pang of guilt at the thought.

Mercer spun her quicker, dipping her suddenly, and when he

bent to kiss her, she yielded easily. Their kiss was long and soft. There were so many things he seemed to be saying with his lips: that they were the same; the two of them were in it together. Davis felt all of her reluctance disappearing, and she gave into the kiss, returning it with equal passion. She ran her hands through his hair and over his chest, pretending to push him away even as she moved her mouth over his.

She heard a movement to her left and opened her eyes, spotting Jan. Davis pulled back, embarrassed. How long had Jan been watching?

The other girl's face was blank, expressionless. "There you two are!" she said brightly. "We were looking all over!" From behind her, two other forms emerged—faces Davis found vaguely familiar but unsettling. Their eyes were a little too bright, almost like they were high, and their grins were perfect, glossy replacements for human emotion. Then she realized: Jan's own eyes were different—they'd been brown when Davis first met her, and now they were a startling green. She'd changed eye colors, but behind the new glittering hue was . . . nothing. The change had somehow wiped her eyes of emotion. "Come on," Jan said. "It's raging inside. Let's get back there."

Davis was about to protest that they had a lot to do—a lot of information to dig up, and they still hadn't made any solid connections—but Mercer was already halfway out the door behind Jan. Davis suppressed a wave of irritation—it seemed like he was way more interested in being home and having fun than in finding out anything about the disease. She'd have to take matters into her own hands. As they approached the ballroom, Davis couldn't help but notice that everyone there had empty eyes and relaxed, neutral mouths. Their expressions were identically blank, like the fire had been extinguished from their eyes. Davis shuddered.

"Is everyone into eye reconfiguration here?" she wondered aloud. Back in Columbus, only a few people had messed with their faces that way. Eye reconfiguration was considered risky; it was a fashion trend that had some worrying effects on long-term vision, and it had a kind of gauche reputation. Here, though, it seemed to be the predominant trend.

Jan laughed. "It's kind of old news. We're moving onto lips and skin now. Check *her* out." Jan pointed to a girl whose skin was luminescent, almost glittery. "Awesome, right?"

"It's a lot," Davis said. Most of the guests, in her opinion, looked like they were wearing garish masks.

"It's just temporary," Jan told her. "It'll be gone by tomorrow morning. And it's such a rush." She laughed. "That's the best side effect—you get a little buzz from it. Wanna try? You'd look *so* pretty with gold irises. The metallic glaze is so in right now."

Davis bristled, backing away. The room was like a carnival filled with performers; no one in the group looked natural or sincere. She saw Mercer accepting a few little yellow pills that Jan was handing him and realized that he, too, would soon cease to look familiar.

Her heart thudding, Davis backed away from the two of them, grabbing a champagne flute from a waiter's tray and downing it quickly. She needed to get information and get out of there. Grabbing another flute, Davis made the rounds, trying to find some of the people Jan had pointed out earlier. But with their facial enhancements, she could no longer recognize anyone. She felt lost, as if in a hall of mirrors: each garish expression was more horrifying than—yet oddly identical to—the one before. She wended her way around corridors hung with expensive modern art, stepping along sterile marble hallways, and for the first time she felt homesick for something she couldn't identify. It had nothing to do with Columbus, or her family. What she was missing was the sense of freedom that had come with living a few months on an island devoid of physical perfection.

She wanted to go home.

No.

She wanted to go home with a cure.

She whirled, moving back toward the settee where she'd left Mercer and Jan. She had to ask Mercer what he'd found out about Dr. Hassman. Jan had shown her a photo of him on her tablet, but Davis hadn't seen anyone yet who'd even vaguely resembled him.

Jan and Mercer were no longer at the settee, but she caught a glimpse of the fabric of Jan's orange satin gown billowing around the corner and disappearing. She moved quickly after it, turning down a long tiled hall dimly lit and glowing blue. The smell of chlorine grew stronger as she approached a long sliding glass door that led to an indoor pool. The pool was empty, except for Jan and Mercer. Davis could hear Jan's voice rising. It sounded like they were deep in conversation, and she paused, wary of interrupting.

When Jan moved toward Mercer, narrowing the gap between their bodies to a mere few inches, Davis gasped. Covering her mouth quickly, she ducked to the side of the door, allowing her heart to steady. Were Mercer and Jan an item? She peered back round the door, afraid of what she might see.

Nothing could have prepared her for the sight of Jan's arms wrapped around Mercer. Jan pulled back slightly, and Davis froze, straining to hear their conversation.

"Wait," Mercer was saying, pushing her away. "Not now."

"Isn't that why you brought her here? So we could try again? With Suen?" Jan said clearly. "You're not like her, Mercer. Do you know that many people here think Narxis isn't a real thing? That's because we've taken precautions to avoid it. Why do you think Columbus is riddled with it? They never took action, never eliminated Imps entirely. It's survival of the fittest, and we took care of this problem before it ever began. Because all Priors is the best way. It's the only way."

Davis stared at them in shock. Jan had mentioned Suen—it was the name of the woman from whom Mercer had gotten Narxis in the first place, or so he'd told her. She squinted, trying to gauge Mercer's reaction.

"I'm not all Prior," he pointed out, his voice low.

"You are," Jan said. "Well, almost. It's just a fluke that you're not, though. Suen screwed up, I know, but you're nearly as good as us, and you're definitely *not* like them. Don't you ever associate with Imps because of this, Mercer. That would be like writing yourself off. Even that girl is beneath you. Anyone could see you're more fully Prior."

Davis tried to move, but her legs were frozen in place. Mercer lifted his gaze even as she tried to move away, and his eyes locked on hers. She gasped and moved from the doorway, willing herself far away from Jan and Mercer and the garish human caricatures swarming the room.

16

COLE

After a quick nap in the barn, during which Cole tossed and turned, barely able to get more than a few minutes of actual sleep, he awoke. He rubbed his hands over his eyes, groaning to himself as his worried thoughts about Davis flooded back.

His stomach clenched. He couldn't train with Mari today. His mind wouldn't be in it. It was better that he just leave. Besides, the Olympiads were the following day.

Cole struggled to his feet. He pulled on his shirt, feeling achy, stiff, and lethargic. He had to snap out of it. Jogging around the south side of the house to avoid Mari, he felt only a little bit like a jerk for not explaining himself or saying good-bye. But time was running out. If he was going to give the fake fingerprinting a shot, this was the time.

He headed back toward Worsley's lab in the Slants as quickly as he could. His feet felt heavy, and he couldn't shake the sense that he'd screwed everything up. With Davis, Mari . . . even with Brent. He needed Worsley's help with this one. But he was going to have to crawl back, after the fight they'd had and what he'd done. He was at odds to some degree with everyone in his life—at least everyone who knew he existed. And he'd betrayed Davis. Every fiber of his being wanted to be with her, and yet he'd acted in a way that was exactly opposed to that. Because he'd gotten carried away, needed comfort in the moment. Succumbed to a moment of weakness.

There was only one way to fix this. Everything—literally everything—rested on the Olympiads. He could give Mari a part of the prize money and finally show her how much he appreciated her training. Her world would open up a little because of that money. He could go see Davis. And when he did, he'd treat her in a way that showed her every day how much he treasured her.

When he got back to the hideaway, making a quick pit stop for a change of clothes and the laser, he was surprised to see Brent pacing the concrete floor. He'd brought Michelle, and the sight of them together gave Cole a pang. He watched Brent plop down next to Michelle on Cole's sleep cot, rest his palm on her thigh. Cole would never have that level of ease with Davis. They'd always be running or hiding or spiriting stolen moments, unless they could get somewhere far, far away.

"Dude," Cole said. "You've gotta stop just showing up here like that." He tried to inject humor into his voice, but it fell flat. He was too tense for their usual banter. Plus, he still felt weird about the friction over Michelle. And there she was.

"We realized this morning, you need to learn a few things about Brent before you go in there," Michelle said.

"What are you talking about? Brent's been in my life since I was a kid. I already know everything there is to know. Right, buddy?" Cole cringed inwardly, struck again by his falsely jovial tone. He didn't have time for this, but he didn't have the heart to tell them that. If they were still willing to support him, the least he could do was play along.

"I'm a man of mystery, my friend," Brent interjected. "There is more to me than meets the eye."

Cole rolled his eyes, but sat down across from the two, keenly aware of Michelle's head resting on Brent's shoulder. "Shoot," he said.

"Where was I born?" Brent asked.

"Trick question. Right here in the ol' Slants," Cole replied.

"Errrrr!" buzzed Michelle. "Wrong."

"I was born in Cleveland," Brent said. "Moved to Columbus when I was three."

"No way. Figured you were born and bred, just like me," Cole said, trying to keep things light.

"Like I said . . ."

"More to you than meets the eye. Next. Shoot." Cole was impatient. How long was this going to take? He wasn't even totally sure they were going to ask identifying questions, and he was certain he'd get all the basics right. The city thing, okay; that was weird that he didn't know it. He'd nail everything else. He *had* to get to Worsley's lab and get the fingerprint ironed out ASAP. . . .

"Favorite food."

"You seriously think they're going to ask that?" Cole had a hard time tamping down his irritation. "Chicken cutlets. Fanciest guy I know."

"Really?" Michelle broke in. "Babe, I thought you hated chicken?"

"Nope. That's turkey."

"And that's weird," Cole told them. "Turkey's a delicacy." Turkeys were almost extinct. It was rare that they got any kind of fresh, non-dehydrated meat in the Slants. In the culinary scene of Columbus, of course, it was different.

"Middle name."

"Gareth. Boom."

"*Gareth?*" Michelle looked amused. "You were basically born to be a nerd."

"How did you not know that?" Cole asked Michelle. "That's our go-to when he's being lame. We blame it on nurture versus nature." Michelle laughed awkwardly, but Brent's face fell.

"Way to pay attention," Brent teased her. But his eyes had darkened, and he shifted on the bed, leaning slightly away from her. "All the important stuff, and you're just checked out." Michelle moved toward him, placed a hand on his shoulder, but he shook it off. "It's *fine*," he said in her direction. Cole racked his brain for something to say to transition from the awkward moment, but it was Brent who spoke up first. "All right, dude, this one's definitely gonna come up. Also the easiest question of the bunch. My birthday."

"May sixteenth. No. Wait. That's Hamilton's." Cole paused, massaging his temples.

"Seriously? How can you not know?"

"I'm sorry! I get you two messed up. You're in the fall. Right? We had that belated celebration last November, which puts you at October. October sixteenth."

"You're kidding me." Brent seemed genuinely put off, and Cole was feeling more and more anxious. How could he not know these things? He was a terrible friend, *and* he was going to blow it at the Olympiads. They weren't going to let him past registration. He stood up, beginning to pace, his pulse quickening.

"That's not right?" Of course it wasn't right. He didn't need to hear Brent's firm no to figure that out. He began to sweat. His head was blank. He felt like he couldn't come up with any facts about his friend just then, even if someone asked him a question that was open-ended.

"Cole, save yourself the embarrassment," Michelle said, straightening up. "I've got this. October eighth." She looked around confidently, but Brent avoided her eyes. There was a brief beat in which no one said anything.

"Tenth," Brent interrupted, breaking the silence. Brent stood up, moving toward the door. Cole watched him, wary. This situation was spiraling fast.

"Oh. I could have sworn it was the eighth," Michelle said, scrambling. "Oh, never mind. That's my dad's birthday."

"No one remembers mine," Cole offered.

"Yours is December fifth," Michelle said. There was another silence; she was right, and they all knew it. Cole cringed and looked away, avoiding Brent's eyes.

"I think I'm done," Brent told them.

"What, you guys aren't going to join me for the hard part?" Cole tried.

"I guess I have a natural aversion to my friend having his skin burned off," Brent said. "But you're the ironman." There was an underlying bitterness behind his words that only someone who knew him well would pick up on. Cole didn't know what to say.

They exited the hideaway, out into the streets of the Slants. Brent and Michelle walked in front of him, Michelle whispering in Brent's ear as she clutched his hand tightly. Cole speculated that she was trying to make up for screwing up his birthday. It must have stung, the fact that she'd known Cole's but not Brent's. She huddled close to Brent, apparently bent on reassuring him, and Cole realized in a flash that theirs wasn't a relationship he wanted. There was nothing easy about Michelle and Brent—all of their interactions were forced, full of deliberate effort and built on the convenience of their relationship. They weren't what he and Davis had been—extraordinary. They couldn't see into each other's souls. Cole thought back to the last time he'd held Davis—the comfort he'd felt in her arms. He'd been unable—was still unable—to imagine a greater level of satisfaction. Everything he was doing was for her.

When Michelle and Brent turned down the path that led away from Worsley's lab and back toward their own houses, Cole pulled Brent into a hug.

"Thanks, man," he told his friend. "You don't know how grateful I am." There was so much more he wanted to say. He hoped Brent would realize exactly how full those words were—how much their friendship meant to him. How badly he wanted Brent to be happy. As he watched them walk off, and Brent looked back to give him a wave, he knew they'd be all right. Brent was more like a brother than a friend; there were few things in life that could destroy a bond like that.

"Cole." Worsley's tone was guarded, and for the first time he didn't look happy to see Cole. A dark bruise blighted the left side of his face. He ushered Cole into the lab—Vera was nowhere to be seen.

"Where is she?" Cole asked, looking around the room. "You didn't send her out . . ."

"She's asleep. I have a back room." Worsley jerked his head toward a curtain Cole had never noticed. "I don't want to bother her."

"I'll keep my voice down," Cole said, wondering why Worsley hadn't already asked him to do so. "Listen, man. I'm so sorry. I am. I've been in a bad place, but . . . I know it's no excuse. I know I have no right to ask, but I need your help. Brent found me a machine that will allow me to simulate fingerprints and take over his identity. You need to operate the machine." He handed Worsley the laser, which he had carefully tucked into his pants, careful to polish it off on his shirt. Worsley took it, eyeing it skeptically.

"This looks dangerous," Worsley said, eyeing the device. "I don't need to tell you that it's not meant to be used for this purpose. And I doubt I need to tell you how little I feel like helping you right now."

Cole looked him in the eyes, abashed. "Listen, Tom," he said. "I get why this is an enormous risk for you. I know that risking your own reputation might mean thwarting all the work you've done on developing the Narxis cure. And I know you hate me right now. But the Olympiads are my only hope. They're tomorrow. We've got to try this. You're the only person I know of who has experience manipulating lasers. And I'm truly sorry for hitting you, for losing control like that. The apology would have come anyway. I just needed to cool off. I know it's inconvenient timing"—he motioned to the device—"asking you for a favor at the same time I apologize. But I don't feel I have a choice. And I am truly sorry. I know you're trying to help Vera. I'll make it up to you any way I can."

"Okay." Worsley nodded, looking reluctant. "But only—and I mean *only*—because if there's any chance in hell Davis survives the disease and you can bring her back, she might have the antibodies I need to create a cure."

"And save Vera," Cole added, trying to keep his voice neutral. Despite what he'd said a minute before, he was still deeply worried for Davis's friend.

"Yes," Worsley said brusquely. "Let's do it before I change my mind. I have local anesthetic, but it's going to be painful as it heals. We can burn away your fingerprint and carve Brent's into your skin. We need to take a mold of his first. And in a few days, after your finger heals, you'll regenerate new cells to replace your natural print. Just try not to let them know you're wounded. You don't want to raise eyebrows. Are you sure?" Cole nodded. Pursing his lips, Worsley readied the machine.

"Place your finger here," he told Cole, after applying a numbing fluid to Cole's right index finger. Cole slid his finger under the machine and braced himself as Worsley lowered the laser to target his fingerprint. "Are you ready?" Cole nodded, gritting his teeth. Worsley flipped on the switch controlling the laser beam, and a sensation of excruciating pain flooded Cole's entire hand, despite the anesthetics. Worsley pinned his wrist down with his free hand so Cole couldn't move.

"Ten seconds. Stay strong."

When Worsley was done, Cole's finger was raw and bloodied. But Worsley had succeeded. Cole's fingerprint had been stripped away, only to be reconfigured into a mold of Brent's print. It would last two days before Cole's own cells started to replace these faux cells. Cole gritted his teeth against the pain, but it was too much. When Worsley applied antiseptic to the wound, he cried out.

"Shhh!" Worsley hissed, glancing over his shoulder. It was too late.

"Cole." The word was long and low, guttural. It sounded almost inhuman, but Cole recognized Vera's voice.

"What—" He looked at Worsley, who fidgeted, seeming uncomfortable.

"It's nothing," he said.

Cole narrowed his eyes, snatching his half-bandaged finger away from Worsley's grasp. "What are you hiding?" he growled, standing up and shoving past Worsley, to the curtained area in the back room.

He pushed aside the curtain and found Vera moaning and thrashing in a puddle of her own sweat.

"Cole," she muttered through white lips. Her belly was distended to the point that Cole thought she must be due at any time, but her skin was pale, almost blue, and her eyes were unfocused. Cole held a hand to her forehead—it was damp, feverish. "Cole," she said again, thrashing in the bed. Cole's stomach dropped. He turned around to find Worsley behind him, watching. Worsley's expression was resigned.

"What is this?" Cole shouted. "She looks terrible. I apologized to you! I said I should have trusted you, and you said nothing! There's nothing in you to trust. You've turned into someone I don't even recognize." His words were bitter, but this time he wasn't sorry at all.

"I didn't know she'd get so sick," Worsley said, pleading. "I was certain it would work, Cole. I was *so sure*. I've never felt more sure of anything. I'm trying to fix it. I'm trying my best to make her better. But even so . . . the sacrifice is nothing compared to the lives we'll save. Don't you see? I'm sacrificing one to save millions. It's not always clear and easy, Cole. You can't just fight your way through life."

"You need to do more," Cole told him. "You can't just give up on her."

"What do you suggest?" Worsley's face was hard. "Go ahead. Tell me how to make this better."

Cole opened his mouth then closed it again. At a loss for words, he pushed past Worsley and ran from the room. Once he was free, he told himself, he'd get help for everyone. He just needed to win the Olympiads to get there.

Cole was so immersed in his panicked, frenzied thoughts that he forgot about taking precautions to stay safe. He just ran down the route he now knew by heart, heedless of his hood flapping down from his head. He was exposed, and he barely realized it. He barely even cared.

The horror of seeing Vera like that made him want to do something destructive. He was tired of trying so hard to keep it all together, and for what? To see all his plans fail, every single time. To watch everyone he loved get hurt, and to know there was nothing he could do about it.

When he heard the voice shouting his name, he almost didn't care. It was the cops; he knew it. Finally, it was all going to end, and there was some relief in that.

"Cole!" the voice said again. He whirled, facing it head-on.

"What," he shouted. "Take me. Arrest me. That's what you want, just do it."

The footsteps pounded around the corner and the owner of the voice came into view. Cole felt like an idiot for not realizing it sooner.

Hamilton.

His brother's face was ashen. "It really is you," he said. "I can't believe it." He ran to Cole, wrapping him in a hug. When they pulled back, tears were streaming down both their cheeks. Hamilton cleared his throat, trying to pull it together.

"How did you . . ." Cole trailed off, speechless for one of the first times in his life.

"Worsley called me. But quick," Hamilton said. "We need to get you off the streets. I was an idiot for shouting your name like that. I just . . . I couldn't believe it." His words came out in a choked sob. "All this time, we've thought you were dead. I thought I'd killed you."

"This way."

Cole led Hamilton back to his hideaway, and the two bolted the door behind them.

"Did anyone see us?"

"I don't think so." Hamilton shook his head. "When Mom finds out you're alive . . . Cole, it'll save her."

"She can't know." Cole's voice was sharp. "Not yet. I have too much riding on tomorrow."

"The Olympiads. Worsley told me. He told me everything. He called me when you left his lab . . . said he was worried about you, that you were distraught. He was afraid of what you might do."

Cole averted his eyes. He *had* been on the brink of desperation only minutes ago. Even now, it seemed so futile.

"I don't think I have a hope of winning," he told his brother. "Sometimes I think I'm deluding myself because I'm too much of a coward to face reality."

"That's not true." Hamilton leaned forward, resting his forearms on his knees. His green eyes shone brightly and his expression was sobering. "I was the one deluding myself. I thought all those riots and protests would amount to something. All they amounted to was more violence and hatred. I was *wrong*. I guess it took you dying to show me that." He let out a rueful laugh. "I wish I'd been smart enough to see it sooner."

"You said Mom isn't doing well," Cole prompted him.

"It's not her health," Hamilton said. "It's that home. The morale. Her grief. She broke when she lost you, Cole. We need you back."

"But how can I come back? The second I show my face it's all over. I may as well be dead, for what they'll do to me."

"You need to win the Olympiads," Hamilton said. "Then we can get away from here, build a new life elsewhere."

"I don't know how realistic that is, anymore," Cole admitted. "I'll be up against Prior champion athletes. I've been naive."

"I believe in you." Hamilton held Cole's gaze. "I never told you when we were kids. I was too tough on you. But you're the one who can save us, Cole. I used to be jealous of you, because you have it all—courage and strength and integrity. Now I just want you to use it. Please don't stop now. If you won't do it for us, do it for Davis."

"What do you mean?" Cole shifted, the springs of the cot creaking beneath him. He was suddenly aware of the oppressive, stifling air in the tiny room. "What do you know about Davis?"

"I've heard things." Hamilton clasped his hands together, moving his thumbs in semicircles the way he always did when he was making a hard decision.

"Tell me."

"There are rumors about TOR-N. That it's a cesspool. The patients are underfed, not receiving proper medications or care. That the doctors are skimming. That . . ." He paused, looking nauseated. "Dead bodies are just strewn about in open air. They aren't even being properly disposed of. No matter what I ever thought about Priors," he said, swallowing hard, "no one deserves that. If Davis is there, and the rumors are true, she needs you."

"Why would her father leave her there?" Cole's voice was thick. The words hurt to say. The thought of Davis suffering caused him physical pain under his rib cage. It made him want to punch something, anything.

"He may not know," Hamilton told him. "They say the staff gives false reports, cleans the facility up for inspections, hides it all. They want to keep it running so they can keep taking money. I only know any of this because I know a guy who runs the ferry. He quit his job because he said he couldn't stand to be a part of it. That was his only source of income. He meant it when he said it was bad."

"If I win the Olympiads, I can go to her. I'll have enough money to travel." Cole felt a surge of determination. He had to, and he would. He'd had a moment of weakness, but he wouldn't let it stop him. Not when everyone he loved needed him most.

"You have to," Hamilton told him, moving to Cole. He wrapped his arm around his brother as he had when they were little, before everything had gotten in the way. "You're the only hope for us all. Be brave, little brother. Braver than you've ever been."

❧ 17 ❧

DAVIS

Davis fled the room, heading out of the party toward the elevator bank. Her heart pounded and she struggled to catch her breath, recognizing the weakness that overcame her body as a sign of shock. She'd trusted Mercer—and he was *using* her. But for what? And was he using Jan, too? Who was Suen, really? There was no cure, no doctors with all the answers—she realized that now. She'd have to return to Columbus with nothing, if she could make it back to Columbus at all before she was caught and shipped back to TOR-N. Everything she'd planned for was falling down around her; in just a few brief moments, all her hope was lost. Davis fought against the tears that threatened her vision and struggled hard to stay calm.

She heard footsteps pounding behind her and she made a dash for the elevator. She needed time alone to think—the last thing she wanted was to have it out with Mercer when she was feeling so betrayed. The elevator door began to slide shut, but just before it closed altogether, a hand shot out, causing it to reopen—and Mercer slid inside. He pushed the *Door Close* button as Davis frantically pushed the button for the lobby.

"What are you doing?" she shouted. "Why did you follow me in here? What do you want from me?"

"Calm down," he urged, placing a hand on her shoulder. She shook it off roughly.

"I *knew* you were lying about something," she hissed. "I can't trust you anymore. I don't know what this is about, but I can't believe anything you say. What else have you been lying about?" She punched the *Lobby* button over and over, even as the elevator made its rapid descent.

"Just listen to me," he started. "Please. Just calm down."

"I don't need to do anything you say," Davis said as the doors slid open. She ran out, down the stairs leading through the front door. She took a left through the massive gated property and rounded a bend to find herself in a small, immaculate garden. She turned, ready to leave—she didn't care where she was as long as she was away from him—but he was already there, facing her and blocking off the only entrance to the garden.

"Please. I can explain," Mercer told her, breathing hard. His eyes were wide and earnest, and Davis wanted more than anything to believe there was some sort of explanation she was missing. But her self-protective urge was kicking in and pulling her back and away from the connection Mercer was trying to make. She wouldn't let herself ignore the warning signs again, or believe someone who would betray her.

"This is a misunderstanding," Mercer continued. "Just listen to me."

"I'm listening," she told him. She'd listen, and then she'd go her own way. She was done with Mercer. She couldn't believe she'd allowed herself to start wondering if he could be something more. She was worried about being deceived, and what she'd done with Mercer was the biggest blight on Cole's memory. Davis flushed, ashamed. It all seemed so clear; how could she have let her emotions overcome her? But Mercer was talking, laying out whatever excuse he had for what Davis had witnessed.

". . . where Neithers can become fully Prior, and—"

"What?" Davis cut him off. She felt her hands clenching into fists. Mercer looked wary, his face flushed with the exertion of chasing her.

"I'm telling you, Jan's been helping me with research. It's a really risky, dangerous process. But we think Neithers can become Prior—at least the ones whose genetic makeup is primarily superior. It's something like ninety percent superior that you need to qualify for an operation. I'm ninety-two percent, but that's how I got Narxis. I tried to undergo a procedure and it failed. Suen—she was the doctor. She lives just outside of the city. You're ninety-three-point-six percent superior—it's what your file said. That's why I wanted to bring you here with me. One of the reasons, anyway."

"Do you know what you're saying?" Davis was shocked.

"I was going to tell you about everything," Mercer told her, reaching for her. Davis pulled back. "You're unique," he pleaded, pushing his disheveled blond hair from his eyes. "You can have the operation and become fully Prior. I wanted that for you. I thought you would want it. I thought once you were here—once I explained everything and you saw how it could be—you'd jump at the chance to go through with it. But now I see that even that was wrong. Believe me," he said, moving toward her again, "I would never encourage you to do anything that would put you at risk." His eyes were wide and earnest.

She wanted to believe him. But something about what he was saying made her stiffen, igniting her natural urge to protect herself. "But when we were just friends, it was different."

"I was stupid," Mercer admitted, tucking his head down so that his hair fell partly over one of his eyes.

"And selfish," she added, realizing she was shaking with anger, with shock.

"Yeah, and selfish."

Davis turned away from him, catching a glimpse of her reflection in the small koi pond in the garden. Mercer drew closer, his own reflection looming behind hers. She watched his face in the water; it rippled as he spoke, distorting his expression into a funhouse version of him.

"I thought you'd be happier with the operation," he explained. "At least that's what I told myself originally. I thought we'd go through it together, then be together as Priors. Isn't that what you want? It's better than this . . . this limbo reality. I'm tired of being invisible. It's not fair that Neithers don't have the same privileges as Priors. Don't you believe in equality for all?"

"I believe in an equality that doesn't force me to change myself to get it," Davis told him, her voice measured. "Why do you want to be a part of something that forces you to be someone different?"

"This is my life," Mercer uttered, his voice thick. He put his hand on her shoulder, urging her to face him. When she did, his eyes were full, impassioned. "Everything in it is true: my friends, my family, all the people I love and have grown up loving. The only thing that's a lie is my genetics. It's the one thing no one can see but the thing that makes a world of difference. Can't you see that? If it doesn't matter, why *not* change it, when it can do so much?"

"I'm so sorry, Mercer," Davis told him. She meant it. She was sorry he was so tortured, had this rage bubbling just under the surface all the time, distorting everything just as his reflection had been distorted in the pond. "Cole must have felt this same way," she realized aloud. "Always inferior. Never able to fit in."

"I can't believe you're still talking about him," Mercer muttered. Davis jerked back, feeling like she'd been slapped. Back when they'd become friends, in the early days at TOR-N, he'd always made her feel comfortable talking about Cole. But she guessed that was because he hadn't yet developed the feelings for her that he possessed now.

"What is wrong with you? You know how much I cared about Cole." She was barely able to utter the words; he'd shocked her breathless.

"Cared or care? He's *dead*. Don't you think it's time to start getting over it? You're mourning a dead Imp. What ever happened to progress?"

His words were putrid. They seared her. Davis stepped away from him, reeling. It was as if Mercer had been possessed by a stranger capable of inhuman cruelty. She couldn't believe he was capable of these kinds of malicious thoughts. She regretted ever mentioning Cole's name to him.

"If anyone believed in progress, it was Cole," she spit out, barely able to force the words past the knot in her throat. "But he believed it came from inside. Not from some stupid, superficial surgery." She turned, unable to face him. He was repugnant to her now. She couldn't believe they had ever been friends.

Mercer didn't respond; instead he stared at her, a look of contempt crossing his features. Davis felt suddenly, horribly sorry for

him. Worse than being afflicted with Narxis—worse than being a
Neither with nowhere to fit in—Mercer was a shell of a human.
Instead of being a vessel for love and hope—as Cole had been—
Mercer was brimming over with self-loathing. That was what
separated them, and Davis saw now that it always would. She could
step beyond her circumstances. He was an exercise in longing. It
made her weep for Cole, with whom she'd been able to be authen-
tic and fully herself, despite everything they'd faced together.

She ran from Mercer, allowing the tears to spill over only when
she was outside the gates of the complex. She'd never felt more alone
than in that moment. She had nowhere to go, no friends in Durham.
She ran blindly through the streets, trying to make sense of all the
emotions that whirled about within her. She took a right turn and
found herself stumbling along a brightly lit street that was teeming
with people spilling out from nearby buildings. She looked up to
see a marquee heralding a theatrical performance, right next to her,
and across the street was similar advertising for another show. The
sky was crisscrossed with bright beacons of light streaming from
the buildings. Davis sobbed aloud, overwhelmed, and ducked her
face as more than a few theatergoers gave her quizzical looks. She was
still wearing her gown from the party, but her face was almost surely
smudged with makeup, from her tears. She was afraid of standing out
among the perfection around her. She had to find somewhere to go to
calm down and clean up and figure out what to do next.

Davis scanned the street, distracted momentarily by the projected figure of a lithe, graceful woman dancing through the air.
She took a closer look—it was a ballerina clad in a black leotard and
a tutu that glittered as she turned, emitting hologram sparks through
the night air with each pirouette. She was breathtaking. At the next
whirl, she faced the streets, dropping into a dramatic curtsy. When
the ballerina raised her head, Davis gasped.

It was a mirror image of Davis herself. A slightly older, more mature version of Davis's green eyes, high cheekbones, and chestnut hair. They had the same lips, the same delicately shaped nostrils and wide-set eyebrows. The only thing that set them apart was the gap in this ballerina's front teeth, which lent her face a playful charm as she smiled. Davis had grown up looking at photos of that same smile.

The ballerina looked just like her mother.

Davis couldn't move, couldn't breathe. Racquelle Eide had told her that her mother was still alive. But it had never crossed Davis's mind that she might find her; half of her had thought Racquelle had been lying. And now . . . but it couldn't be. Could it?

Davis felt her legs moving woodenly toward the entrance to the theater. There was a door in the back, a nondescript metal one that seemed to lead into the building, away from the crowds—the kind of door that only opened from the inside, or from the outside with a key. Davis waited until someone slipped out of the door—it was a workman carrying a stack of large boxes—before she slipped in after him, navigating the hallways backstage. She passed a curtain and peered through it. The stage was empty and the crowds were just beginning to disperse; the performance must have recently ended. Tinny strains of music were just winding down as sound technicians messed with the equipment, but Davis could identify Mahler's Third Symphony, one of her favorite pieces to dance to. She felt a surge of hope well up within her.

She turned from the stage, moving toward an adjacent hallway lined with various doors covered in photos of the ballerinas' smiling faces. She scanned the photos until she found pictures of her mother, and before she could give it more thought, she knocked gently and pushed into the room.

The ballerina's back was to her. Her shoulders framed a strong, sculpted torso. She was blotting her face with makeup remover, and

when she lifted the cloth from her cheeks, Davis could see her reflection full-on in the mirror. The ballerina met her eyes. It was her
mother; Davis knew it beyond a shred of doubt. The look the woman
gave her in the mirror said it all. Her body stiffened, and she lowered the washcloth to her vanity.

At the same time, a stage manager rushed the room.

"I'm so sorry," he told the dancer. "I'm not sure how this girl got
in here."

"I'm her daughter," Davis said quickly.

"I don't have a daughter," the woman snapped, and Davis felt pain
shoot through her chest. Was it just her, or did she see a brief flash
of regret in the dancer's eyes? "It's okay, you can let us be," the woman
told the stage manager, recovering.

The manager gave Davis a skeptical look but backed from the
room, shutting the door behind him.

"How did you find me?" her mother asked, turning to her. Her
face was stony—any emotion Davis thought she'd seen had disappeared entirely, leaving her mother cold and impassive. "How did
you even get in here? Neithers aren't allowed in Durham."

Davis wasn't sure what she'd expected, but this chilly reception
wasn't it. She fought back tears, struggling to formulate a worthy
response. "I have friends who let me in," she said. Then, "So you did
know."

"Of course I knew." Her mother turned back to the mirror and
began removing her false eyelashes with careful, rapid movements.
Her face was beautiful, but her expression was so devoid of warmth
that it bordered on grotesque. She pursed her lips, but Davis saw
the tendons in her neck pulse, and her jaw clenched subtly. She was
rattled. Still, her eyes remained empty. Davis was filled with mount-
ing dread; still, she moved closer to her mother. She'd been searching for her in one way or another her entire life—and now that she'd

found her, she couldn't pull herself away, no matter how much darker the world looked, the closer she moved toward her. No matter how much she wanted to flee and hide somewhere safer, away from her mother's orbit and its oppressive lack of love.

"So you came from Columbus, then." Her mother's voice was confident; Davis didn't bother to correct her. "Now there's a city I don't miss."

"What do you mean?" Davis stood near the door. Her mother's voice was absentminded, almost as if she barely realized Davis was still there. Davis was afraid to move, afraid to jolt something within her mother that might cause her to dismiss her like she'd done so many years ago.

"I mean it has a way to go in terms of progression," her mother elaborated. "Your father's notions of a forward-thinking society are so backward. They always have been. Sure, I fell for him—back when I was young and idealistic and would have drunk up anything he said. But ultimately he's never been strong enough in his convictions. That's why we never could have worked out. Columbus will never rise to greatness when it still allows Imps within its walls. Durham is so much better; it allows us to flourish without the hindrances of imperfection."

Davis absorbed her mother's words, which had been spoken without a hint of irony, and as she did, her stomach dropped. Her mother was almost merciless. She knew Davis was a Neither, and yet her words were designed to cut deep. She was without any empathy at all.

Davis took a breath, fighting to steady herself. Tears threatened her vision, but she squared her shoulders and blinked them back. She wouldn't let this hurt topple her. She was strong now, much stronger than she used to be. Her mother's memory had chased her for years, but she wouldn't let the disappointing reality of it crush her as it once would have.

"Did you ever remarry?" Davis asked. "Do I have any brothers or sisters?"

Her mother paused, and her mouth turned up in a smirk. "No," her mother said, as though it were obvious. "I've never wanted to. Children only would have held me back. Look at me," she said, gesturing around the small dressing room, until her gaze came to rest again on the face in the mirror. "I'm achieving my dreams. Did you see those people out there? They're there for me. Another pregnancy would ruin me for good. A marriage . . . well. Marriage isn't what it's cracked up to be. It's better you learn that now. Compromise means giving up your dreams. And frankly, there's no one worth it. I refuse to settle. After what happened with you, especially. I'm not going through the horror of that scenario again."

"The horror of having an imperfect baby," Davis echoed. She gripped the side of the vanity, needing to steady herself. She'd dreamed a thousand times of having the chance to meet her mother, somehow. Now she felt as though she'd been hollowed with a knife. She squeezed the side of the chair, balancing her weight atop it. Her knuckles turned white.

"Well, you're hardly an Imp," her mother said. "But yes. The fact that you weren't a full Prior was devastating. It took me a long time to recover from the shock, get back on my feet. I can't allow for that kind of personal derailment again."

Her mother was a monster. Davis felt it—a total void where love should have been. Her heart shattered. Even if she could put it back together, there would be nothing left to fill it with. Acknowledging the double loss of Cole and now her mother—whom she'd once thought was the answer to everything—left her trembling.

She couldn't stop herself from feeling devastated. But she could get answers.

"What happened to Leslie Eide?" she asked, afraid of the answer even as she uttered the question. "Why did she have to die?"

"Leslie was a waste," her mother said, her voice hard. "I did Columbus a favor. Leslie was making babies imperfect on purpose."

"What? You mean I would have been born a Prior?" Davis reeled. Leslie was responsible for this?

"If Leslie hadn't interfered, yes. She purposefully neglected giving you your prenatal procedures because she thought they would make you susceptible to a deadly virus."

The implications were terrifying, and Davis sank into the chair that had been supporting her weight. Her legs felt cold and leaden. Leslie Eide had both ruined her life and saved it.

"Narxis," Davis whispered. If she'd been a full Prior, she'd be dead.

Her mother met her eyes for the first time, looking amused. She reached for her water bottle on the vanity and took a long sip before answering, as though it were any other casual, leisurely talk. To Davis, who now rested her head in her hands, it was earth-shattering. So much of her life had been left to chance.

"Yes," she said, "If it actually exists. Half of me thinks it's just a product of the revolutionary imagination. Fodder for riots. Propaganda. God," she laughed, waving a hand dismissively, "every time I think of the trouble that goes on over there, I'm thrilled I defected to Durham. You couldn't pay me to go back to that sullied city. Even if Narxis is a real thing, it would be better to die perfect than live imperfectly, wouldn't you agree? From the look of things, these years haven't been kind to you, have they?"

Davis froze. "Are you asking me if I'd rather be dead?" Her mother's question was unfathomable.

"Wouldn't you? Look at the way you've suffered, you poor thing. What Leslie did was a crime. She deserved to die. You'll make your own decision. When you realize how ugly this world is when it's tainted with imperfection, you'll see how little your own life matters. Now fill my water bottle, would you? There's a filter in the hall. I'm parched."

Davis rose with effort, repulsed. There was something else there, though, something she couldn't quite identify.

Davis nodded, giving her mother one last look. Without emotion, her mother was a lovely shell. But her hateful words made her something worse, more sinister. Davis realized how lucky she'd been to grow up without her mother. And then she put her finger on the feeling that had begun to germinate when her mother spoke of death: pity. Her mother was the emptiest person Davis had ever met.

She thought of her father and Fia, who were truly loving, and something inside of her shut down—the parts of her that had felt incomplete without her mother. The parts that had idolized her mother and had striven to be just like her one day. All of it was gone, wiped out, as though it had never existed, hadn't propelled her through every single challenge for years. What would make her happy, now that she wasn't searching for her mother?

Love and kindness and the true connections she had left. That's what would get her through this.

"I'll be right back with your water," Davis said to her mother, leaving the room and shutting the door resolutely behind her. Instead of stopping at the filter station, though, she kept going through the hall and left the theater altogether, letting the metal door slam shut behind her, never once looking back.

18

COLE

Olympiads registration was at eight a.m. The shuttle ride over had been strange; the city had changed since the Imps had gone on strike. It was grimier—a film of dust covered almost all of the buildings, and trash was strewn about the streets. It also felt eerily empty—Narxis had taken so many victims that a number of the buildings were practically vacant.

Cole hadn't known how big the Gen turnout would be, but there were only five of them. He recognized one of the guys from FEUDS when they boarded, and he kept his face down and sat on the back to avoid being recognized himself. The others—a muscular girl about his age wearing athletic shorts and a tank top, and three other, younger guys he didn't recognize, all in sweats—chatted among themselves, seeming to know each other. Cole had shaved his head and grown out his facial hair in an attempt to alter his appearance. As always, he kept his hood up and his head down.

He was relieved when the bus pulled up in front of the arena, so he could disappear into a crowd of Priors. He was more likely to go unnoticed among Priors; they didn't know him, and they likely didn't care too much about tracking down an Imp fugitive whom everyone presumed was dead.

There were guards, though, at every corner. The arena was intimidating in scope, encompassing an entire city block, a behemoth structure of concrete and chrome with a domed ceiling made of metallic sheets that appeared to be partially retracted to allow the morning sun to filter in. He recognized it from when Davis had pointed it out—it was where she'd done her Qualifiers—but he'd never been inside it before.

Cole queued up at 7:45, scoping out the competition from under the protective disguise of his hood. The Priors, he noted, all had flawless facial features and sculpted figures. They were all wearing brand-name athletic apparel: patterned Lycra and colorful sports bras, the signature striped shorts of a fitness label. He guessed they were sponsored, and a wave of hot anxiety flashed through him. This would be the stiffest competition he'd ever faced. Still, he'd trained hard with Mari. He had what no one else had: a knowledge of both sides.

When he approached the registration desk, his chest seized. All the dates they'd stumbled over the night before mixed into one indecipherable medley, and he prayed he'd know how to answer any questions thrown his way. Having to face a Prior head-on—and communicate with her, even look her in the eye—made him feel cornered. Being out in the open was terrifying, like being fully exposed for the first time. For so long, he'd been hiding. This was the first time he'd been forced to show his face in public, and it felt unnatural, like he was naked.

"Brent Kayson," he told the person managing sign-in. The name rolled uncomfortably off his tongue. She pushed the ID monitor his way.

"Pointer finger, please," she told him, and he pressed the altered finger—mangled and swollen—onto the monitor. A light flashed and the laser scanned his index finger. Time seemed to stand still. The process was painless, but for all the terror he was feeling, it may as well have been a high-risk surgical procedure. The staff member didn't seem to notice the state his finger was in, and after what seemed like a catastrophic moment in which Cole feared everything was about to end, the machine lit green to indicate that his name matched his print. Cole breathed a long sigh of relief.

"Just a few questions before you go in," the woman said. He flexed his palms a few times, trying hard to relax his facial features so he didn't appear tense. Under his white hoodie, his T-shirt was drenched in sweat.

"Birth date."

"October tenth," he said, praying he was remembering correctly.

"Street address?"

"One Halsey," he said, and the woman jerked upward, examining his face.

"Imperfect," she stated.

Cole froze. For a second, he thought she meant his answer was incorrect. Then he realized she was just identifying him, and adrenaline rushed through him, causing a curious mixture of relief and indignation. "Is that part of the verification, or are you just curious?" Cole's voice was hard. The woman rolled her eyes and motioned him into the other room.

"You're clear. Just go in."

Cole nodded and accepted a towel from the woman's assistant. The woman had already turned to the next contestant, eager to be rid of Cole.

"Thanks," he said to the girl with the towel, pushing past the waiting crowds, which stood four or five people deep, into the prep room.

"Good luck," she called after him. He nodded in thanks. He would need it. It was official: he was *in*.

Cole stripped down to athletic shorts and had just begun to tape his wrists, his hands shaking more than a little bit, when a burly Prior approached him. The guy was wearing a name tag identifying him as one of the judges, and for a second Cole's heart stopped. He was sure he'd be caught, and he tensed, ready to bolt.

"Relax," the guy said, reading his expression. "You've still got prep time. Just wanted to let you know you have a visitor."

"Prep time," Cole said. "Right."

The guy raised an eyebrow. "So, can I show her in?"

"Yeah." Cole's voice caught, his relief threatening his composure. For a brief second he found himself hoping wildly, irrationally, that the "her" in question would be Davis.

Instead, Mari walked in, and Cole tried not to feel disappointed. It was brave of her to come; the journey, crossing in from the Slants, was treacherous for Cole, who'd done it a million times by now, but for someone who had never done it and didn't have clearance . . . it could be disastrous.

"You shouldn't be here," he said, standing. He looked over his shoulder to see if anyone else noticed, but the other competitors in the room were consumed by preparations for the games.

"Is that any way to greet a lady?" she asked, offering him a small grin. "Anyway, they think I'm competing. Imps are allowed to compete, remember? Or are you having another identity crisis?"

Cole smiled, feeling the return of his affection for her.

"I don't like the way you left with no explanation," Mari continued.

"Mari, I—" He'd meant to tell her he was sorry. But she held up a finger to quiet him.

"I came here because I have a few things to say," she informed him. "I'm not interested in hearing you 'mansplain' the situation to me. We've become friends. It took a while. I understand you now. You know that. You're strong, brave, loyal. But sometimes you act like a real dick. I put everything I had into your training, and I deserve better if I'm going to let you be my friend."

She was right. "I'm an idiot," he said. She raised an eyebrow, nodding in agreement. "Thank you for being so honest. I'll probably still be an idiot occasionally, as that seems to be my way. But," he continued, "I'll have you know that I'm not a complete numbskull. There's no way I could have gotten here without you."

"You bet your ass you couldn't," she said with a smirk, her eyes lighting up in mischief.

"So I'll be a better friend," he told her. "And I can't wait to give you half my winnings—because I fully plan to win."

Fifteen minutes later, Cole was poised on a swimmer's block with a half dozen other swimmers, ready to jump into the cool water in front of him. He tried to ignore the crowd in the arena, which was packed to capacity. He'd heard the arena seated one thousand. He breathed, focusing on the task before him. The pool was manufactured by top Prior engineers to simulate open water, and the competitors had been warned in advance that it would behave as natural water might—whatever that meant. The water itself certainly wasn't clear. It was murky and choppy, splashing him gently as he stared into its surface. Cole felt ready for release.

"Part one in the extended triathlon is the open water swim," the announcer intoned over the arena loudspeakers. "Each competitor who fails to reach the finish line will be eliminated from future events. Last one standing is the winner, folks! And our competitors have been warned that they'll face certain . . . surprises." The crowd roared and booed as one.

Cole stared at the lapping water, forcing everything from his mind but the goal: the finish line. He had to stay mentally strong. Adrenaline surged through his body, and when the judge blew the whistle, he jumped in and swam with a great tide of energy, primed to destroy his opponents.

By lap three, though, his energy started to wane, and each stroke required more effort. He pushed on, fighting through the pain of it, and pushed back his growing desperation as he watched two other swimmers—well behind when they started—push in front of him. Panic welled up in his chest—for the first time, it seemed entirely possible that he might lose. Still, even thinking that was a kind of defeat, so he forced it away and pushed forward, his lungs burning.

When the water started teeming around him, Cole at first thought it was natural tides caused by the swimmers next to him. But as it pushed against him and gained more force, he realized: the pool had been designed to take on a life of its own, its currents resembling a river. At first he panicked further, flailing among the powerful currents as he felt himself being dragged down and pushed aside by the waves. He looked up, gasping for breath and halting his forward momentum altogether. The scene around him was chaos: the other swimmers were being tossed around like debris at the mercy of the currents. They were no better off than he was. In fact, they looked worse—completely at a loss about how to handle the simulated experience of navigating the rhythms of a natural body of water.

It occurred to him that ninety percent of the contestants were used to man-made water, had only trained in sterile environments. He was likely the only one who had had river experience. *He had the advantage.*

Channeling all of his experience swimming with Mari in the pond behind her house, Cole took several deep breaths and channeled everything he knew about moving with, and not against, the current. He fell into an easy rhythm that complemented the rhythm of the water, and he swam that way, outpacing most of the others, who were still struggling to understand the water's patterns. Cole pulled ahead of the two guys who had passed him only moments before. He was closing in on the lead, with only a few swimmers ahead of him now.

As Cole swam, small tentacles reached from the bottom, simulating pond reeds. They rose toward him, angling toward his legs. What kind of "surprises" had they meant? Could this be something live and potentially poisonous? There wasn't time to consider it. The tentacles rose higher and higher, as if they could grow to infinite heights. With a renewed surge of confidence, Cole easily dodged them, shaking them off deftly as they wrapped their slimy fingers around his ankles and calves. He navigated the ever-dimming water like a pro.

Opening his eyes to peer under the water's surface, he noticed that the pool was completing its transformation to pond even as he moved. Very little light filtered down to its depths, and some of the other swimmers—who were likely unable to comfortably open their eyes underwater, never having done it before—were no longer swimming in a straight line. Cole watched as bodies collided and people struggled through waves and in and out of weeds—but he stayed his course. He was nearly in the lead and just a half mile or so from the finish line when he noticed the frantic flailing of the swimmer next to him.

Cole looked back as he swam, waiting for the swimmer to shake off whatever he was fighting and regain control of the situation. But his movements grew more panicked, and he drew in long, hacking gulps of water. Cole halted, then turned back. The guy looked like he was in serious trouble. Cole could go on and finish the race . . . but no one else seemed capable of helping the other swimmer. As the guy sputtered and coughed and swallowed another long gulp of water, Cole made up his mind.

With a heavy heart, he swam over to the drowning swimmer, giving up his lead. He locked his arms under the swimmer's arms and pulled him onto his back.

"Stop struggling," he shouted at the guy. "Just relax, I'm going to drag you in." In his panic, the guy's eyes were glassy, and he seemed not to register Cole's instructions. He fought against Cole, threatening to bring them both down. Desperate, Cole lifted a palm and slapped the guy across the face, stunning him into silence. Then he swam him over to the end of the massive tank, hauling them both out of the water and handing him off to one of the waiting coaches. In the stands, the crowd went wild. Cole couldn't tell whether they were cheering for him or heckling him . . . but he didn't care. It was over. Cole watched as a rogue wave tumbled through the tank, plowing over several swimmers in its path. He stood at the side, unaffected.

Cole vaulted off the side and pushed back into the race. There was no way he'd win it now, but he would at least finish with his head held high. Cole fought through the waves, adrenaline infusing each of his movements with intensity. When another wave, stretching nearly six feet above him, threatened the course, he dove underneath, cursing inwardly. They'd designed the pool to resemble some sort of hybrid between lake and ocean, he realized. Which meant all bets were off—literally anything could be up next. When he resurfaced, he saw that several of his opponents had taken the same strategy, only to find themselves entangled in the long, twisting weeds. Cole looked at the course spreading out before him and realized that he was back in it. He glimpsed the edge of the pool—the finish line—which wasn't too far off, if only he could swim with the water and not against it. He dove forward, easily dodging the weeds and reeds that ensnared the others. He moved his body with the current, allowing it to fuel his progress. He stopped fighting against the tides and worked with them in the same way he would if he were back in the river with Mari, training behind her wilderness house.

When Cole hit the tape that designated the finish line, he was caught in his own world. He lifted his head to a stunning onslaught of noise. He felt a coach hoisting him up out of the water, but barely registered it when the same coach slung a gold medal over his neck and lifted his arm high in the air, signifying his victory.

Cole had done it. He had won. He looked around him at the audience's stunned expressions and caught Mari in the front row of the crowd nearest the finish line. Somehow she'd slipped in among the observers. He shook his head at her, laughing to himself; the girl was so small and swift that she could sneak around just about anywhere. She pumped her fist in the air and flashed him a broad smile.

Cole was past the first round. The first round, as Mari had told him, was especially designed to weed out the weakest competitors—but he had done it. Cole let himself be ushered from the arena, the cacophony behind him fading only slightly as he moved into the men's locker room.

"Congratulations," the coach who'd led him out there said. "Not bad, for an Imp."

"Not bad for anybody, I'd say," Cole told him. He wouldn't let anyone detract from this victory.

"We'll see how you do in the triathlon. You've got ten minutes to prep."

"What? I thought there was a requisite hour break between events."

"The schedule's been altered," the coach told him with a smug grin. "We'll see how tough you are with no rest at all."

Cole tried to contain his fury. He strongly suspected the schedule had been altered for the purpose of putting him at a disadvantage. His race had wrapped up later than the other morning events, he saw from the status boards. He and one other guy were the only Gens entering the triathlon.

When Cole was ready, he followed the signage to the roof of the auditorium and took his place among a good twenty competitors.

"Why are we up here?" he wondered aloud to the girl next to him, who only shrugged. There wasn't any space up there to do any major events, so when the judge blew the whistle and announced the long jump, Cole furrowed his brow.

"We're jumping across that gap," the girl told him, indicating a wide expanse of air between two buildings.

"You're kidding. We're at least twenty stories up."

"That's right. Piece of cake. Oh wait, Imps don't go roofing, do you?" the girl said, her face alight with a cruel smile. "Too bad." Her words cut deep. Cole watched as the first two contestants readied themselves on the roof's edge, preparing to leap.

Roofing. Cole had forgotten. He had experience with exactly this. It hadn't been easy, but he could do it—he'd done it once before, with Davis. He closed his eyes, imagining Davis there next to him, urging him on. With her there, he could do anything. He breathed in, channeling her presence.

Cole ran for the roof edge, imagining Davis right next to him, laughing with him, telling him to pick up the pace. When he leapt, he cleared the gap by a good distance. He bent to his knees, the fear of having sailed over a death trap finally hitting him. As it turned out, lots of Priors had fallen—there was a net strung up two stories below—but lots had cleared the gap easily. Cole was the only Gen left in the competition . . . but he hadn't even made it to the top ten competitors. He only had two more events in which to scramble back into the winners' bracket.

Cole moved over the deck of the next building toward a low-lying, enclosed space, as per the judges' instructions. He raced into the space—which seemed not permanent, from the look of it, but constructed for this event—and tried not to worry about what might await him inside. When he burst through the door, he found himself in a hall of mirrors. They stretched out all around him, and on all sides he saw the other contenders climbing through mazes of charged wiring, contorting their bodies to bend through and around the live electric ropes. Because of the mirrors, at first it was impossible to tell where the ropes were suspended. From where Cole stood, people were reflected climbing above him and at his feet. When one slipped and was subjected to the wires' resulting shock, a scream echoed for minutes around the room, and his body looked like it hurtled for miles. Cole closed his eyes, warding off panic. Then he forced himself to block out all manufactured stimuli—strobe lights, pulsing music—and feel his way to the course.

As he pulled himself through the ropes, focusing on the coarse, uneven strands of the nonelectrified holds and avoiding the sleeker electrified supports, Priors dropped out all around him. The course seemed easy to Cole; he was surprised that so many of the others were dropping like flies. Then he realized.

Just as flies are drawn to light, the Priors were drawn to the mirrors, moving toward their images—and the small, mirrored panels that decorated the electrified cords—to the point of distraction.

They were too distracted by their own reflections to pay attention
to the ropes.

Cole finished easily, only a little dizzy and disoriented from
the top-is-down, funhouse quality of the race. He and only three
others—all Priors—made it through. Cole noted that Landon,
the crowd favorite and his stiffest competition, was still in it. The
last race would determine everything. Cole squared his shoulders.
He'd come this far, and it seemed like every portion of the contest
involved a code he could crack. He'd do it again for the finals.

"Five-minute break!"

Cole watched as the moderator approached with water. When
he arrived at Cole, he also placed a small yellow supplement in his
palm.

"What is this?" Cole asked, taking the water but ignoring the
supplement.

"Performance enhancer," the moderator said. "We're giving them
to all the standing athletes." Cole looked at the others; sure enough,
Landon was downing his own enhancer with a huge swig of water.

"Do I have to take it?"

"You won't be eliminated if you don't," the guy said, raising an
eyebrow. "But you'd be foolish."

Cole hesitated, considering the options. He'd never taken an enhancer. But Priors already had the physical edge. Without one of
these pills, he'd almost definitely be screwed.

"Two minutes!" the moderator called out. Cole took the pill from
his hand and, without further thought, washed it down with the
water.

As they lined up for the final portion of the contest—a balance
and dexterity competition involving rotating, vaulted beams—he felt
the drug kicking in. His sense of smell was heightened, as was his
hearing. He heard the wind—which he felt against his skin as a soft

breeze—like a freight train in his ears. Small blobs moved in his periphery, obscuring his vision. Cole panicked. He shouldn't have taken the enhancer—his genetic makeup was different from the others', and he wasn't used to it, on top of that. He felt loopy, high. He opened and closed his eyes several times; each time he opened them, the world rose toward him in a frightening configuration of unfamiliar, leering shapes.

Stepping before his beam, he closed his eyes again. He knew what he had to do.

Keeping his eyes closed, he felt the beam rotating beneath his feet. He recalled the night with Mari, in the abandoned stone house, where he'd had to shut out all the obstacles that threatened his mental endurance. That night when they raced he'd had to look deeper inside himself, filtering through the chaos to focus on the simple things: the acoustics of the house, the way his senses inter-acted. Now he focused on the movement of the beam beneath his feet. He took his time, allowing the beam to set his pace as he moved forward, faltering more than once.

Everything else faded away: the crowds roaring below him, the others competing next to him, the surreal quality of the course as seen through his new "enhanced" perspective. He blocked all of it out until it was just the beam and his feet gripping it deftly, propel-ling him forward. The voices of his competitors, trying to distract him with catcalls from where they already stood safely on the other side, faded into nothing.

When he reached the other side, Cole collapsed. He felt stron-ger than ever before, but the world spun in heady circles around him.

Landon leaned over him, his face so close that Cole could smell mint on his breath.

"You'd better watch yourself in the finals," he told him. "I'll die before I let an Imp win the Olympiads."

Cole pulled himself to his feet. Landon backed away, but the very real threat hung between them. Cole could tell Landon had meant every word.

It was up to Cole, then, to see Landon to his death.

19

DAVIS

As the sun came up on Durham, Davis wended her way through the streets of the city, uncertain where to go. The shock of her mother's betrayal was still fresh. It frightened her that her mom had been as emotionless as she was. It horrified her to have such coldness in her blood. What had her mother been like when she and her father first met? Had she changed over time, become so consumed by physical perfection that the most important thing—human connection—died out altogether?

Davis's thoughts turned to Cole, and how close they'd been. She wondered if her mother and father had ever experienced that level of closeness, and the thought that they hadn't made her sad. For all his faults, her father loved her—everything he'd done in his life had been for her and Terri and Fia. How much of that was a result of not feeling loved himself? Everything she thought she'd known started to fall apart as she examined it more closely. Her father had never revealed her mother's true nature—if he had, would she have been better off? Davis gazed up at the buildings looming above her. The city suddenly seemed sinister and threatening, and as she looked upward the buildings seemed to tilt as if about to cave in. Her palms sweated and her heart began its frantic race, making her queasy. All she wanted was to be in Columbus already, with her family.

Davis was so lost in her panicky, splintered thoughts that she didn't see the tall, uniformed men approaching from behind her. When a set of strong hands wrapped themselves around her wrists and clamped over her mouth, she was too startled to try to wriggle away. Her body was seized by terror, and all the times she'd narrowly avoided capture rushed through her head. She'd come so far, only to find herself again in the hands of the enemy.

"Ms. Morrow? Ms. Morrow. Relax," one of the guards said, bending close to her ear. Davis bit down on his hand and he grunted, swearing and pushing her away. She stumbled along the sidewalk, ignoring the curious looks of passersby. She scanned the rows of buildings for an out, but she knew even as she did that it would be impossible. There were two guards that she could see, maybe more lurking somewhere. They were almost certainly from TOR-N. She had no recourse. Still, her flight instinct had kicked in. She darted through the crowds, knocking into pedestrians as she went. An elderly lady cried out, stumbling, and Davis was overcome by a flash of shame. When the guards seized her again, she didn't resist.

"I'm not her," she said desperately. "You have the wrong person."

"We're here on orders of your father," one of the guards said. "Mr. Robert Morrow."

"My . . . my father sent you?" Davis was breathless. "How could he have?"

"So you *are* Davis Morrow."

Davis swallowed hard, caught in her lie.

"Get her ID," one guard, a trim man of average height with a small mole just below his left eye, instructed the other. The second guard, redheaded and lean, patted her down, pulling out the fake ID she'd brought into the city. Davis cringed as his hands wandered briskly over her body.

"Right person," the redheaded guard said. "But this ID is about as real as my grandma's teeth. How the hell did you get in here? Never mind. Let's go." The guards ushered Davis into a nearby building; the one with the mole hummed the whole way. They stepped onto an elevator that ascended to the rooftop at lightning speed.

"Where are you taking me?" Davis fought to keep the fear from her voice. They'd said they'd come on her father's behalf, but the helicopter waiting for her on the rooftop was very real, and their words could easily be nothing but a lie to ensnare her.

"We're going back to Columbus," the redhead said, holding open the door to the helicopter. "Get in. Now."

"How do I know you're not lying?" she said. "How can I be sure you're not taking me back to quarantine?" The other guard stopped humming and sighed impatiently.

"Ms. Morrow. With all due respect, it doesn't matter whether you know for sure. You can get in of your own volition, or we can forcibly take you. We have no orders other than to bring you back to your home in Columbus. Do you have another option?"

Davis gritted her teeth but climbed into the waiting chopper.

"Columbus," the guards told the pilot. For the first time, Davis began to allow herself to hope it was true. Still, her anxiety didn't subside. She wouldn't be able to relax until the chopper touched down in Columbus. Every part of her told her to stay alert. She wouldn't feel completely safe until she was there, in the arms of her family and friends. She realized with a horrible flash that she didn't even know whether they were all still alive. What horrible surprises awaited her there? She took a breath, trying not to think about it. She couldn't; it was too terrible.

"But how did you know I was here?" she asked, once her heart had slowed and her breathing had returned to something resembling normal.

"Reports came in a couple of days ago that you'd escaped TOR-N along with a young man. Since Mercer Wells is from Durham, we put people on it. There have been flyers distributed all over town. Alerts were sent out to everyone's tablets. Someone called in a tip last night around eleven p.m."

The party. Someone must have spotted her there and given her away. Had it been Mercer or someone else? Had he betrayed her a second time? Her heart raced, and shame filled her being. If it wasn't Mercer—because it was too painful to think that he had lied again—who could it have been? Had people from TOR-N located him, too—and if so, would he be sent back?

Three hours later, the helicopter hovered over the roof of Davis's building. Columbus spread below her like a dream; she was overcome by excitement at the thought of returning home. But imagining the city without Cole provoked a wave of fresh pain. There was something different about the city, too, that she couldn't pinpoint from so high above. It was almost as if she were seeing it through a different, foggier lens. Something felt off. When she peered closer, she realized what it was. The buildings didn't shine as brightly as they used to, or as the buildings in Durham had. The streets were empty, yet somehow cluttered. Broken tree limbs lay about and cars rested abandoned on the sidewalks, their doors hanging open. Very few people were walking about. She fought off a pang of worry. A roar from behind her caused her to swivel in her seat, and as the chopper rotated slightly, preparing to land, she gasped, realizing at least one reason why no one was in the streets.

The arena where the Qualifiers had been held, and where the Olympiads were held every year, was jam-packed. The biodome was retracted, as it was only once a year, for the games—and she could see straight in. The games were in full swing, and from the sound of the crowd, it was a close race. A small part of Davis couldn't believe she wasn't there herself, competing. A larger part of her could hardly believe she'd ever thought it possible, or that that had been her life. There was something about the scene that felt larger than life—the athletes at their prime; the course designed for an entire year by Columbus's brightest innovators; the way the entire city turned out for the event. It was hard to believe they were all under the threat of death. From the air, they looked invincible.

Her thoughts fell away as she identified several small figures waiting atop the roof. It wasn't until they touched down on the roof of her building that Davis really allowed herself to believe she was home to stay.

Davis barely waited for the helicopter to fully touch down before she leapt from it and crossed the roof, leaping into her father's arms. Her dad scooped her up, whirling her in a circle like he had when she was a child, and after he set her down, she was shocked to see tears in his eyes. Her father had always been stalwart; now he was overcome.

"Sweetheart," he said, drawing her close again, his deep brown eyes brimming over. "You can't know how much we've missed you.

Having you home . . . it's like a dream come true. You don't know how happy it makes me." She leaned into him, breathing in his familiar, oaky scent and allowing her own tears to spill down her cheeks.

She wanted to stay like that forever, soaking up his love, but the feeling of urgency inside her was overpowering. "Dad," she said, pulling back, her voice thick with tension. "You've got to do something. TOR-N isn't what you thought—they're abusing patients, they're stealing money, no one has good food or care—"

"I know," her dad told her, and her mouth dropped open in shock.

"Then why—"

"I didn't know when I sent you there. I thought it was the best of the best. But when you ran away, and they reported it, they tried to keep me at bay. I got suspicious. I had always wondered why you never answered my videos. It all seemed weird, the way they wanted to keep you away from me. So I sent people out there to check it out. They told me what it was like." He grabbed her shoulders, looking deep into her eyes. "My baby," he said simply. "I'll never forgive myself for sending you there."

"We have to do something," she told him. "You didn't know. But now we do, and we've got to fix it."

"We've removed all the patients to the hospital here in Columbus," he assured her. "They've been made comfortable."

"Made comfortable." Davis pulled back. "I don't understand. Aren't they receiving treatment?"

"They're getting treatments to ease their discomfort, sweetie," her dad told her. "But most of them are near death. Only a dozen cases have survived, including you. Everyone else is dead or dying. But the good news is, the scientists think it's contained. Even if there's no cure, the disease should eliminate itself soon."

"By eliminating the people it's infected," Davis said, her voice stiff. Her father frowned. She could see in his eyes how helpless he felt.

She realized then that he looked more tired than when she'd seen him last. His skin was sallow and his eyes were less bright. "I'm sorry," she whispered. "I know you've tried."

"Davis," he started, his face tortured, "apologizing isn't enough. I know that. I sent you into danger. I didn't give you a choice. I'll never, ever forgive myself."

Seraphina's face flashed through her mind, and the faces of the others from TOR-N: the old lady who liked to help out in the craft room; the boy who'd taught them all yoga. Were they still alive or had they succumbed to the disease?

"I forgive you, Dad," Davis said, wrapping her arms around him once again. "You were just trying to save me."

"I was. But I should have done more. I'm your father. It's my job to protect you." He kissed the top of her forehead, and she leaned into him. It was such a simple gesture, one she'd taken for granted her entire life. "I'll never forgive myself for letting you out of my sight," he told her. "Especially after what happened with Vera . . ."

Davis drew back. "What do you mean?" she asked, her voice panicked. "What happened?"

"She's gone, sweetheart," her father said. "I'm so sorry. I don't know why I thought . . . of course you wouldn't have known. I tried to find her," he said. "We both did, me and Terri. We called her parents, went to their house. They say she ran away and they can't find her. No one can. Everyone assumes she was paranoid about the disease. We have no idea if she survived. I'm so sorry." He pulled her into a hug again, kissing her on the forehead. "We're so glad to have you back, honey. We'll keep searching for Vera."

It wasn't until her father walked her down to her old bedroom and she closed the door behind her—seeing her mother's medal for the first time in months, seeing pictures of herself and Vera tucked into her gilded bedroom mirror—that she collapsed with emotion.

She cried because her friends had died, and her mother had turned out to be someone unrecognizable, and she'd lost the one person she'd ever loved beyond measure, and the world was falling apart around her. Davis looked around her at the objects that had once held meaning for her but that now seemed foreign, and she realized she no longer knew where she fit. She didn't know how to stop feeling sad.

She was so caught up in her thoughts that she didn't hear the door open. It was only when Fia climbed up onto the bed next to her that she realized her sister had entered the room. Their dad stood in the doorframe, smiling tenderly.

"Looks like someone else missed you," he said.

Davis shifted on the bed, winding her arms around her little sister. She breathed in her familiar, baby powder scent and buried her face in Fia's fuzzy black hair. Her heart lifted.

"Fi pea!" she exclaimed, wrapping her little sister in a hug. The sight of Fia—looking even taller and older after just a few months apart—made her smile, when she hadn't thought it was possible. She wrapped her arms tighter around Fia's narrow, birdlike frame, so grateful to have her sister alive and healthy and sitting beside her.

"I thought Daddy was lying," Fia whispered in her ear. "But I made you a welcome home cake just in case. Mommy helped me." Davis laughed, burying her head in her sister's dark hair.

"That was sweet, honey," she said. "I missed you so much." Her words didn't begin to explain how she felt. Everything had looked so bleak a second ago, and it still was. But Fia was a golden beacon of hope. A reason to keep going. She was lucky, and she knew that if Cole and Vera were there they would both agree. Davis lifted her head to see Terri standing a few feet behind Fia. Her smile was warm and her eyes brimmed over with tears.

"Davis," she said, her voice unsteady. "We're so happy to have you home." Davis stood, releasing Fia, and moved toward Terri. Terri, who had been there for her for the past four years, loving her as if she were her own. Terri, who had made her snacks before ballet and taken her to lunch, just the two of them, and talked to her about boys and growing up. She'd always taken Terri for granted—resented her simply for being the woman who had replaced her mother. Now she saw Terri and realized that the whole time she was searching for her mother, a mother had been right here, waiting for her to accept her love.

"Thank you," she said to her stepmom, pulling her close. Terri looked startled at first; then she smiled.

"There's nothing to thank me for," she told her.

"You've always been such a good mom," Davis said quietly. "And I've never told you how much I love you."

"I love you, too." The intensity in Terri's voice brought fresh tears to Davis's eyes. "You're my daughter. I love you and Fia both more than anything."

Davis felt the emptiness that had always existed somewhere within her begin to fill. For the first time, she felt nearly complete. The void Cole had left with his death, of course, would always be there. And Vera's disappearance had caused her more devastation than she knew how to handle. No one would ever replace Cole—not Mercer, not any other guy she might one day begin to care about. Today would have been the happiest day of her life, if only her love and her best friend were there to share it.

An hour later she sat eating cake with Fia and Terri. Her father had already left for the Olympiads, where, as city prime minister, he was required to make a speech. Davis had wanted to go, but her father had ordered her to stay put and get some rest. She didn't have it in her to argue. But now that she was here, once again doing nothing, thoughts of Narxis were plaguing her. Her dad had said the scientists had given up. How could that be possible? How could they be sure the disease was no longer a threat? It was troubling. Davis smiled at Fia as she chattered, and she complimented her little sister's baking, but her mind was racing.

"I have to go rest," Davis said, standing up. "I'm not feeling well," she amended, when she saw Terri's look of concern. "This news about Vera is overwhelming. I need to lie down." Terri nodded, but she looked worried. She wrapped a protective arm around Fia and gazed up at Davis with concern.

"We'll be in the rec room," she told her. "We trust you, Davis. We only just got you back. Please don't jeopardize that."

"I wouldn't." Even as she said it, she felt a pang of guilt.

Davis squeezed Terri's hand and pecked Fia on the cheek, then hurried to her room. Once there, she composed a note to Terri. She didn't want to worry anybody, but she wasn't sure how long she'd be gone, and there was no way she could put them through the agony of wondering whether she was okay—especially after she'd lied outright. But she had to get to the Slants, to find Thomas Worsley. She was certain there was a cure. Even without Cole and without Vera, she had to find one. They'd want her to. All hope couldn't be lost—not when she still didn't know whether Thomas had stumbled across any developments. Even if he had, it was likely that the Priors would have ignored them. She needed to see his progress for herself.

She waited an excruciating half hour before she snuck downstairs, laid the note on the kitchen counter, and slipped out the door. The movie they were watching—a classic Disney film from long ago—was playing loudly in the other room. She was confident they hadn't even heard the door latch shut behind her.

The trip to the Slants was different from what she remembered. It was both more ominous and less treacherous. The banks of the river were no longer guarded at all, but they were overgrown and strewn with garbage. Davis approached a raft stored up along the side of the riverbank and, seeing no one around to claim it, climbed in and rowed herself across. She was struck by how alone she was; the last time she'd done this, Cole had been with her. The memory seared its way under her skin, making her feel more alone than ever. And yet she was proud of herself for carrying on. It would be so easy to give up—to crawl into bed and sleep and sleep until this whole nightmare was over. She had even more strength than she realized. She was able to hold it together. She wasn't giving up on figuring out how to cure Narxis. She no longer had any care for whether she was doing something wrong. She had to get across, and quickly.

The atmosphere on the other side was like a free-for-all. People swarmed the streets, and the state of affairs was more desperate than before. Skinny children wandered in ripped clothing, eyeing her curiously. Davis didn't stand out as much as she used to—that much she knew. She'd lost weight at TOR-N, and she was wearing a nondescript sweat suit. Still, she was clean and relatively strong. Some of these children looked abandoned, like no one had cared for them in months. She promised herself she'd talk to her father about it later. What had happened to her city? How had Columbus, once a superpower, fallen apart so quickly?

She wove her way toward Thomas's lab; if anyone would know anything, it would be him. But as she approached, she was overcome by a sense of dread. The buildings leading up to the lab were no longer intact. Piles of charred wreckage were everywhere. Something awful must have happened—a fire or a looting. Her dread mounted as she turned the corner and faced the remnants of Thomas's lab. It was completely reduced to rubble.

Davis felt her throat tighten. Was Thomas okay? What had happened? Where was he, and where was Cole's brother, and the rest of his family and friends? Could they have died in the riots? She felt horror and shame for having been gone so long. She should have been there, making sure that Cole's family was okay in his absence. She should have forced her father to do something. Surely, there was something she could have done.

"Lookin' for Worsley?"

The voice was harsh, craggy. Davis turned, frightened.

"Yes," she said, trying to sound brave. "How did you know?"

"This was his lab," the old man said. "No one stares at a pile of junk like that unless they're missin' what it used to be."

"Is he okay?"

"Worsley's fine," the man said, leaning heavily on his cane. "Has a new lab now. North of here. In the old parking garage. You see that scaffolding?" He hobbled to the corner of the street and waved northward with his cane. Davis squinted. She couldn't see anything.

"That there. Peeking out from behind the yellow house. Here. Move to your right." Davis took a few steps toward the man and peered in the direction he was indicating. Sure enough, there was a gray cement structure rising up about a mile away, farther back toward the outskirts of town.

"You're sure Worsley's there," she said doubtfully. "How do you know?"

"Take it or leave it," the guy said with a shrug. "Everybody knows Worsley. He's the only doctor we got. Surprised you need the advice in the first place." He raised an eyebrow, and Davis bit her lip, afraid of giving herself away.

"Thank you, sir," she said to the man. "I really appreciate it."

"Happy to help," the guy said, turning to hobble back inside his shack.

Davis made her way to the parking garage, a little nervous about what she might find. She wandered through three levels before she spotted an old office in one corner of the fourth level—the kind that must once have been used by valets and parking monitors before everything became automated. The door to the office was slightly ajar and the window was covered with an opaque metallic shade. A narrow beam of light leaked from the gap between the door and the door frame, and as Davis approached, she heard low voices. One of them was feminine. Davis moved closer, her heart beating ever faster. The voice was lilting and soft. It was as familiar to Davis as her own.

Davis burst through the door to find Vera and Thomas Worsley sitting opposite one another in a small, sterile room lined with medical equipment. She paused, sucking in a breath. Vera was pale, drawn, and very pregnant.

In the space of a few seconds, everything fell into place: Vera's disappearance, her parents' silence, their reluctance to search for her. Davis drew a hand to her mouth, stunned.

"We had a conversation," Davis started, thinking aloud. "Just before I was taken away. You said you had news."

"Davis," Vera breathed, struggling to stand up. "I wanted to tell you." Thomas offered Vera an arm, and Davis rushed to her friend, wrapping her up in a hug.

"You're okay," whispered Vera.

"*You're* okay," Davis replied. "I'm such a fool. I can't believe I didn't think of it sooner, you being here . . . being pregnant." None of it felt real. Shock roiled across her, and she struggled for air. She'd hoped against hope to find Vera, but now that she had, her friend seemed like a product of her imagination. She was thinking this through her tears, when she realized her arms reached only partway around her friend's formerly petite frame.

"But are you healthy?" Davis asked, her voice anxious as she moved away again to examine Vera's belly. "You're pale, Ver. You look a little thin, aside from your belly. I'm worried about you."

"She'll be fine," Worsley broke in, holding Davis's gaze. Davis nodded, wanting with all her being to trust him. She couldn't think of the alternative, now that she'd found her friend again.

"I was going to tell you," Vera said, frowning. "I wanted to so badly. I was just frightened. And then you were gone and I didn't have the chance. I'm so, so sorry."

"No," Davis said. "Please don't be. I'm just glad to be here with you now. And I'm so happy for you, Vera. I just can't believe it."

Vera smiled shyly, looking down at her belly. She rested a hand atop it, massaging gently. "Would you like to feel?" she asked, looking suddenly hopeful. "Sometimes the baby kicks."

Davis laughed. "Of *course* I want to feel," she told her friend. "Are you kidding?" She placed a palm on Vera's belly. Her friend's skin was taut and smooth and blessedly warm feeling. Sure enough, the baby kicked—a little impression that nudged Davis's hand for an instant, and then it was gone. Davis had never thought she could feel so much joy in the midst of so much turmoil.

"Vera, is it . . ."

"It's Oscar's," Vera told her, her face darkening. "Have you seen him?"

"No. I only just got back. My God, Ver. How are you? Are you feeling okay? Are you healthy? How is the baby? My God," she repeated, shaking her head. "I just can't believe it."

"Vera needs to rest," Thomas interjected. "Davis, I'm so glad you're well."

"Oh, Tom, I'm sorry," she said. "I just . . . it's such a shock." She turned to him, giving him a hug. "You're right. Vera, we can talk more tomorrow. Now that I've found you, we have all the time in the world. I'm not letting you out of my sight."

Vera smiled, clasping Davis's hand in her own. The simple gesture brought tears to Davis's eyes. She led Vera back to her narrow bed and helped her lie down, tucking her in. Vera's eyes were already closing as Davis adjusted the blanket around her. She looked, suddenly, like a ghost to Davis.

"Tom, you've got to tell me. Why is Vera here? Is she okay?" Davis spoke in a low whisper, careful not to disturb Vera. She felt her heart sink as Tom bit his lip and looked down at the ground, avoiding her gaze.

"She's sick, Davis," Tom said. "I thought I could help her. I thought I could use her baby to create a Narxis vaccine to save her and eliminate this awful disease. It's . . ." He ran a hand through his hair, clearly distressed. For the first time, Davis noticed how puffy and bloodshot his eyes were. It looked like Tom hadn't slept for days. "I just don't know what to do," he finished. "I was so close to figuring this thing out. I thought I could save her. But my experiments failed. Something's missing; I can't figure it out. She's not doing well."

"But she'll be okay?" Davis waited for him to reassure her, and when he didn't, fear took hold of her heart. "Tom, will she be okay?"

Tom shook his head. "I don't know," he said quietly. Davis paled, her entire body turning cold.

"The baby?" she asked.

"It's too soon to say," Tom said. "But it doesn't look good for either of them. Still," he said, "I'm glad to see you're holding up. I'd heard what happened to you."

"I'm cured," Davis said.

Worsley's eyes widened in disbelief.

Davis took a deep breath, steadying herself. There had to be a way. There could still be a way to beat this thing. Silently, she cursed her father's guards for finding her before she could find out anything real about Narxis. She racked her brain. There was very little she could do, but she could tell Tom everything she knew.

"No," he said when she was done. "It's not possible."

"It's true," she insisted. "I'm no longer contagious."

Worsley stared at her, his face flushed.

"What is it?" she asked, leaning close. He furrowed his brow, thinking intently. He held up a finger, motioning for Davis to give him a minute. Finally he raised his glittering eyes to meet hers.

"I think I understand now," he whispered, breaking into a grin. "I can use *your* DNA strands—cured of Narxis—to create the vaccine. Since you've developed antibodies and I have both your old blood and your new, healthy blood, it should work. I can save the baby. But I'll save the baby *and* develop a cure. Davis, don't you see? This is what we needed. It's your blood that's special. I never thought I'd see you again. I never knew for sure there *could* be a survivor, and I certainly thought no one with Narxis would ever make it home. But if you're really cured as you say you are, then you must carry the antibodies in your blood."

"It must have been what Hassman needed," she said.

"Hassman?" Worsley looked confused. "Dr. Hassman, the famous researcher?"

"Never mind," Davis told him. "It isn't important. What's important is that you can save Vera," she told him, her voice urgent. "And develop a cure for Narxis here."

"I don't know. But this is the first time in a while that I've thought there's a chance. I'd hoped . . . well, I wanted you home. I thought it was nearly impossible, but I hoped for it." Davis nodded. It wasn't enough. Nothing would be enough until she knew Vera and her baby were safe. But it was something to hinge hope on.

Her eyes were drawn to a flash across the small TV set mounted on the opposite wall. What she saw sobered her. There it was again, and this time Davis leapt from her perch on the floor and raced over to the television set, eager to adjust the volume.

The Olympiads banner flashed across the screen, followed by the faces of the remaining competitors. Cole's face was among them.

"What is this? Tom? What does it mean?" She felt panicked, shaky. Her legs gave out from under her, and she reached for the wall to steady herself, but it was too late. She sank to her knees on the floor, hugging her stomach.

"You didn't know," Worsley stated in astonishment, wonder crossing his face. "You thought he was dead?"

"What are you saying?"

"Cole is very much alive, Davis," Worsley told her, crouching beside her and placing a hand on her shoulder. "He's been competing today. He assumed his friend Brent's identity to enter."

"Alive." Davis whispered it, and Thomas nodded. "He's just about to start the ropes." Worsley joined her in front of the set. She couldn't process what he was saying. Cole was alive. It was everything she'd dreamed of. He was there, only a few miles away from her, and she had to get to him. There was no way he could compete against Priors on the rope course and stay alive. He was lucky just to have made it through the other lethal tests the Olympiads were famous for. If she didn't get to him, she'd lose him again. She knew it with as much certainty as she knew she loved him. The Olympiads were not designed for Gens . . . unless they were designed to *kill* them. Davis's hands went cold. To see him like this, to know he was alive, and then to lose him . . . she wouldn't survive it. The rope course was nearly impossible for the average Prior, let alone a Gen.

"They misreported his death," Worsley said as photos of Cole and the headlines for the event results flashed across the street. "He's managed to lie low."

He'd been alive all this time. The whole time she'd been mourning him, he was okay. Davis gasped, and Worsley pulled her into him. Then she struggled away from him and to her feet. There wasn't a second to lose. There was hope for Columbus. Never had she thought there would be hope for her to be reunited with her love.

She had to get to him *now*, before the rope course began. Davis felt happiness and fear flood through her in powerful juxtaposition. Cole was alive, and he needed her help. She had to go back to the Olympiads. She had to save him.

⊰ 20 ⊱

COLE

Cole's palms burned each time he heaved his body upward. His hand, swollen from his fingerprint surgery, throbbed. The coarse ropes stretched from the tenth story of one high-rise to the twentieth of another. So far, Cole had made it to the fifteenth story, but his muscles burned and his arms threatened to give out. There were no knots on the rope to help him propel his body forward. He had only brute strength, but he knew there was no way he'd make it to the end. His lungs were heaving, his arms burning and shaky. And Landon was at least two stories ahead of him, climbing the ropes like a monkey might climb a vine.

Cole stopped, panting. He had to last at least until Landon won. He couldn't let go—literally couldn't, or he'd plummet to the pavement fifteen stories below. There were no safety nets this time; the stakes were life or death. Worsley had told him that, for the Olympiads to keep running, there had to be fewer than three deaths. There hadn't been any deaths that day. The audience was restless. Cole guessed the sponsors had felt free, then, to remove any precautions, heightening the stakes for the crowd.

Landon moved deftly ahead of him, fueled by seemingly endless reserves of energy. Cole faltered, watching him, and his grip shifted on the rope. Cole's body weight dipped sideways, and his feet scrambled for a hold. He cried out, terrified, as the rope swayed precariously. For a split second, it seemed futile. He was certain he was going to fall. In his panic, he fumbled for the rope, his sweaty palms slipping across it. It may as well have been slicked with oil, given how impossible it was to retain a grip.

Cole could hear a collective gasp from the distant crowd. He knew they were watching a projection of the events, but without the immediacy of it, some part of him had been able to pretend he and Landon were alone on the ropes, engaged in something more than a performance bent on regenerating a city he no longer felt any loyalties to. It was a city he'd only loved for Davis.

Davis's face flashed through his mind, producing adrenaline. He couldn't give up, not while she was still out there somewhere. He had to stay alive for her, to take care of her. The thought of dying like this—never being able to see her and hold her and touch her face again—was unfathomable. Cole used every last ounce of his strength to right himself, listening to the jeering cries of the crowd. He knew they were cheering against him, not for him—still, they seemed more hostile than usual. He steadied himself, trying not to look at the sheer drop below. He couldn't let himself think of how close he'd come to falling.

He moved forward an inch and looked up at Landon again. Landon was now mere feet from the finish line. It was all over. Cole swayed in the breeze, on the rope, feeling his future slip away from him with every rocking motion. Part of him had wanted to let go, he realized. He wanted to stop struggling. It had only been Davis's face flickering through his mind that had prevented him from giving up altogether.

Landon looked back at him and laughed, outwardly mocking him. He hammed it up for the cameras, hanging from the rope with one arm, then pulling himself up again. The crowd was going wild; Cole could hear them cheering loudly, egging him on. Landon pointed at Cole, then moved into what looked like a side plank, with one arm and one leg balanced on the rope. He grinned and waved in the direction of the cameras with his other hand as he swung into a one-armed pull-up.

Sweat trickled into Cole's eyes, obscuring his vision. In that moment, he hated Landon with his whole being. Landon, who had been given every advantage and had done nothing to deserve it. Cole had simply been born without. That was it. He'd worked so hard, and he'd come this far—almost to the finish. But "almost" wasn't enough to win the prize and save everyone he loved.

The breeze picked up and the rope swayed beneath him. It felt good—calming—against the heat of his body. It wrapped itself around him more powerfully, causing the rope to rock. What was happening? Cole gripped the rope tighter between his arms and legs, feeling unsteady. When he heard a roar from the crowd, he assumed it was because Landon had finally reached the finish line. The wind had really picked up by then, and Cole held his ground, moving only to look up toward Landon.

But the screams of the crowd grew louder, and Cole squinted to see Landon dangling by one arm, his body being whipped around by the wind as if it were flimsy as paper. Landon struggled, flailing for the rope with his other hand. Cole moved forward, bent on helping him, but the ever-stronger wind made him clamp his body firmly in place, holding on with all his strength. A weaker person than Landon, in his same position, would have fallen already, Cole realized. He heard a whirring sound and looked up to see an emergency chopper heading their way. Landon just had to hang on for a few more seconds.

But the wind gusted harder, and Landon's fingers slipped, releasing the rope.

He screamed as he fell, passing mere feet from Cole, who reached out a hand in a desperate attempt to grab him. Landon's fingertips brushed Cole's, and for a split second, his eyes met Cole's. It was enough time for Cole to register the panic of a doomed man. Cole turned, steeling himself against the sound of impact fifteen stories below. There were screams from the crowd, and then sobs.

The Olympiads were over, Cole realized.

He was the winner.

The breeze quieted, and Cole pulled himself slowly along the rope, aware of the eerie, oppressive silence that surrounded him. His arms still burned and he gasped for breath, but without the need to quicken his pace for a competitor, he was able to inch his way to the finish line. Once there, he hoisted himself up and flopped to the ground, gasping for breath.

A line of four or five imposing men and women stood before him, arms crossed over their chests. But they didn't bear the official Olympiads crest. They stared at him, their mouths hard. Cole pulled himself to his feet with some difficulty. His eyes narrowed in confusion.

"I've won," he said. "I'm the winner, right?"

"Cole Ethan Everest," one of the men said. It was all Cole needed to realize what was happening. He'd been identified. "It's over. Turn yourself in."

"No," Cole said, backing up. "No. I won. I fought to be here. I won my right to be here. Where is my prize money? I deserve this." His voice rose, panicked, but it was met with silence. Cole took another step back, then realized: any further and he'd plummet to his death right behind Landon. There was nowhere to go but forward, into the lion's den. Again, he thought about death. He'd struggled so long and so hard. But the thought of abandoning Davis was too much. He stepped forward, holding out his arms. That's when he saw the Taser. They were going to take him, he realized. They would arrest him now and do who knows what to him later.

"What's happening?" he asked, faltering. "What are you going to do?"

"You've been convicted of kidnapping and impersonation," one of the guards informed him. "The penalty is execution."

"What about a trial?" Cole's heart stopped. He eyed the glittering Taser gripped tightly in the arm of the man next to him. Another guard, a woman, was closing handcuffs around his wrist.

"You've been found guilty already," she told him. "As a fugitive, you have no recourse." Two firm hands gripped his shoulders, pushing him to his knees on the ground. Cole cried out as the man next to him raised the Taser in the air and commanded the others to surround him.

And then the truth of the situation landed within Cole's gut, solid as lead. He still had an out. He would die either way, but he could still determine the nature of his death. He could die with dignity, on his own terms.

Cole braced himself and prepared to roll.

❧ 21 ❧

DAVIS

Davis ran faster than she'd run in months. Her lungs burned, but she pushed through it. She was half ecstatic, half terrified. She'd arrived at the Olympiads to see a large projection of the guards congregating on the rooftop as they waited for Cole to make his slow ascent. She saw their guns and their handcuffs, and she'd turned from the spectator stands, pushing her way back to the streets, toward the building where they stood.

It wasn't just about Cole making it through the ropes alive anymore. He'd been identified, likely by someone in the crowd—some dirty old Prior gambler—who'd recognized him from the FEUDS. He was so close to making it to the end—a minor miracle in itself— but for what? She knew what the guards would do if she didn't get there in time. The thought of being given a second chance and having it ripped away was too much to bear. Fear kept her legs moving faster than she'd run since before she contracted the disease. She prayed Cole would move slowly, that even the promise of money— which is surely why he'd risked the Olympiads in the first place— wouldn't enable him to quicken his own pace.

She had to get to him before he got to them.

Cole. Her Cole, whom she'd loved with her whole heart and had never stopped loving. Only one thing mattered to her then, and that was reaching him in time. She would die herself before she lost him again.

She'd recognized the building from the advertisement looming above it. She'd passed that very sign—an ad for luxury apartment buildings—every day on her way to her dance studio. She'd memorized the outline of the swimming pool, of the laughing, canned faces of a young family posing happily. It was a half mile from the border of the Slants. It may as well have been a hundred miles. She felt, as she went, as though she were running in place. Every second felt like an eternity, and yet her lungs burned and her legs begged for relief. Her still-weakened body fought against her mind and heart. But every time she wanted to stop, Cole's face flashed in her mind.

She'd never met anyone like him. He was determined, stronger than his limitations. He was brilliant and sensitive and kind. He was doing it all for her; she'd seen that. All this time, he had to have known she was still out there—and he was pulling himself across that rope straight to her.

Or straight into the hands of the policemen.

She couldn't let it happen. She couldn't allow it to end this way.

It took her four minutes to reach the building from the spectator stands. Four long minutes in which she felt Cole's life slipping away even as it was just restored to her. Then she was there, riding the elevator to the top, racing up and down the hall on the top floor as she searched for the entrance to the roof deck.

Thankfully, it was well marked for staff and judges. The hallways were eerily still. Where was everyone? Her heart in her throat, Davis pushed her way up the stairwell and onto the roof.

There were twenty or thirty people obscuring her view. Judges, civilians, fallen competitors. Gasps and cries rippled through the crowd of onlookers. What were they gaping at? Were they staring at Cole's slain body? Davis shouldered her way through, elbowing and shoving everyone in her path without caring how it looked or whether she hurt them or whether anyone tried to stop her. She nearly fainted from relief when she saw Cole kneeling, still alive, in front of several guards. She paused just long enough to take in the scene.

One guard lifted an arm high in the air. He was wielding a Taser. "Go!" he yelled, and three other guards formed a semicircle, blocking Cole in against the edge of the roof. They, too, drew Tasers from their belts. Davis saw Cole's eyes darting to the open air behind him. She knew in an instant what he planned to do.

"Cole," she cried, hurling herself in front of the crowd, then in front of the guards, who didn't register her presence fast enough. "Cole, no." She threw her body onto the black tar surface of the rooftop, shielding his body from the guards. She braced herself against the pain that was sure to follow. She wasn't afraid of the Tasers. She didn't care what happened to her, as long as Cole was safe. She shut her eyes, trembling, shutting out the roaring cries from the people surrounding her. Waiting for the shock and the ensuing current of pain to rip through her body.

"Davis." She heard his voice, low and tender, next to her.

She opened her eyes to find Cole's eyes locked on her own. His were full of feeling, wide and disbelieving. He reached toward her, touching her cheek lightly, as if she were a fragile thing that he couldn't quite believe was real.

"I never thought I'd see you again," she whispered, tears spilling down her cheeks and over his fingertips. Together they looked up to see all four Tasers angled down at them. And yet, no one shot.

"Look," Cole said, reaching for her. She looked up into the mouths of the guns. There was a firm hand gripping the arm of the guard who'd barked the command to pull the Tasers. The hand was adorned with a government-issue signet ring. Her father. He'd stopped them for now, but his eyes were fraught with doubt.

"Dad," she said, pulling herself to her feet, careful to keep her body between Cole and the guards.

"Davis. You need to step aside."

"He's not a kidnapper, Dad," she said. "He hasn't done anything wrong. All this time, he's been taking care of Vera in the Slants. Vera and her baby. Vera's pregnant, Dad. That's why her parents threw her out. And they're working on a cure for Narxis. Vera's baby is going to save us all." She stopped, aware of the way her sentences were running into each other, making little sense to anyone.

"What are you saying?" her father said. Then, to the guards, "Lower the Tasers, for God's sake."

"Cole and his friend Tom are developing a cure for Narxis," Davis said again. "He wants to help. He's not a bad person, Dad. He doesn't deserve this. I . . . I love him." She held her father's eyes, trying to convey through a single look the depth of emotion she felt and the truth of her words.

Her father swallowed, saying nothing. "Cameras off," he finally said. "*Off*," he bellowed again, when nobody moved. There was a general chaos as Priors scurried to obey his command and onlookers muttered to themselves. Davis turned to Cole, wrapping her arms around him.

"I never thought I'd see you again," she wept into his neck. "I was sure you were dead."

"I stayed alive for you," he told her. "All of it, every day, was for you." His forehead rested on hers and his breath was hot. Through her chest she felt his heart pounding. Without hesitating, she drew his mouth to hers, kissing him passionately. His lips against hers made her feel whole, complete again in a way she had forgotten. She felt bigger than life, and her heart soared with his above the rooftop and her father and the crowds and the Olympiads. Together, they were so much more than they were alone. They were invincible.

"Well," her father said, his voice rough. "There's certainly not a lack of love here."

"Dad—" Davis started, but her father held up a hand, silencing her. He turned to address Cole.

"I watched you out there today," he told Cole. "I saw the way you fought. You had strength of character. You fought from inside, without trying to derail anyone else. And you saved a competitor's life earlier. I respect that. I'm not going to have someone executed for trying to live with integrity."

"Sir, I—"

"Not a word," her dad said wearily. "We have a lot to talk about. But let's do it back in my office." He put his hand out, helping them both to their feet, then he led them from the roof, past the few officials who had lingered to watch it all unfold. When they descended to the ground floor and climbed into the waiting taxi, Davis wrapped her arms around her father.

"Thank you," she told him. "I don't know what to say."

"Everything I do is because I love you," he said to her.

"I know, Dad," she said. "I understand that now. I know all about my mom. And I see that you were protecting me all along. I know why you hid her from me."

Her father's eyes were sad as he spoke. He squeezed her tighter, and she breathed in his familiar scent of cigars and vanilla aftershave. It was a scent she'd known her entire life, and it immediately calmed her. "I'm sorry, sweetheart," he told her. "I can't help but feel like I should have told you the truth. I couldn't bear to hurt you. But maybe it wasn't the right way. I'm human, just like everyone else. I spent my whole life teaching you. But it's a new world, and everything's changing. Maybe I could use a few pointers from you."

"No," she assured him. "I'm grateful for it. I wasn't ready to know the truth until the moment I did." Her dad smiled down at her, squeezing her shoulder, then turned to Cole.

"What's this you say about curing Narxis?" he asked as the car sped back to their apartment. "Is what my daughter said true?"

"It's all true, sir," Cole said, his face grave. "We've been working for months. We're close to developing something that may work."

"We have a lot to talk about," her dad repeated, gazing out the window. "And I'd like to help. I'll provide your friend—the one directing the experiments—with anything he needs. Just tell me where to find him."

"I can do better than that," Cole said. "I can take you."

"No." They pulled up in front of their building, and Davis's father nodded toward the door. "I want you to stay with my daughter. I suspect you two have some things you may want to talk about."

Davis smiled gratefully. "Thanks, Dad," she said, leaning over to give him a kiss on the cheek. "You have no idea what this means to me."

She climbed out of the car while Cole gave the driver detailed instructions to Worsley's lab in the Slants. She waited for him, and when the car pulled off, they walked hand in hand into her building. Cole had never been to her home before, she realized. He'd never been allowed. The feeling of freedom was intoxicating.

Cole felt it too, she realized. He squeezed her hand, drawing her to him. This time, when they kissed, it was a promise.

"I'll never leave you again," he told her.

Everything from now on—their devotion to each other, and what they chose to do with it—was up to them. Freedom was powerful. It was invincible. It was their destiny.

22

DAVIS

Davis completed thirty-two *fouettés en tournant* and slid to a graceful stop, padding lightly to the window of her studio. It had been ages since she'd nailed the thirty-two *fouettés*, but this week she'd done it three times. She was free of Narxis, having tested an early version of the vaccine, which was in the production phase. For the past month she'd been building back her strength and training for her role in the New Atlantic Ballet Company's *Cinderella*, due to go on tour that month. Cole had promised to attend the opening performance. Davis wasn't the prima ballerina in her new company. But she'd realized belatedly that it was better this way; she was dancing for the love of it, and she was working hard, but she no longer felt the pressing need for perfection.

The window of her studio overlooked the Slants. Formerly an eyesore, the Slants were being built up—and her father was at the head of the plans. Integration was moving full speed ahead, now that her father had passed the bill that allowed Priors and Gens to intermingle at all points in Columbus, and required equal plumbing, electricity, and housing standards in the Slants as well as in North Columbus.

A new bridge linking the Slants to the city proper had already been erected, and from her position at the window, Davis could see construction commencing on several modern apartment buildings. The estimated time for completion of the project was one year, with displaced Gens living in temporary housing in downtown Columbus, smack in the center of the town. It was no longer uncommon to see Gens and Priors intermingling, and according to her father it was happening more steadily and quicker than any other integration in history—largely due to the Gens' recent contributions to the medical field. Ever since Thomas had perfected his Narxis vaccine, he'd become a local celebrity. Best of all, TOR-N had been shut down for good, and proceeds from the lawsuit against doctors who'd been skimming had been put toward the care of remaining patients and proper burials of the dead. Dr. Grady had finally gotten what was coming to him: he was in jail for a minimum of five years, even after paying reparations. The island itself had been turned into an animal sanctuary. Davis liked that.

Furthermore, a dialogue had been opened about just what was

preventing Gens from attending top colleges, and why. Columbus had banded together to rebuild the city, and everyone was encouraged to contribute. The stigma still existed, but after only two months, they were making enormous strides. Davis felt pride, looking out at the Slants and knowing that just a few months ago there had nearly been a civil war. She and Cole—and their love—had helped bring about the change.

Her DirecTalk beeped loudly, interrupting her blissful haze. At first she worried it might be Mercer—they were in the process of rebuilding their friendship, after he'd professed his love for her, post-Olympiads. Davis had always known he didn't *really* love her—not her essence, just what she represented for him. But she was glad he was in the process of finding himself, that he'd stopped trying to hide from what he was. Still, things had been tentative between them.

She picked up the new heart pendant Cole had given her—purchased with part of his Olympiads winnings—after she had abandoned the chain that reminded her of her birth mother.

A message from Tom Worsley—not Mercer—was projected into the air. "*Hospital,*" it read. "*Come quick. Rm 314.*"

Cole was already waiting for her when she arrived at the hospital ten minutes later. Davis dashed inside, barely able to form sentences due to her excitement and the fact that she'd sprinted over as fast as she could. He smiled broadly and greeted her with a kiss on the cheek.

"Did you come right from work?" she asked, indicating his brown contractor's uniform.

"Nope, I've just taken to wearing this thing around," he said, rolling his eyes at the baggy tunic and matching pants. "Yeah, of course I came from work. Had to negotiate an early lunch, no big. You know I wouldn't miss this for the world."

"I wish you *would* just wear it around," she teased. "You look pretty cute." She pulled him in for another, longer kiss on the lips. She'd meant it. Cole was healthy and rugged looking, now that he spent his days in the sun working on building up the Slants. He wrapped a muscular arm around her waist and pulled her against him. She leaned there for a second, listening to his heartbeat where her head pressed against his broad chest. He smelled like sweat and linen and something else all his own. She loved his smell. She loved that it had become familiar to her.

She pulled back, realizing there was something else that was different about him. Then it hit her: the worry that had once darkened his features was gone. He smiled at her, and it occurred to her that he smiled so much more now, and he and Davis had taken to teasing each other and laughing a lot. What had once been a relationship built against the odds now felt easy. She'd never been so happy, and she thought he could probably say the same.

Hand in hand, they ran toward room 314, in the Delivery wing.

"How is she?" Vera's health had been on the upswing since Thomas had perfected the vaccine. Still, he'd warned them that because of the physical toll the disease had already taken on her body, the birth would be high-risk. The thought of her friend in labor had put Davis's nerves into high gear. Plus, she was two weeks early. Thomas stood outside the room, looking grim, and her heart sank. Then he broke into a smile.

"Both mama and baby are perfectly healthy," Worsley informed them. "We've got a little girl on our hands. Our little miracle baby."

Davis brought a hand to her mouth, and Cole wrapped his arm around her shoulders. "Can we see her?" he asked.

"She's awake now," Worsley said. "She's been asking for you two. Go on in."

Vera looked tired, but her smile glowed as she looked up from the little bundle in her arms to greet Cole and Davis.

"You came!" she said. "I'm so glad."

"Of course we would," Davis told her, rushing to her side. She gave Vera a kiss on her forehead and clasped her hand, gasping as she stared down at the baby's lovely face.

"Vera. She's incredible," she said, meaning it with all her heart.

"Isn't she beautiful?" Vera asked. "Davis, I would love her no matter what. But it makes me so happy to know that none of her peers will be . . ." She trailed off, catching Cole's eye.

"They won't feel superior," Cole finished. "They'll all be the same."

"Not the same," Vera corrected. "Just not perfect. Your dad made the right decision, banning in utero treatments. Hope is going to grow up in a world free of all this awful pressure and prejudice."

"Hope," Davis repeated. "I like that."

"It's fitting," Cole agreed. "She's a special little baby."

"Would you like to hold her?"

Cole nodded, and Vera placed Hope in his arms. Davis watched as he cradled the infant, his face full of emotion.

"Cole," Vera said suddenly. "How's the girl you're friends with? The one who was with you that day when you found me at the abandoned house?"

"Mari's doing well," Cole told her, staring down at Hope's upturned face. "So's her father. Davis's dad helped them relocate to a safe commune."

"It's fully integrated among Neithers, Gens, and Priors," Davis added. "We've visited them there—they seem happy." She smiled and leaned into Cole, bringing a finger to the baby's cheek. Hope's skin was soft and new. She was beautiful.

"That's wonderful," Vera said, leaning back against her pillow. "I'm so happy to hear it."

Davis was just happy. She'd never imagined she'd be able to stand freely in a room in Columbus with Cole and Vera like this. She leaned over and squeezed Vera's hand. Cole caught her eye and smiled, pulling her close.

"Little Hope," he whispered to the baby, just loud enough for Davis to hear. "You'll heal us all."

He was right, Davis realized, her heart filling at the sight of her best friend and the little baby that had brought them back together. Hope was a harbinger for a new kind of Columbus, a city centered on peace. She wrapped her arms around Cole, staring at the baby's bright blue eyes and tiny, shell-shaped lips.

Hope *was* perfect.

ACKNOWLEDGMENTS

I would like to thank the entire team at St. Martin's Press—in particular Jen Weis and Sylvan Creekmore (tireless, dedicated, and all-around wonderful)—for their efforts at making this book special both in content and design. As always, I owe a big thanks to Lexa Hillyer, Laura Schechter, Angela Velez, Tara Sonin, and the talented Alexa Wejko of Paper Lantern Lit. I am tremendously grateful for your perpetual support.